SHAMBLES

OTHER BOOKS BY DEBRA MONROE

The Source of Trouble

A Wild, Cold State

Newfangled

SHAMBLES

a novel by **debra monroe**

southern methodist university press **dallas**

Copyright © 2004 by Debra Monroe
First edition, 2004
All rights reserved

Requests for permission to reproduce material from this work should be sent to:
    Rights and Permissions
    Southern Methodist University Press
    PO Box 750415
    Dallas, Texas 75275-0415

Cover photo: "Brenda, 1976" by Luther A. Smith
Jacket and text design by Teresa W. Wingfield

Library of Congress Cataloging-in-Publication Data
  Monroe, Debra.
  Shambles : a novel / by Debra Monroe.— 1st ed.
    p. cm.
  ISBN 0-87074-486-0 (acid-free paper)
   1. Mothers and daughters—Fiction. 2. Women social workers—Fiction. 3. Maternal deprivation—Fiction. 4. Adopted children—Fiction. 5. Single mothers—Fiction. 6. Texas—Fiction. I. Title.

PS3563.O5273S53 2004
813'.54—dc22   2004045342

Printed in the United States of America on acid-free paper
10 9 8 7 6 5 4 3 2 1

to the memory of **arlene louise wedell frigen tyman mcelligot**

Nighttime—when the sun bails out—hums with danger. Or so I thought. Light shrinks. Hate spreads like mildew. I've been afraid of the dark, ghosts, murderers. Most people outgrow this.

I didn't.

When I was five, I woke after a nightmare caused by some Sunday School teacher's complicated lesson about the end of the world. Holding a blue globe that was the planet where we lived, she'd pointed to our town, Stites, Idaho—a speck here, she'd said—and told us that one final night trumpets would blare and the planet would crack. She tapped an egg on a saucer, its slick contents glopping out. Like this, she said. I didn't believe her globe idea. The world seemed flat with dents and hills. The other children were thrilled—like it was a story, better than *King Kong*. She passed the saucer around. The goop in the egg spilled like the earth's goop, she said, but inside the earth was acid like acid from our insides, which, when we vomited, made our mouths burn, like our bodies would when we got swept away. Buried dead people would spill out too. Maybe she said their bones would ram against us, or that's what my hair-trigger imagination made up. But late that night I woke from my dream in which the Sunday School teacher's idea had figured; my father was in the living room cleaning his tools. I screamed, like my daughter screams now after a nightmare. She can't stop until I carry her through the house, pointing at toys. That night I woke thirty years ago, I thought if I described my dream I'd bring it on.

My father picked me up.

I looked at the blue linoleum I sometimes pretended was a lake, at lit dials on the stove that seemed like a far-off city. I told him I wanted to go outside, to see the sun, sand from the road I sifted with a scrap of window screen. My father said it was too late. Neither of us could bring back the light, I realized. I asked, "Is there a way to skip the end of the world?" He said, "What end of the world?" I told him about cracked earth, sinking dead people. He said, "At the end of the world we live with animals in heaven." He was mistaken or lying, I felt. I went back to bed with a hunch that the longer you lived the likelier it was you'd suffer, and no surefire safe zone afterward.

I think about the next phase—when we come back as stars or souls, or fertilizer, or our kindness outlasts us, or friends miss us so we live on like that, or dust and stones soak up our DNA. If it's daytime, I stay calm. I don't believe in God as insurance. I can't stand changes, threats—living, not dying—if I don't believe. But at night I picture skin-burning waves, bones rolling.

My dad's view—everybody with animals in heaven—was too nice. I didn't buy it. People have direction only if they picture a hellhole to sidestep. Besides, my Sunday School teacher's story was organized—geography, lava, egg yolk, bile. Details combining into a nerve-wracking big plan with fear built in. Back in Idaho, there's a park built by a man who fought in the Civil War, then married a Nez Perce. He used concrete to make forty-foot statues of William Jennings Bryan, Adam chopping wheat, Eve in labor, Custer's last stand, rebel soldiers. He built a tomb with a pane of glass so that you could see his mummified corpse. He'd rotted in the neck, the guide said, because the tomb had leaked. The point of this park is that the wages of sin is work. I don't understand the fine points; it was his autobiography, not mine. But I understand hoping for a pattern where there might not be one, and there might not be one in any darkness or future we can't fathom. Today, a letter to the editor of the local newspaper here, the *Port Town Sun*, said the reduction of arms between the U.S. and Russia took place the same year Port Town built the Slippery Zip Water Park, and now the big slide contains nuclear warheads. "My secret informant, Keith, briefed me on this volatile subject," the letter-writer said. Conspiracy theories, everyone's got one based on what you saw too much of or how you've been stinted. Me? I don't know, but a feeling that a shadow or grid hangs over us, putting us in categories, the Good and the Not Good Enough, keeps me careful. What passed through here? I wonder, surveying my own scattered odds and bits. We act our worst and best, tallying up hunches. We try hard in the face of bad outcomes, being afraid of worse. Good work, unfortunately murder too, is based on that.

ONE

Port Town smells like sulfur. Because there isn't a port, you see?

Just swampy land and an inkling of the ocean, fifty miles away.

I had random thoughts like this, getting out of my car. I'd stopped expecting a smell like water. I moved here six years ago from Boise, where I had a job taking kids from parents who weren't always pure bad, chaff as opposed to wheat. I pried this one boy loose—he'd have been dead from pneumonia if I hadn't—and his mother lay facedown in the snow, weeping. Some parents are bad. In the old days we'd have said evil. Well, the state cut our funds. The pay was already low. My supervisor, who'd worked there twenty years, lived in a travel trailer a mile from the office. He quit. A freak cold year. I nailed blankets over my windows and looked for a job in a warm place. Port Town, Texas, needed a social worker to float between the regular school and the vocational-residential. I got here and saw bars and pawn shops. Exxon, a blinking castle or prison. And down the road looms Houston, which I dream about as an expensive, mapped-out place to visit, and I'm not exactly welcome there, but it's hard to leave too—I lose my car and steal a Moped, or I borrow a bicycle from a gay man who says, "Girl, you can just make it out." I was sleeping in fits then, on the couch near the baby, never asleep herself except in the automatic swing, tick tick all night. I thought about her feedings, the texture of her shit, what the babysitter said, the sound of her breathing, the name she came with (Esme), her plummy smell. Not the advice from everywhere that didn't add up. Be firm. Be flexible. Quality time is stupid. You'll be so close, you two. *You have no idea the trap you're in.* Work I couldn't block out either—teenagers lately turning up high-risk for school shootings. I was on my way to meet my new intern, who might help. But I didn't want some Pollyanna saying how seamless life was so far—reverse snobbery, I know, this cold shoulder for people unmarked by grief.

Which is caused by mistakes—parents' maybe. Then our own, when we react.

I had a student once named Labia, no kidding. I wouldn't have picked out the name Esme. Still, I knew of a kid they couldn't place, too old, hospitalized twice already, named Nicholoasdemus.

I unlocked the doors and went into the school. My dad used to teach on the reservation near Stites. In Boise, I went to schools if a teacher or principal called. They all smell the same—chemical disinfectants, the underscent of sweat. The blinds in my office were drawn; they had been since the last day of school. I turned on a light and looked for a fax that said who my intern would be. Dannie Lampass. In Texas, that's a girl. The "ie" ending tips you off. I threw away the papers on my desk, urgent messages from two-and-a half months ago, situations better or worse by now, repaired or escalating. Then I got an intuition, which can be wrong, haywire—like maybe I haven't slept much, or I drank the night before. But sometimes it's dead on. Like that night I bought a ticket to Cleveland because of a private circumstance. Anybody would have been nervous. A strange city. Unknown factors once you got there. No one on the phone knew of a decent motel. An airline clerk read fares available in the next twelve hours. I drove to the airport at 4 a.m. I got my message, my clue, on the bridge crossing into Houston, cars slipping past, distorted sound, streaks of light crackly and unreliable. For a minute I felt like three people. One driving and, unbeknownst to me, *miscuing, blundering.* Then a message from myself already in the future, saying: Don't head this way. But I was also a person who knew the mess in front of me was mine; I earned it. The feeling left by the time I got to the terminal, bought a ticket from a guy who said I looked tired. I went to get on the plane but I got paged—*Delia Arco, pick up the white courtesy phone.* I went back to the counter, returned my ticket. But ended up flying to Cleveland two days later anyway. Two days that passed like a flood, or illness.

I got a hint like that at school, only mild. The air-conditioning roared. Walls and corners seemed close in. I hadn't eaten. I'd gotten the baby fed, washed, dressed, took my shower, drove fifteen miles to the sitter's, work still to come. I heard the big doors open, then shut. Last year a custodial woman got attacked with scissors by a man who'd been sleeping in the school on weekends. But there'd been inspections since. Next, I heard muted clopping, thick-soled boots in the hall. Then someone at my door. Short hair, Wrangler jeans, plaid shirt, a belt with a rodeo buckle. And lots of makeup: eyeliner, blue eye shadow, frosted lip gloss. "Howdy, ma'am," she said. I waited for a facetious comment, like: I'm going through a cowboy phase. Or: I've been watching too much *Gunsmoke.* Understand, I work with fourteen-year-olds.

Style is visualization. Image, an attempt to influence what happens to you. And it does, sort of. Dye your hair blue and given conversations follow. Dress like a Madonna-influenced Tejano singer, black leather bustier and spike heels, new invitations materialize. This is a variation on the Cinderella story, where, if you have a dainty-shaped foot or whatever, the right people notice. Checking out Dannie Lampass—sun creases at the edges of her eyes, she looked maybe five years younger than me—I wondered if she'd struck the pose so long she couldn't see it.

Then I glanced at my own black dress, black shoes, and black hose, smudged already with chalk, omnipresent in a school as coal dust in a mine. Cheap clothes look less cheap black, see. And everything matches. I do own colored things and wear them on, let's say, Easter, but most days No. The last time I did wear something pink or yellow the kids talked about it so much I got fed up.

"Are you the little lady I'm supposed to see?"

Odd to have Gabby Hayes in drag in my office asking me questions? Yes. But I've seen stranger getups. A boy pierced in nineteen places—upper and lower lips, tongue, eyebrows, chin, nipples, forehead, etcetera. He takes his studs out every afternoon to go to his job at Baskin-Robbins.

"Are you Dannie Lampass?"

"I can't wait to help the little critters," she said.

For a second I thought there'd been a mix-up—she'd been assigned to the animal shelter.

"Young people," she added.

"Hmm."

Next she said her sister was visiting from Atlanta, and they went to a bar and her sister didn't see how people in tight jeans sat down. Then the guidance counselor, Sage Hearttsock, walked in. The phone rang. "Delia." The voice on the phone was Caroline Blakely, Lee College. She never says hello, just my name in a southern clip. "I wanted to chat before you met your intern."

I said, "She just walked in."

Caroline said, "Then you can't respond, I understand. I did want to tell you that she's brilliant, though not quite sane. She has a genuinely horrifying story. We all want to see her graduate."

I thought: We do?

Sage held up a package wrapped in teddy bear paper, FOR BABY. She works with GED test scores, not students. Dannie Lampass grinned. Caroline Blakely said, "Her IQ is off the chart."

And I got jaw-grinding mad. It happened all the time back then, no sleep. Also this Mormon man I used to work with said it was a sin against nature and God, which was the same thing, he added, for a mother to be away from her baby for even an hour. The governor of Texas had said close to the same thing when he ran for president. *Stultified*—either the working mother or the neglected baby was. I felt like pitching a fit, this stylized screaming you see on talk shows, which kids emulate, so you see it at school too. Wave your hands, bob from the torso, yell in stripped-down grammar, a cartoon imitation of black street talk. Don't shove your shit off on me, bitch! Then I thought about Esme on a pile of goose-down blankets at the sitter's. She slept the whole time, Luann said. Resting up to stay awake all night for me. I waved Dannie into a chair and stared at her face while talking behind her back on the phone; I hoped the eye contact would throw her off. I said, "Caroline, in regard to that topic you brought up when you called."

Caroline said, "Topic?"

I said, "For a minute I thought we were talking about a ten-year-old kid." I shoved a candy bowl toward Dannie, also magazines—*Teens Today*, and the Spanish-language edition of *People*.

Caroline said, "Delia, are we still talking about Dannie Lampass?"

I said, "I'm not talking about a ten-year-old, a client, a student, someone else to take care of."

Caroline said, "She is going to need . . . support."

Support hose, I thought; my mind flitted around like that then. I said, "I see."

Caroline was far away now. "Thank you." She hung up.

Sage stood next to me. I couldn't tell if she knew I'd had a bad conversation, or she was chomping at the bit to describe some deep thought she'd just had. I said, "Meet my new intern, Dannie."

"Sure am pleased to meet you," Dannie said, thrusting her hand forward. She looked like someone you knew already—a little boy playing cowboy, or an over-the-hill guy who used to be bona fide, then got elderly and couldn't see that cowboy suits didn't flatter him anymore. I waited to see how Sage would react. If she'd give me a look like: you let *this* in on your watch? But she blushed a little and said, "I'm pleased to meet you. You won't get bored working with Delia."

What the hell.

Dannie said. "Good thing. Hate to be bored."

Sage said, "She gets the most arresting cases." Then she turned to me. "I want to tell you about what I started doing this summer—my hobby. And I can't wait to hear about your summer."

I said, "Let me finish up with Dannie." I explained about Project Promotion. I opened the blinds and pointed out the old airplane hangar across the field that was the boys' dormitory now. The new pole barn up the highway, the girls'. The cinder block building we were in—classrooms and offices— was just five years old. "The state pays the kids a dollar a day to attend, a fifty-dollar bonus at the end of term for students with perfect attendance who've never been to DAC."

"Dack?" Dannie said.

"Detention activity curriculum."

Dannie said, "Damn, I thought the whole thing was detention—you know, last stop before jail."

I said, "Some judges treat it that way. But a lot of kids just can't make it at the other school. They don't know English so well. Or they don't have a place to sleep or eat. We get them ready for jobs. We have classes in auto mechanics, computer keyboarding, business math, TV and VCR repair, child care. And on-site training—we send them out to real work situations, supervised."

"Like they sent me here," she said, her voice obvious-eager, a Shirley Temple tone, heartwarmingness.

"Yes," I said, "except you're about to graduate from college."

She said, "My sister's an artist."

I waited to see where she was going with this. Nowhere apparently. I tried to make the conversation near-normal by saying, "We'd like to be able to offer commercial art classes here some day."

"But she only sketches Duane Allman's grave."

I said, "She gets paid for that?"

"No," Dannie said. "I don't know what she does for money."

I couldn't help it; I glanced at Sage, who looked like she had motion sickness or slowly-getting-annoyed syndrome. I said, "Project Promotion is a decent enough idea, just underfunded."

Dannie pointed at the name tag on my desk. *Delia Arco.* "My mother was from Arco."

This tripped me up. Was there an Arco, Texas?

"Arco, Idaho," she said.

I'd seen the road sign once—when I was camping at Craters of the Moon National Monument, which is volcano remains, lava and ash beds. My real last name is Frigein, rhymes with migraine. But I married this guy for eight months, Stephen Arco, who grew up in Boise, nowhere near Arco, though Arco the town was named after his dad's third cousin. Having married an Arco who had relatives in the town Arco and never getting around to resuming my maiden name, I'd felt a jolt—my town! me, prodigal daughter—the day I saw the sign, ARCO 24 MILES. I never went there, though. It's above the deciduous tree line, where the trees don't drop leaves in the fall and push out new shoots, regrowth, in spring. Pine. Pine everywhere. Unscientific to say so, but people who live north of the deciduous tree line all year (which in Idaho is summer, winter, winter, winter) tend to be severely drunk, or crazy. I said, "I know where Arco is." I considered whether my ex-father-in-law's third cousins might know Dannie's mother, but decided not to pursue this—small world after all, and so on, which is the way people from one-horse towns talk, a habit I'm breaking. So far I hadn't even admitted I was from Idaho. What I mean to say is that Dannie seemed like a nut, and I thought: I can't go around being a paramedic to everyone.

Or I can, but it's my day job. I need nights and weekends off.

Dannie said, "She was a pioneer gal from the North with real grit. I used to call her Little Hoover because she vacuumed a lot. She came down here and married a long tall drink of water, my daddy."

I followed this. It wasn't exactly incoherent. I myself vacuum every other day. But I must have gone a long time without talking, because Sage shifted her weight, cleared her throat. "Uh huh."

I said to Dannie, "I've got a lot to do. I'll see you tomorrow."

When she left, Sage said, "I'm not against hiring people who seem unstable, but it's counterproductive for her to work here when we put so much emphasis on appropriate social interaction."

"She's not so bad." A minute ago I'd been yelling at Caroline Blakely. Saying to myself that Dannie was over there in her oddball mindset, me here in mine, separate, never the twain to meet.

Sage said, "She got personal too fast. She doesn't understand boundaries."

Boundaries. Tag. You're "it."

I have trouble standing up to Sage with her how-to attitude, also her negative stance about Port Town. I myself see Port Town as a southern Boise, which is like Cleveland only western—highways, cloverleafs, Wal-Marts, 7-Elevens, billboards, houses, manufacturing. Not twisty, snowy roads and bait-tackle-liquor stores, and roadhouses named Merv's or Bert's, and maybe a windsock at the end of one driveway, and down that road a swastika on someone's barn. City streets lead to public places with people, witnesses, and one or two are mean, full of revenge, but the rest aren't. In the country, though, you better watch where the fork in the road leads. And there's another reason I get edgy with Sage—it started at a stress-management clinic in Houston for social workers, including two Sage knew. Every night we sat in the hotel bar. Sage said, "I'm doing time in Port Town." Some Heidi of the Swiss Alps who wouldn't know sarcasm if it bit her in the ass said, "You don't like it?" One of Sage's friends said, "It's been an adjustment?" Sage said, "In college everyone talks about how to improve the world, and respect for women and minorities is built in. Then you get out, and people went to college but didn't absorb the altruism." Sage's full name is Samedi Sage Hearttsock. She grew up in a suburb, and her dad teaches logic. She said, "Delia handles it better than me." She looked at me. "You're stoic."

At the time I knew that stoic had something to do with Spartans, but I couldn't remember who they were. I went home and looked it up. Sage meant Port Town isn't a place decent people would like. Me? When it turned out not to be a resort town—and why would a palms-waving, frosty-drinks, and suntan-oil kind of place need a social worker to float between the regular school and the vocational-residential, which is what people used to call reform school?—I decided that no matter where you go, you're the same except for details. What I got from being called stoic, not being too miserable in Port Town, is that my weirdometer doesn't go off. I can't tell if some place—worse, person—is subnormal, a nagging handicap in my career, if you call it that.

And in front of those girls at the hotel, Sage said, "Of course you'd been out of college awhile."

I had gone to a junior college close to two years.

"So you went to college in Idaho?" Sage asked.

Before I could answer, Sage's friend said, "I love Idaho. My husband and I ski there."

That's one way you end up with secrets.

I didn't want to talk to Sage about Dannie, how she didn't stay inside her boundaries. Maybe it was up to me to show her how? But you can't air-condition the world. This is a saying I got from my boss, Hector Jaramillo, who knew when he hired me I didn't have a degree. It wasn't against regulations. He read from a handbook. "Nowhere does it say college degree required. My own education, Miss Arco," he said, "was by hook and by crook, and whether or not you have a degree isn't going to come up much." He placed his hands on the table. "But you won't help your case or mine by telling people you don't." He dresses like a thug, a *pachuco,* because boy students appreciate it, or it's the only way he knows. So he helped me create this false identity. Besides, I slept with him—not to set up a scratch-my-back and vice versa scenario. Just misguidedness, like an otherwise repented crackhead lighting up after an emergency-level bad day. Not once but twice, four years apart. For him there'd been no one else in four years, no one in practically forever. Second time we fucked, he started talking, *te amo.* I gave him a few days, apologized, said I wasn't in the market. Unkind, careless, I mean me.

So that day at school, I changed the subject away from Dannie. "Sage, why are you here?"

She said, "Same as you, reacclimating, getting used to school starting."

"What's your new hobby then?"

She pushed her glasses up her nose. "Creative writing."

I didn't have an opinion. Someone had come by Project Promotion last year and pitched creative writing here. They had a grant. And theories. Finding words and phrases to match what the students feel but don't yet understand will lead to autonomy. For bilingual students the acquisition of English becomes suddenly relevant. Hector Jaramillo sent them packing. "You teach a class in how to fill out job applications, you're relevant." They ended up at the regular school.

Sage said, "I took a class at University for Man."

University for Man is a nonprofit outfit in Houston with classes for no credit. "What do you write?"

"Whatever we want. I'm writing about going to City Park on Sunday— bamboo, lizards, palm trees, and later the same day eating ripe tomatoes off the vine. My teacher is a Jungian." She frowned. "He studied Jung, I mean. But he works at the post office. He said my themes are religious."

I thought about my own Sunday. This is my Body Broken for You, a scrap of cracker dissolving on my tongue as I think *repair.* Contradictory, cannibalistic. Then I go home and clean.

"His point is that religion doesn't have be gruesome." We looked at each other, nervous, like we weren't ready to have this little-known-splinter-sect-of-religion talk. Sage and me, who usually converse like: have you seen the stapler? Sage said, "Anyway, tell me about getting your baby."

I'd saved up a long time for her—the envelope budget. Every month I label envelopes: Rent, Phone, Electricity, Water, Trash, Gas, Food/Miscellaneous, Installment Plans. I put a piece of paper inside with a reasonable amount written down, then pay each bill and subtract. Leftover sums are decontrolled. If one bill is high, I find money somewhere, usually Food/ Miscellaneous. In spring and fall, when I don't pay much for heat or AC, I splurge. Or I pay extra on the couch or refrigerator, once or twice on a plane ticket. This helped me save $130 a month, which in five years became $8,000. People said I should save for a house down payment. But single mothers all over raise kids in rent houses. People also said to get a kid from the state because they don't cost a thing. The state pays you. But I work—I can't be a stay-at-home mom. I don't have a dad for the kid. I didn't want a baby removed so many times already from parents who did terrible things. Social workers don't get kids out fast enough. I wanted a basically undamaged baby. I got Esme, two months old. Her mother had put off filling out the papers.

But with only eight thousand dollars to spend and living in this neighborhood, Pesquera, which means place of fish, and is, Sage said, the barrio, I had my ups and downs with the adoption process. Conversations with birth mothers. One who thought she'd get a wad of cash—you know, sell the baby. One who pretended to put her baby up to freak out the baby's father. Another was eighteen and had four kids already, but when I got to the hospital she was lying in bed with the fifth and the baby's father, crying. This other—we talked on the phone four times, and I was packing my car to drive to San Antonio because they were inducing labor. That same day she talked her sister into taking the baby. The man at the agency who worked with me always wanted to talk shop, bond over our professions. But he acted rude to the birth mothers. I told Sage about him. "He came to the adoption agency on Sunday night for the signing of papers wearing a Mickey Mouse T-shirt and shorts. He was about fifty, but his skin looked tight, stretched out. I found out later from a person who fired him that he'd had two face lifts. He brought his new wife with him—she seemed about sixteen, braces on her teeth. Her name was May."

Sage frowned. "Was this a reputable agency?"

"I guess," I said. "His name should have been December. Get it?" I was reliving that night. Thinking about the old guy and his teenage wife was to avoid thinking about the tattoo on Esme's birth mother's thigh: marijuana. But the doctor said it was no big deal. "In the prenatal context," he said, "give me marijuana any day over alcohol." Also, Esme was a rape baby, and that meant there was no father to fill in those blanks. Esme's mother had checked NO in every category. No history of diabetes, no heart disease, no drug or alcohol abuse, no cancer or allergies or mental illness or cystic fibrosis or gingivitis in any branch of any member of her family, no. The whole other side unaccounted for, except the father was a rapist. The specifics of the rape, I don't have. Seemed insensitive to ask. Though it did worry me in my dark dreams. Also, those first months of Esme's life—what had she seen and felt? not seen and not felt? In my mind, this worry mixed up with news I'd had about one of my students, Vanessa. Her parents went away—in July—and Vanessa and her sister were tending the younger kids. They had a party, and someone lit a firecracker indoors and a piece of it flew like shrapnel and settled into a holding pattern near the baby in his bouncy seat, in between his legs. He had third-degree burns.

Not that Esme wasn't healthy, so far so far.

"You named her Esme," Sage said, handing me the gift.

"She was named Tandela-Esme." It'd seemed like a big name for a little baby the mother never meant to keep. "I shortened it." I'd felt bad about dropping the Tandela, but it felt clumsy to keep saying this long name over and over. I opened Sage's gift—a fuchsia sleeper with fake fur.

"I shopped hard for that," she said. "I wanted something that would look good with her coloring."

Dannie Lampass burst back into the room.

Sage ignored her. "Do you worry about the birth mother?"

"Like she'd change her mind?" In fact, Texas law is cast-iron. That's why movie stars like Sharon Stone adopt kids here. And anyway no law saves you from the other ways someone leaves.

Sage said, "I thought there was an official policy against adopting interracially—of course there couldn't be, because you see these mixed-race families. But I read that once, in school."

The Black Social Workers of America voted they were against it in 1972. Cultural genocide, their statement said. It's posted on the Internet, still official. "The idea," I said, "is that babies should be with parents who are like them. But there's too many babies, not enough parents."

Dannie spoke up. "I have a present too—on account of you having been to Arco."

I turned to her. "What?"

"I got it at a monastery."

"A monastery where?"

"In Blanco," Dannie said, "which is in Texas. They got a little Virgin made of wood who weeps real tears for people's sins. The Weeping Icon— they scrape off her tears and put them in jars."

I opened the jar and sniffed. "Sandalwood," I said.

Sage said, "The Virgin Mary weeps sandalwood oil?"

Dannie said, "You look just like her."

Sage did? Sage looked like the Virgin Mary? I started laughing.

"You," Dannie told me, a rattled look on her face. "You look like my mother."

T W O

I thought: I *am* someone's mother. And I didn't adopt Dannie Lampass.

But people will look for a stand-in mother, a sub, if theirs is missing. I know.

I once saw a kids' book my grandma bought when the library sold books they didn't want anymore, about a lost bird asking other species: Are you my mother? They snub him. Dannie Lampass operates like that. She'll say, "You hate getting stopped at that long traffic light near the railroad tracks, and your air conditioner's not working, and some old man misses the light, so you do too, and you want to smack him from behind." *You* means her, me, all mankind. *Your car* means all cars with AC on the fritz. People do feel hateful in jammed traffic here, sticky, murderous. So I nod yes, as in *finish up this detailed part and cut to the chase*. And it's like I said, yes, I think about smacking people. She said, "You and I are made out of the same raw material, Delia." Not exactly, but my car, a cheap hatchback, does have bad air-conditioning. I bought it on a five-year note, which was what I could afford when I was married to Stephen Arco, who had a lease-to-own deal. He got to the end of his lease, and they told him to pony up more money or turn the truck in. He turned his truck in and bought a Dodge with 150,000 miles on it, no tailgate, dents all over, which someone wrote in with Magic Marker: Ouch. In six weeks he's driving my car, beating it, but I'm still paying the car note and driving his old truck. I objected. I objected with Caroline Blakely at Lee College too. No fair, I'll say. But if the other person doesn't see the unfairness—or in the case of Stephen Arco, saw it and still felt blasé—I don't argue.

I said as much to Dannie. We were in my car. I felt I needed to explain why it was a rattletrap. When I was bailing out of my marriage, I told her, I still had four years of payments left and my ex-to-be agreed I should take the car. Dannie said, "When I got divorced I worried I wouldn't get to keep my truck." I started thinking: Dannie, divorced? Considered saying so. But thought: do I want to get so buddy-buddy? How had I ended up with her on my day off anyway?

I'd been in my living room, holding Esme, who'd been crying, her face mottled, sweaty.

It was Sage's fault—Dannie stopping by, I mean.

On the one hand, Sage says, work relationships should stay focused on work. On the other, she complain—a hobbyhorse she rides when we have staff meetings—that we have lousy rapport. We should hang out more. Why that's not out-of-bounds and Dannie talking about her sister or mother is, I don't know. Then we got this set of tests we rate together—everyone reads fast and without being too analytical decides A, B, C, and so on, and the grades get averaged out. Sage said we should do it in a relaxed setting and bring food. I'm away from Esme five days a week. I don't want to be away more. So everybody—Sage, Hector, Mason Pratt, the shop teacher and head of extracurricular, and the DAC supervisor, Creola Wheat—came to my house on Sunday. No plans to invite Dannie. But Creola, who sees Dannie every day, said, "Have a good weekend, honey. See you Sunday night." Dannie asked, wide-eyed, "Where are we going?" Creola flashed me a worried look. "Dinner at Delia's, where we're going to rate tests, right?"

Sunday night Dannie nit-picked, and not obvious problems, not spelling, not this one test, a section that was supposed to be like a letter, that started: Dear Assholes. About the best test, she said, "This boy uses words to show off." Hector Jaramillo snapped, "Big words are not a handicap." Sage said, "We're not assigning the Pulitzer here." A few minutes later, Dannie said, "Who the hell wrote these questions?" Hector said, "I did." Dannie had a point. Hector's not a great sentence-maker. So I asked Dannie to run errands—go to the store. She came back and I sent her to the post office, where I have a mailbox, because when I moved into this duplex—stone exterior—there wasn't one and it seemed easier to get one at the PO than hammer into rocks. But then I got Esme. Just to leave home, you feed her, dress her, pack a bag with diapers, spit-up rags, put her in a car-seat carrier, strap it in, hum "Amazing Grace." I wasn't picking up my mail often enough. When Dannie got back, we were eating. She did fine, complimenting people on their bean salad (Creola), mashed eggplant (Sage), microwave tamales (Hector), chicken (me), chips and dip (Mason). Creola and Mason went home, then Sage. Hector and Dannie sat down. Esme, who'd fallen asleep as soon as she realized she wasn't alone with me, woke and cried. She didn't want any new faces. She was still adjusting to me and Luann the baby-sitter, having said good-bye to the people who'd tended her or not her first two months of life.

I went into her room, sat in a chair, gave her a bottle. Hector stood in the door, Dannie behind him. I said, "You need to stay out." This should have been a clue: Go home. Hector shifted his weight, like he belonged. Dannie angled for a view and said, "She sounds like a little puppy."

Hector said, "She's . . ." He patted his chest. "*Constipada.*"

Dannie, "What? No way. She has a chest cold or something."

Hector said, "That's what I said."

Dannie said, "Close enough."

"What are you yakking about?" I said. Esme sounded this way every night. I took her to the doctor when I got her, and he said she was fine. I had a baby care book, *What to Expect*, but I couldn't read it much because I'd start thinking she had roseola, diphtheria, hand-foot-mouth disease. All mothers worry, but most have other babies for comparison. Or a mother-in-law for advice. And on top of that, most mothers don't wonder where their baby's been, contaminated how.

"We wouldn't want to overstimulate her," Dannie said.

"Exactly." I walked Dannie and Hector onto the porch. Lupe, my neighbor, came out and looked at Esme. When Hector and Dannie got into their trucks—both black Fords, but Hector's had big mufflers and Dannie's had dogs in back—Lupe said, "He's not good enough for you."

I said, "Hector? He's my boss."

She said, "You should meet a black man."

"I can't just drum one up," I said. Lupe was always worried I was single.

"For *la bebita.*" She pointed at Esme.

I held Esme toward Lupe. "Does her breathing sound okay to you?"

Lupe listened. She said, "*Gripe.*"

Sounded like *greepay*. I didn't have a clue what she meant.

Lupe touched her nose, throat, chest.

I went inside and put Esme in her bouncy seat and made bottles for the next day—Playtex most like mother herself except for sterile baggies and nipples you boil. And thinking about *greepay,* whether it was usual or life-threatening, I spilled formula, maybe six dollars' worth. By the time I mopped it up and made more, the clock said midnight and I wanted to sleep, but Esme woke then. I fed her. And I couldn't sleep, thinking about her lungs, each the size of a walnut maybe.

But a week passed and she sounded better. I meant to keep her awake that Saturday so that she'd sleep all night. I sang. I tickled her feet. She gave me a moony smile, hunkered down, and snored—delicate, tinkly sounds like I imagine a watch with diamonds makes, ticking. So I put her in bed. In the middle of the night, I always put her in the swing, where she doesn't sleep but doesn't fuss either. I needed diapers, I thought, and groceries. Dannie's pickup pulled up. Lupe's husband, Arturo, sat in a chair outside. When I went out onto the porch, Lupe stood in her doorway.

Dannie came up the sidewalk. "Howdy."

"Don't wake the baby." I didn't want Dannie inside. As far as boundaries go, the curb is one, I thought, the front door is one. All the same, I wished Esme wouldn't sleep so much in the daytime.

Dannie leaned forward and whispered, "Your outfit's all topsy-turvy."

I looked at it. I was wearing a bathrobe—inside-out though.

"I came to see if I could run your errands for you again."

Lupe said, "We planned already I should stay home with *la bebita* while Delia shops."

I said, "What?"

Lupe said, "Go to the store."

I saw her point. If I went to the store, Dannie would leave.

Lupe came inside with me. I got dressed, warmed a bottle for Esme.

Lupe said, "She's still out there."

I went outside and Dannie said she needed things at the store too. A firmer person, Sage, or Hillary Rodham Clinton, would have given her a thin-lipped smile and said, "Some other time." I thought this as Dannie got into my car. Next time I'd say: "Some other time." People know you mean No, Never, When rats fly. But I didn't think of it soon enough. I said, "Where did you grow up?"

She said, "Port Arthur."

I paused, sorting this out. Port Town, famous for Exxon. Port Aransas, where surf bums go, like ski bums in Idaho, rich kids taking a year off. Port Arthur is unemployment and Janis Joplin's birthplace.

Dannie said, "It was like *Mad Max,* the Deep South, and *Hamlet* all mixed together."

I said, "Port Arthur was?"

Dannie said, "My cousin still thinks he's an avenging knight. Someone raised him to think, you know, it was too coincidental one family had two lesbians. He obsessed about my parents for years, kind of like Hamlet waiting around wondering if he was supposed to kill his uncle."

I puzzled this through. The cousin obsessed about her parents because they had two lesbians in the family? He thought they caused this? And Dannie had some other relative who was gay?

Dannie said, "And I've always been close to my cousin. See what a position that puts me in? I wish someone *could* indoctrinate me about sex. It's damned inconvenient being queer. If you ask me, Freud was a trouble-maker, saying everything has a deep-seated early childhood cause."

I tried to think of an answer, but we were at the post office. I ran in and got my mail. On top lay a manila envelope from my dad—a ball-point pen drawing of eagles and mountains instead of a return address. Inside, on the back of a calendar page, the kind you rip off every day, he'd write something like: "Dear Delia, Taking wannabe hunters out at dawn. Snow expected. The enclosed, for your edification." He'd end with a quote from Chief Joseph or Kahlil Gibran, or once the insane wife of a famous writer: "It was sad to see you going off in your new shoes." He encloses newspaper clippings. Maybe about Boise schools putting in metal detectors. Or next year's cars because I said mine was old. Once I needed to buy a lawnmower and he sent an article on sod. Apart from my dad's letter I got the JC Penney catalogue, the phone bill, a postcard from Lake Charles, Louisiana, from Mike Cleary, who special-izes in rain collection and environmentally correct septic systems. I met him at the public library. He doesn't live here, but when he passes through we rent a movie, kick back with drinks, and I sleep with him, or used to. My new plan, a bit rigid, is that I won't have sex until Esme leaves for college.

At the store Dannie bought Mountain Dew. "You drink a lot of that?" I asked. Big caffeine content, explained how antsy she was. When we got back to my house two things were going on—three, if you count Lupe on the porch holding Esme, who wailed in that low-pitch way no one registers ex-cept me, and even through car windows it got to me. First, my landlord was standing in my yard. And this woman from across the street—Regan Janeway or Janeway Regan, I can't remember—had gotten stalled backing her Ford Explorer out of her driveway because—you got the idea from her pursed face in the driver's window—Dannie's truck was parked across the street and, insult to injury, Dannie's dog, Jackson, was snarling at the Ford Explorer like it was a Tyrannosaurus Rex. Janeway, or whatever her name is, has a sign in her yard that says *Namaste,* which means, she told me once, "The Divinity in Me Acknowledges the Divinity in You." I always think of that gluey-white Christ-mas candy. Mine in me detects yours in you.

Janeway Regan or vice versa rolled down her window. "Tell your guests not to park across from my driveway. It affects my clearance. I have to take my friend to the airport. She's from L.A."

Big deal, I thought. And what did the landlord want? I feel the same way when a boss, even Hector, asks to see me. Or if I spot a cop. Not that I break the law now. Also, the baby was crying; I couldn't think. Then Dannie jumped out of the car and did a half-bow in front of Janeway's Ford Explorer and said, "I'm so sorry. Please don't mind the dog. He's had a hard life."

Janeway glanced at me, rolled her window up, and drove away. Dannie left too.

I grabbed my groceries. Lupe followed me inside. When Esme sensed it was me, she howled. No one could miss this. I put the perishables into the refrigerator. "What's up with the landlord?"

Lupe said, "I told him I wouldn't talk. He wants to see you."

When Lupe's scared or mad she pretends she can't speak English. Or it fails her. It does fail Arturo. Once when I had plumbing problems at my place, I took a shower over there. Lupe left for the store. When I got done, ready to go home, the bathroom doorknob fell off—most of it on the other side, on the living room floor. I banged on the door and yelled. I knew the word: *Abra.* I wondered if Arturo had gone somewhere too. I stayed stuck in the bathroom until Lupe got home an hour later. "*Nervioso,*" she said when I asked why Arturo hadn't let me out.

But standing at my front door now, the landlord was knocking. "Can we talk?"

I threw my mail into a drawer, hoisted Esme on my shoulder. "Yes."

"In private?"

"I'll come see you in a while," I told Lupe, who went home.

The landlord sat at my table—pine, five-piece, tile-top. I got it from a catalogue. "I have to sell," he said.

This seemed too *Perils of Pauline.* All the same, I found this place in a newspaper ad, the second one I'd called.

He said, "I'd like to sell the house to you."

I couldn't think of what to say next.

"As far as your credit goes, I'm impressed. I've seen enough. I'd need about three thousand dollars down."

"I don't think so."

He raised his eyebrows.

I didn't exactly love this house, but I didn't want a worse one with bad neighbors. I said, "I have a baby. I pay for child care, formula, ten bucks a can. I couldn't come up with three thousand dollars to save my life."

He said, "You could borrow it."

"I couldn't afford to pay it back."

"You pay your rent on time."

"But I'd have my house payment then."

He shrugged. "You don't want to know the price?"

"No." He didn't matter now. He was giving us the boot. "How long do I have?"

He said, "If you're honestly not interested in buying, I'd like you to stay while I show the place. Your half looks great. It'd give people an idea of how the other side could look with a little work."

Putting down Arturo and Lupe's decor because he'd been too cheap to remodel. I said, "They're a little old to be scraping and painting so you can knock—what?—ten bucks off the rent."

Rude, yes. I didn't care. I remembered one landlord I'd had in Idaho—the place was fine in the summer, but in the winter my dishes froze in the sink. I called him a motherfucker when he wouldn't fix the furnace. He said, "Don't take that tone with me, young lady." I tell you he didn't call me young lady when he was asking me out, saying put on a swimsuit and ride in his big boat.

But this landlord said, "They never brought up repairs. It's not in their ken."

Ken, I thought, Barbie's boyfriend. What bullshit.

"If someone makes an offer, you'll have thirty days. They might let you stay. But they might raise the rent. I think you should sleep on it. It's bad business to dismiss an offer right off the bat."

When I talked to Lupe that night, she wasn't as calm as me. She'd lived in this apartment twenty-two years. This was the third landlord she'd had here. "He raised rent but he fixes things."

"Not the bathroom doorknob." I jiggled Esme.

She waved, scorn. "He sprayed bugs. He bought an air conditioner."

I looked at Arturo, drinking beer, watching channel 45, Telemundo. "Does Arturo know yet?"

Lupe said, "This is what he does with trouble, puts it to me." She slammed a cupboard door. "They kill your love for them. Maybe it's fine you don't have a husband. Stick to that gun."

When I left to go, she leaned out the door. "Delia, we don't know how the next will be."

I put Esme in her Snugli stomach carrier, $24.95, and I turned on the outdoor hose. I thought: another new yard, new flower beds. I'd put bulbs in here. You can dig them up and take them, but I didn't see myself doing that with Esme strapped on, not with school in session. Esme squirmed in the stomach sack, so I lifted her out and sat on the porch. I'd meant to take a bath today. I'd picked up my mail and bought groceries—that was it. Across the street, Janeway got home from taking her friend to the airport, her garage door rising silent and royal like some techno-gadget in *Star Wars*. She disappeared inside her big Spanish-style house, which she'd bought and restored, she'd said, because property values in Pesquera were going up. I like Pesquera—green, pink, aqua houses, a store that sells nothing but bean bag chairs, a used-vacuum-cleaner shop, three churches, a thrift store, a bakery (*panaderia*). Janeway is ahead of the curve, or thinks she is, because she studied for a real estate license. But she doesn't sell houses. She inherited the local newspaper and once a week writes a column on summer safety, or a pat on the back to Exxon, or why we should cough up money to restore the Bijou. Her door opened and she came out into her yard, then to the street, pausing for a car with booming music to pass. "I saw your sprinklers," she said in the same chirpy way you'd say I see you're receiving callers.

She sat down and babbled to Esme—fuzzy wuzzy this or that. Some people love babies. Some would just as soon step on one. Once I had a dream that drove this point home. People who didn't like babies were animals, but you had to look close to notice. I'd been watching *Sesame Street,* which emphasizes interracial friendship. And they show a deaf person hanging with someone who can hear, or someone in a wheelchair married to someone who isn't. Yet never a mother and father or mother and kid who aren't the same race, too controversial. Animals crossbreed, though—interspecial dating. A frog will marry a fox in a big church wedding. In my dream, I'm on a date with a man who's been to college so he knows not to blurt about Esme not looking like me and where is she from. But you can see he's struggling with the idea of dating any woman who smells like spit-up and hasn't washed her hair. I'm thinking: no future here. I notice his temples, cheekbones, his wrists below his sport coat sleeves, normal but a little spindly, alien. He's a cricket, I realize suddenly. In the dream I tell Esme this, telepathically. I set her car seat on the floor, and someone trips over it. I look around the restaurant and see tables and tables of diners: disguised bears, rabbits, birds, bugs, a few humans mixed in. That's how you know who to trust. What was I thinking when Janeway sat down? Cricket.

I said, "Hi, Janeway." I wondered again if it wasn't her first name. I'd feel odd if she came to me and said: Hi, Arco. So I said, "Is Janeway your last name then? I never got that straight."

She didn't answer. She said, "I saw Chuck was here."

"Chuck?"

"He owns your house."

I'd always thought of him as Landlord.

Janeway said, "I've known him for years."

I wondered if she'd fucked him. Beside the point, and nosy. But this is the way my kids think. A janitor drops in, they say: "Are you two married?" Or the district superintendent, Hal Hollie, who people call Hollywood Hal because he's handsome and overpaid. "Miss, is this your boyfriend?"

Janeway said, "He mentioned he wants to sell you the house."

I thought: Wasn't that a little anticonfidential on his part?

She said, "I'd love for you to buy it."

I couldn't imagine her saying this to Lupe.

"I've always liked the house. You'll need to do something about that paint someone spilled on the roof—I can see it from my bedroom. I actually offered to pay Chuck to clean it up. I'm sure the inside needs work. And get rid of that shrub—people don't landscape like that anymore."

I was daydreaming, picturing myself as owner. My house I just bought, I could see myself saying. I was supposed to get a raise at the end of the year—$209 a month. But I'm stretched thin now. I'd stopped giving ten dollars a week at church and give five. I eat macaroni, split pea soup, tuna loaf. I'm good at saving unless I drink. It's not the price of vodka. Drunk, I go to a cafe and order steak. Or, hungover, head for Wal-Mart or, God help me, a mall.

Janeway said, "Who was that gay girl you were with earlier?"

I thought you weren't supposed to say that now. Gay girl. Black man. Mexican gardener. Not unless you'd say *white* and *straight* the same way. I said, "My colleague." I'd never used that word before. It gave me a kick. Sage was my colleague, but that didn't sound so funny.

"What's her name?"

"Dannie Lampass."

Janeway said, "Is she from here?"

"Port Arthur," I said. I was thinking about Janis Joplin—how tough she was, to a point. So I didn't focus when Janeway spoke next, her face clarifying as she sighed, expressed herself. *"Ah, the Lampass murder,"* she said. *"Have you seen the true-crime book?"* Or I did focus, but the information came to me wild, mangled. Maybe she said *read*. Had I *read* the true-crime book? I held Esme close. Lightning flickered. I wanted Janeway to go. I said, "Those books scare me."

She stood up. "I thought she looked familiar. That's why I asked."

Six weeks passed then, and I was driving toward home one day with Dannie, Esme strapped in the back. "I'm yammering, I know," Dannie told me, "but last night I dreamed I found a girl, a pretty thing with slanted eyes like I always want, not bossy like my ex, and we're holding hands in a car and I kiss her, and she stops me, she says, because my mother and father are in front my daddy steering, my mother watching, and I tell her, 'You'll get used to them. They're dead.'" Dannie had come by just when I'd finished getting Esme ready to go to a fair with clowns and music and crafts, ART FOR KIDS. I was on the porch; I'd stopped to water my bougainvillea. If I hadn't, Dannie would've come by, eyes confused and bloodshot, and Esme and I would've been gone already. I wouldn't have ended up here, Sunday afternoon feeling like Monday, and Dannie in the passenger seat with her Day of the Dead talk. Dead, I thought. Who killed them?

I didn't need to know, I decided. Dannie was a person, not a movie. I don't watch murder movies anyway; I don't care about Janeway's book. Who-done-it, who *cares*? But I did want to know how you get by afterward. Not just hours and days, but life ever on and onward.

I parked the car and started to unload Esme. Janeway came across the street with her friend from L.A., Marla. "Marla works on the TV show *The Simpsons,*" Janeway said, an introduction.

"Damn," Dannie said. "Are you Madge's voice?"

Marla wasn't Madge's voice, Marla said. Marla was assistant to the producer, which sounded secretarial. I hate *The Simpsons*. Nothing personal, just that Stephen Arco used to watch it, then skateboard. I'd come home from work and find him—thirty-some years old and jobless—out in the road with kids. Janeway glanced at me. "How are you holding up?" Holding up making the big home purchase decision, she might have meant. Holding up as a new mother. Or holding up spending all my time with a sexually ambiguous lumberjack. I shifted Esme in her car seat to my other arm. I wondered: were Janeway and Marla gay, thinking Dannie and I were? If I were, I'd hope to have different feelings from what I have for Dannie. She makes me sad. I can't help her. Who else will be nice to her? Where is she supposed to go on a Sunday, which is lonely for anyone? Janeway seemed gay, I thought, because she'd been sure Dannie was. And she stood half-claiming us, but you could see she'd rather not. "How am I?" I said. "Fine."

After supper, I sat on my porch. Janeway crossed the street and tossed a book down. "Don't you want to see the pictures of Dannie?"

"Where's Marla?" I asked.

"Catching up on her sleep. Really, don't you want to see the pictures of Dannie?"

"Why?" I meant why see them.

"She's in here because she was a key witness. Before that, a suspect. She was close to the murderer. He's her cousin. He's in Huntsville on death row. The book mentions the funny way she talks."

The book lay half on the porch swing, half in my lap. The word *tome* popped into my head: a big book, sometimes published in volumes. This one, *The Fall of the Bingo King,* wasn't so big. It weighed less than Esme. I said, "I get bad dreams." I wondered if every woman does—every woman who doesn't sleep with a strong man at night. Janeway didn't, but she has an alarm system that beep-beeps down at the police station. I said, irrelevant and slightly disloyal, "Dannie's not my girlfriend." And I tried to think why Janeway was so het up about this book.

She said, "True-crime books are trash, but they're my vice. If I pick one up, I can't put it down. I looked at the pictures again after talking to you— they're all together in a section in the center."

Maybe because the photos were glossy, heavier than print pages, the book fell open that way—front and back spread-eagle, the photos clustering erect, fanning. Before I made myself shut it again, I glimpsed the first photo, its voodoo, cheerful mood. Dannie's parents, Mack and Lorinda Lampass, drinking champagne on a gambling boat. Lorinda was from Arco, Idaho. I'm from Stites. Arco's my last name. As parallels go, that's it. Still, a few months later—before I went on another trip to Cleveland, third fucking time I'd book tickets to Cleveland, and this time hold Esme in the dark plane the whole way, spit-up soaking my clothes—Dannie came to my house and gave me her mother's rosary. "To keep you safe on this trip," she said. I refrained from saying: but your mother didn't keep safe. I said thank you. Dannie left, and I put it in a drawer where I keep my car title and birth certificate, also mittens, a little-used drawer because you don't wear mittens in Texas; I'd brought these from Idaho. But I remembered Esme's adoption papers were in that drawer too, and I couldn't bear the jinxed crucifix anywhere near them. I hauled it, sealed in an envelope, bound with string, contact with my hands minimized, to a shed where I keep my lawnmower. I went to Cleveland with Dannie's mother's rosary in my shed.

I once gave Dannie a doily my mother crocheted when she was young. Why, I can't think now, except it didn't match my furniture. But when Janeway's book opened that day and I saw the photo of a woman, hair pulled back to accentuate the wave and pomp around her forehead, her dark-stained lips, I thought how I have hair pulled back and dark lipstick too, that I work hard to look not-of-this-era, from another time, and I decided that me reminding Dannie of her mother wasn't crazy.

I turned the page.

The book was planned this way, to make the reader think "happy," then "heinous."

The flip side of the riverboat photo was the crime scene—forty stab wounds in my facsimile, her husband gored too. In black and white, blood looks slick, oily. I shut the book fast.

In photos of my own mother, she had big eyes. Also bad taste in men, according to my dad, himself excluded, he said, which is why she left him, a null-and-void explanation, since she left everyone. But the one time I saw her alive I understood that in the flesh an angel mouth and deer eyes add up to a face that quivers too much: all reception, no broadcast. If someone sent brute signals, she got them. In photos she looked tougher than that, tilting at the camera like Patsy Cline. She could have been someone, Dad said. Luann, my babysitter, said the same about her dead husband, who built toys, for example, a pulley for a kid to hoist himself into a tree—that he could have had a business, toys, but he drank too much. People who die sad maybe go to a station between the living and dead, not heaven and not hell, but like a tunnel in an airport where you buy newspapers from a stand and cross from Terminal A to Terminal C—the not-quite-dead riding a train in an underground hallway, down and back again, sipping coffee, waiting.

Janeway said, "If you don't read true-crime books, then maybe I've been . . ."

She didn't finish.

We sat there until dark. I went inside and checked Esme's breathing.

T H R E E

Dense, humid air I took in—hearing a girl, Miranda, saying her mother cried, and her dad worked all the time and left Miranda to help her mother with the crying and the housework. I told Miranda about family counseling, how we could find some that didn't cost much. Miranda said, "Miss, it doesn't work, because someone told my mom my dad needed it, and we put notes about it in his lunchbox, and he ignored them." The Hebrew word for wind means *God's breath,* my preacher said. We get gulf wind here, hurricanes. I sleep with my windows open; I do this to save on AC. The sound outside was blusterous, squally. Above my head was my headboard made of white-painted iron, beyond that a screen separating me from the night. It didn't sound like God outside but a dying dog. Dogs pant hard at the end. Or maybe it was a man wanted by the FBI who hitches up and down highways from here to Illinois and killed eight people already with hatchets and rakes. The deep part of my brain thought this, but the shallow part went off like a pager: ache ache. I woke and took account of my headache, the metallic leftover taste of vodka. I was thinking about wind, bad weather, so when I rolled over and hit thickness I thought of a levee. It was Mike Cleary. I woke all the way up. I got out of bed. I thought: Esme. Had she slept the whole time I'd been drinking and fucking, which, after months without it, felt like an appointment for the relief of pain? It was like I'd mislaid her; in my dream about Miranda, I wasn't even a mother. I looked at the baby monitor on my nightstand. It blinked green/calm. I picked up my dress off the floor. I went to Esme's room and laid my hand on her, her breath raspy.

I stood there thinking. Mike Cleary had sent me that postcard, good move. I'd set it—a picture of a house in front of the ocean—on my desk. Nice reminder: some guy somewhere wanted me. That's what he wrote. LOOKING FORWARD TO OUR TIME ONE-ON-ONE. BE THERE ON THE 5TH. But days had run together, and last night I walked up and down the street with Esme, who stared at the palm trees above us glinting, blooming under streetlights, and I looked up and saw what she saw: jewel-like, green fronds flailing, glittery. I wouldn't sleep either. Yet after an hour she did, and I carried her onto the porch, but she sensed the change, the threshold, and woke up. I sat on the porch swing and held her and, when she finally did sleep, I moved her to her crib and turned the phone ringer off, the answering machine down. I was turning the volume button low when I heard the tape click on. I picked up and whispered, "Hello."

"What's up?" Mike Cleary wanted to know why I was whispering.

I told him I had a baby, and she was asleep.

"What do you mean you had a baby?" he said.

"I have a baby," I said. "I adopted a baby."

"You mean from work?" he'd said, confused.

"What do you mean work?" I was annoyed. Like I took a student's baby and hauled ass home with it.

But right now he was standing in the door of Esme's room, wearing pants, no shirt. "Stay out," I whispered. "Get out of here before she wakes up." Frantic, yes. I didn't want it to be like one of those times—to my dad's credit, few—when I'd be eating cereal and thinking, he must have had a late one or he'd be out here tending the woodstove. One day he was next to the stove, and I thought, well, he got up early, stoked the fire, and is sitting here deciding what job to go to. And he turned, bleary, drunk, and I understood he hadn't been to bed yet. Most nights, he had, though. And only a few times in sixteen years did a woman come out of his room. One tried to talk to me, and he yelled at her: hurry, get your shoes, get in your car. Of course, Esme wouldn't be up at dawn, staring. She wouldn't remember Mike Cleary when she was fifteen or fifty.

"We both have to work today," he said. He went back to my room and dressed. I stood at the sink, gulping water, swallowing Tylenol, when he came up behind me, pressed himself against my back—I felt his belt buckle, car keys—and put his hands on my tits. "Call you," he said.

He seemed like a fly in the room, a dunce. And honked when he drove away—like to wake up Arturo and Lupe. I held Esme and turned on the TV. I like PBS—shows about sharks, polka music, school prayer. My dad never let us have TV, a daily danger, he said. I understand now it's not what TV might do to us: make us dopey. It's ideas other people might get from TV and take out on us. Regular channels don't have much truck with people like me, who don't get it right the first time, unless it's to put us up there and stare and holler, *The Jerry Springer Show.* If people like me show up on regular TV, we're oddballs, expendable. Even with PBS, you see it happen. Last week I watched a program about the Korean War, and it showed this woman knocked over, shot, her son beside her (an old man now if he's alive), jumping like he'd been electrocuted, struck twitchy at the thought he has to live in rubble now and his mother can't move or breathe anymore than a clump of mud. What cameraman filmed that, I wondered, and how did he stand it? Just thinking about it, I felt like crying, slinging snot. The show on now was about making quilts. I looked at the clock, 6 a.m. I needed to feed Esme and take her to Luann's.

It's normal to have mixed feelings about your babysitter; I read this in a how-to book. I like Luann, but she does seem to have bad luck so steady I worry it's contagious. When I got there, I set Esme in her lap. "You looked peaked," she said. "Don't you feel well?" I didn't. She said, "That feeling that you're a baby-tending robot will go away after awhile." My problem was my hangover. Still, I do sometimes feel like an automatic nose: detecting sweat, shit, panic. Being a mother isn't hard, just routine. Unless I'm overlooking some major duty. I wouldn't know. Besides my dad, who's not exactly a wisdom font, the only person I talk to who was ever a parent is Luann, and she had different circumstances (having to gather firewood with her baby strapped on her back, not being able to afford the doctor and riding the bus to wait hours in the free clinic). Next, I got mesmerized by Luann's ninety-one-year-old mother, a skinny replica of a human—her hair coifed to look like a brown, crinkly dome, her stickman legs, her eyes, nose, and mouth in all the right places but sunken too deep. She has strange ideas about words. She spells Luann's name L-U-A-N and calls her "Lew-un." "The word A-N-Y is pronounced 'annie,'" she said once. Luann said, "Mama, that's not right, otherwise the word *many* would be pronounced 'mannie.'" Her mother said, "If you know what's good for you, you'll say it that way."

I told Esme and Luann good-bye and left. I drove to the regular school—Friday morning motivational speaker, attendance for all students and faculty required. At least they don't have it on Monday, Sage pointed out once. Before I headed to the auditorium I stopped by the cubicle they gave me—Sage and I share a corner of the coach's office. On my desk I have a locked box with a slot on top where kids who want to see me leave private messages. I had one from a boy, Sean.

I'm not good at expressing feelings so judge gently. Fun is not fun. Romantics are depressives who make it out of the shit hole their alleged friends dug. I don't get this emphasis on challenge. Would you want hard times? I was pretty sure I knew Sean—smart, skinny, ninth grade. His sister, in tenth grade, has an older boyfriend, unemployed maybe, who drives them to school. I met her because a teacher kicked her out of class for answering her cell phone.

On the way to the auditorium, I ran into Sage. The only speaker we've had here who seemed motivational was Hollywood Hal, his flashy clothes implying an education makes you cool, whereas teachers, after a year or so, have bad clothes and bad moods. I looked around. Project Promotion is small; you can see trouble coming. But Port Town High is big—nine-hundred hormone-stoked bodies, tough, geeky, vulnerable, poised. I only knew students who came to my office. Who else was out there? I wondered. I had the clamoring sense I better find Sean. But I read somewhere that low blood sugar causes anxiety. Maybe I needed a snack. Meanwhile, Sage yanked on her bra and said her underwire drove her nuts. Then she said, "Who's the girl dressed like JonBenét Ramsey?" I told her to hush. The student wearing anklets and a babydoll dress could hear. Besides, I said, JonBenét Ramsey was a person, not a tarted-up corpse on *The X Files.* Dead people are in a different place, and we're headed there. I try to be respectful.

The speaker got to the end of his story about the time he lost a golf game but found inner strength, and the principal told us to leave in an orderly fashion, a plan helped along by the class change officers with their orange vests and walkie-talkies. If there's bad trouble, they radio the police in a squad car in the parking lot. Small trouble we handle ourselves. Sure enough, one girl jumped another, and the crowd parted as they rolled on the floor, purple and navy blue fingernails flying. Boys hardly ever fight—always girls. The class change officers pulled them apart, pushed them toward me. We headed to my cubicle. I locked Coach's door and got to the bottom of the problem: love triangle. I told the girl who got jumped to walk away. I kept the jilted one with me and told her to focus on a new boyfriend and grades, or she'd end up working at Spanky's Drive-Through Liquor Barn for a boss dumber than her, but she'd have to tell him Yes Sir.

"That won't happen, ma'am. I'm going to own a hair salon and a Lexus."

I said, "You can't shut down a hair salon to fight. Right now your job is school."

Next I arranged to pull the kid named Sean out of class to ask him what he meant about romantic depressives and so-called friends, but after waiting for an aide to look him up on the computer and bring him to me, the aide came back and said, "He isn't here." So I pulled his sister out of class. She plopped down in a chair and said she didn't know where he was. He'd come to school. Her boyfriend drove them. "Do you know what might be bothering him?" I asked.

She rolled her eyes. "He masturbates too much. It causes your penis to go crooked—tissue damage."

"How do you know?"

"I want to be a nurse."

"I mean, how do you know he masturbates?"

"Duh, I change his sheets. All of a sudden he likes three-hour baths?"

I looked at her file. "Your grades are decent."

"Uh huh."

"Could your mother come to school for a conference?"

"She works all the time."

"How are you otherwise?" She seemed clean, well-fed.

She gave me a surly look. "Fine. Why?"

"Tell Sean I got his message," I said. "I'm looking forward to seeing him."

Next was my class for expectant mothers. My lesson today was about protein, how many grams a baby needs, but the discussion shifted to why it's not good to stay up all night if you have school in the morning. And that nobody has the right to hit you. A girl named Bree said, "Some women beat up their husbands." I said, "Never hit a man. Nine out of ten will hit you back, and they're stronger." A girl named Nelly asked, "Do you have children?" I said, "A brand new baby girl." Nelly looked me up and down. "You must have done those sit-ups." Then class changed, and I walked down the hall in a tidal wave of students, class change officers floating like orange buoys. I ran smack-dab into Miranda. I said, "I had a dream about you last night."

She smiled, shy. "Was it a good dream?"

"You were a little worried," I said.

"Miss, I've been needing to see you."

We spent an hour in my office. Miranda's mother cries because—Miranda told me this last year—when her mother was little her dad had messed with her. Now her mother goes on about sex. "Do you still have your cherry? I'm going to take you to the doctor to see if you have your cherry." Miranda needed money once and her mother said, "Walk up and down the street and ask people to let you clean or babysit. Sex is the last resort." It'll never come to that, I told Miranda, who makes As and Bs. But now Miranda's dad had bought a stolen money order, and her mother cashed it—six months ago. When Miranda's mother went to get her driver's license renewed, the police arrested her and wouldn't take Miranda home. She spent the day in jail with her mother. A man who mopped floors bought them sandwiches. I thought: Would it have killed some cop to drive her home? I didn't say so. I said, "How are you feeling?" Miranda said, "She wants a divorce." I had an opinion. "Threats are one way some people get problems out in the open." I said, "Miranda, concentrate on school. The next three years will pass, and your parents will be the same as now, but you'll be better or worse depending on how hard you work."

Before I left, I called Project Promotion to say I'd be there in the morning. Hector Jaramillo answered.

"This is Delia," I said.

He paused—being suave maybe? "Your intern didn't show up," he said then, angry.

"Why?"

"Because she's a fuck-up? I don't know. Creola took the call."

He transferred me to Creola, who said, "She called at noon. She was supposed to help Mason's shop class."

"What did she say?"

"Honey, when she starts talking fast, you know you're the only one who can follow it—something about staying awake for two days and buying a sleeping potion at the health food store."

I left work. I drove to Luann's. Luann's mother and Esme were still asleep. "Do you want to sit a minute and drink tea?" Luann asked. And she told me about one of her sons. She could tell by his face he was in bad trouble. What kind? "He hasn't told me, and far be it from me to ask," she said. "I had the idea to pray to my dead father and ask him, 'Please look out for Will.'"

I got home, starving. But I wanted to hold Esme. I put my face near hers, made a surprised O-mouth, and she smiled back, pink, gummy. Then I heard talking outside. When I have company that comes or goes by way of the front porch, Lupe pulls back her curtains and looks. So do I. Nosiness is human. My boss at Child Protective Services in Boise used to say gossip as a root cause of social connectedness is underrated. I looked out the window and saw Mike Cleary holding gladiolas and a six-pack. I don't think I told Mike this, but I love gladiolas. When I got the call to go to the adoption agency to meet Esme's birth mother and maybe bring Esme home that day, I stopped by the store to buy a plant and saw gladiolas and told the man to wrap them up. Then I thought about their tall, gaudy look, that it wasn't a gladiola day for Esme's birth mother, just sad, so I got her a potted plant, purple heather, but I didn't give her that either when I went to the agency and saw her eyes, smart, flicking around the room, sending the message she'd seen too much already and would be looking for less in the future. Mike Cleary with his tall red and purple flowers is too slick, I thought. He was laughing at something Lupe said. I went outside with Esme. They hardly noticed me. I didn't know what they were saying in Spanish—Mike giving Lupe a few flowers and Lupe beaming and blushing as Arturo came outside.

In English, Mike said, "My client had these in her hothouse."

"Nice. Nice young man." This was Lupe. Never mind Mike Cleary has gray hair and a droopy mustache.

"Do you like your new neighbor?" Mike asked her.

Lupe looked up and down the street. "Who?" Mike pointed at Esme. "Oh, *la bebita*," Lupe said. "Funny. Ha ha." She looked at me. "In the long haul," she told me, "a sense of humor is nice."

Arturo grunted.

Mike Cleary turned to me. "So this is your papoose." I thought: He sounds like my dad. My dad once in awhile sleeps in a tee pee he ordered from a catalogue, even though he's Jewish-Mormon, one parent from each religion. He loved that Kevin Costner movie. I told him I was forming a club, the DLDWW. Doesn't Like *Dances With Wolves*. He'd said, "A club with one member."

Mike Cleary said, "What are you doing for dinner?"

I looked at Lupe. She smiled. Esme stared at the murky, orange-gray-purple horizon. Janeway should write about it for the *Port Town Sun*, I thought. Thank you Exxon for complex sunsets.

Lupe said, "You maybe don't see it, Delia, but *la negrita* is more happy these days."

La negrita? Little black thing.

"So happy lately," Lupe said, "*la bebita*."

Esme *was* happy. "I agree," I said. Come to think of it, I was too. I invited Mike inside.

We ordered a pizza. Mike said, "After I left your place this morning, I checked into a motel." I thought: at 5 a.m.? I would have napped in my car. He went on about Super 8, such a good value. "You don't talk," he said, handing me pizza. "I'd like to say, 'penny for your thoughts.'"

I dove in, famished. "Better not."

"Why?" He cracked a beer and drank.

"I have rude thoughts."

He looked worried. "Right now?"

But no more than when anyone else talks, I thought. I said, "I think only mildly rude things when you're talking." This didn't seem to relieve him. "It's a bad mental habit I picked up."

He shook his head—like a dog flicking off water. My theory is that relaxed people are forgetful. They hear something they don't like, presto it's gone. This is a gift. Also a technique to use on little kids. A baby gets stuck on a thought, divert to a new one. I said, "Getting back to the subject of the Super 8 Motel, maybe it's a good price but it's still a lot for a few hours of sleep."

Mike said, "I always get motel rooms when I work out of town."

"I'd think it would cut into profits." Not that I should care as long as he didn't want my money. Esme reached for a rattle; I handed it to her. I'd had the impression he stayed with me when he was in town because he didn't have anywhere else. I hadn't thought where he stayed otherwise.

Mike said, "If I came to town on business and didn't know you, I'd get a motel."

"But you'd be there all night—it'd be worth the money."

"But you don't want me to stay overnight here anymore."

"Right." I was thinking about one of my kids, Gabby—one time her mother's boyfriend slammed her mother's head in the toilet, and Gabby stood in the doorway screaming for him to stop.

"Either I pay for a motel room and . . ." He paused. "I'd miss one of our sessions." Sessions? I thought. "I'd get my money's worth for my room," he said, "but I'd rather have it all, a little R & R." He put his hand on my thigh. R & R? I thought. "Unless I've offended you?"

"No." I went to feed Esme and rock her to sleep. I like putting her to bed when we're home alone, the two of us silent in the half-light, simpatico. Or not. Who knows what a baby thinks?

Mike came to her bedroom door. "This is cool," he said, holding a big envelope.

"What?"

"The drawing in the corner."

It was the package from my dad. "My dad thinks he's a cross between Euell Gibbons and Chief Joseph."

"It's a letter from your old man then?"

"More like a note with newspaper clippings. You're not helping the baby sleep, standing there."

"Sorry." He went back to the living room.

When Esme did settle down, I wound up her mobile—black and white clowns twirling, good for ocular development. Her chest rose and fell. I went back to the living room and sat down.

Mike said, "So how come you didn't open the letter from your dad?"

Don't butt in, I thought. But maybe he didn't know what else to talk about? We usually rent movies. "There won't be much of a letter inside," I told him. "Look." I pulled the package open and, sure thing, on the back of a receipt from Ace Hardware was my dad's blue-ink hieroglyphics, maybe four sentences total. I showed it to Mike. I pulled out the other stuff—an owl feather, a recipe for beef jerky, a travel brochure about Belize, a business-sized envelope with a fancy return address, red and blue block letters. I read the note: "Dear Delia, Sending this to U which came in a $10 package from the PO, express mail. I couldn't fit it in here without removing the cardboard. Am 2 old 2 spend winters here. Catch you up later on my idea of heaven."

Mike said, "Delia Frigein." He was holding the white envelope with the fancy return address.

"My maiden name," I said. I was remembering what a teacher once said. Maiden means virgin.

He nodded. "This letter looks official. You'd better open it."

I looked at the envelope. It was from Cuyahoga Credit Union, 137050 Bagley Road, Cleveland, Ohio 44130. I thought: Credit Union? And words formed in my mind, volunteered themselves. Cleveland doesn't have much to recommend it, ticky-tacky houses and twisted iron smokestacks. I said so to Mike. "Cleveland isn't one of our more scenic American cities."

He looked puzzled. "You have family there?"

"Used to."

"This letter is from a credit union."

"I know. I learned to read," I said.

He didn't react. "Why don't you open it?"

"Later." I stuffed the things my dad sent back into the envelope. I thought how in the past Mike Cleary got to town maybe once a month and that was perfect—regular but not full-time, a temp-boyfriend. Sage once said that she was alone, not married, because she had fear of abandonment. Not me. It's love-nailed-down that gets me nervous. A husband could make your life harder, not easier. Still, I couldn't be dragging boyfriend after boyfriend through Esme's life. A plan hatched. Esme wasn't old enough to notice him now, so I could see him until the end of the school year and decide then whether to settle down or just make a pact for getting laid discreetly. If I could, I thought, I'd be less short-fused. Who are these people who don't like sex? I wondered. Even if it is a stretch to stop freaking out and have it—lose the worry-spasms about work, also unpaid bills, anger, your sore neck. And focus on feeling good, better.

In my bedroom, Mike set his beer on my nightstand and undressed. I stared for a minute at the lump on his back. You didn't notice it through clothes—it's above his belt, so his shirt tucked in his pants juts out just a little there. I didn't see it the first time until we were half-naked, and in the hazy light coming from the lamp with the pink-colored shade it looked bumpy, monstrous. I had a second of thinking, No way, I didn't bargain for this. But it's not a fatal flaw to rule him out. There'd likely be a flaw like that later, but—count on it—you'd never spot it in advance. Anyway, the first time we lay down, I put my hand on it, steady, sure. If I didn't, I'd obsess the whole time about accidentally touching it and jarring us to a halt, awkward if we'd gotten to the In and Out. What if Mike Cleary froze up? He was forty-nine, an age when men sometimes have what Bob Dole calls dysfunction. Besides, I could tell by touching it, it was benign. The only other semi-old guy I'd slept with, in Boise, had one too, only smaller. Lots of men his age did, he said. He'd been to the doctor who'd said it was a cosmetic problem. When I touched Mike Cleary's that day, he said, "I've meant to have it taken off. Never had a reason to before."

Right now he was saying, "Lupe said you might buy this house."

"Bullshit." Not something I'd talk about in bed.

We lay still. "Funny thing, I usually avoid kids like the plague," Mike said.

I tensed up. "What's your point?"

"I didn't do a good job with my own. When my daughter was fifteen, she made a big speech. She stood in the driveway and told me to rot in hell. I should have been around more, but my ex-wife didn't encourage it. My daughter and me—we've made our peace since. But I never want anyone to talk to me that way again. And it's not been easy avoiding kids either. Most women have them, so they're looking for a father-type. Or they've got a biological clock problem."

So he was a lousy dad. And that business about women looking to palm off their kids on him, like we're all strange in the same way, extraterrestrials sort of. I met this woman once who said extraterrestrials live among us and are gentle and unassuming. I didn't feel horny now.

Mike said, "This is a scenario I wouldn't have imagined."

Would he shut up?

"Meeting someone who wanted a baby and got one on her own. You said you wanted to adopt, but working for the state, pinching pennies . . . I thought it was talk. You seemed like a cheapskate."

Was this a compliment? I'd sort it out later, I decided. I put my hand on his dick. Then the phone rang. I'd forgotten to turn the ringer off, down, all that. I jumped out of bed and got it.

On the phone, Dannie said, "Delia, I messed up."

Save it for Monday, I started to say.

"Three men in twelve hours. I had sex with three men last night."

I didn't process this right away. I thought: Men, three. Hours, twelve. Eight p.m. to eight a.m. maybe. One every four hours. Like aspirin. When I did speak I said, "But you're a lesbian."

She said, meek, "I know it."

Without thinking, I said, "How would you even be able to line up three men in twelve hours? That would take monumental effort for a straight woman." I'd raised my voice, I realized.

As for Dannie, she had on her apology voice, sad and trembly, like Opie telling Andy Griffith he lost the fishing pole. "Having split with my ex-wife," she said, "I thought it was a good time to try. One was my friend, not the one I punched. People like me shouldn't drink. I can't sleep."

Esme woke, crying. "Get in bed," I told Dannie. "Read all night if you have to." I hung up. I shut the door on Mike, who snored. I took his empty and threw it in the wastebasket. Once Esme fell back asleep, I'd wake him up, send him on. Holding Esme and thinking how babies pick up on their mothers' moods, or books say so, I tried obliterating the thought of Dannie with three men and why she called me, what I could do, how to talk to her on Monday, and then all the rest of my life, my chores and obligations, seemed like power lines strung too tight over too many counties, shaking in gusty weather, threatening to cross, clash. I held the baby and stared out at the dark, which stretched on and on, except now and then a lit porch or window, brightness.

36 |

F O U R

Sunday morning, a candle guttered. *Guttered* was the word my grandma used when she went to temple, which is what Mormons call church. So do Jews. My dad's dad was the Jewish one, and he'd been dead a long time, so we never went to Jewish temple. I wasn't exactly raised Mormon either. When my dad and I visited my grandma, we went to Mormon services with her. She always made the two of us sleep on a rollaway in the basement. I'll take the couch, I'd say, and she'd say the basement was the guest room and she wanted us there. But when my dad was out of earshot, she'd ask: Does he touch you? I'd say, No. He'd roll over and his arm fell on my back maybe. Neither of us liked sleeping on that striped mattress next to canned goods, and my grandma's question made me sorry for my dad that she thought such trash about him, also grossed out to the point I was glad when she died. Candles guttered, she used to say, if your prayer was selfish.

We say church. My preacher, a short woman with curly hair, says church belongs to everyone no matter what condition we're in. When I got here today a greeter came up. This one rubs me the wrong way with his pricey clothes but with a homemade necklace, a cross made of pipe cleaners. This is like showing off he's humble—he could afford decent jewelry. And just before the sermon you get a chance to talk—fifty people in church, most of them quiet, and this guy every week has something to say about how hard as a rock his faith is. I would never in a million years draw attention to myself in front of strangers. Anyway, he came up when Esme and I were settling in a pew—pacifier, spit-up rag—leaned over and said, "Hi there, little baby." I must have been worn-out because I snapped, "Don't wake her." I didn't want to end up taking her to the cry-room with its damp smell and ripped couch and the preacher's voice through a speaker. I needed to be here, praying. Hallowed be thy name. (Don't swear.) Thy kingdom come. (Try harder ASAP because you don't have forever.) Thy will be done. (Yield to the future, even bad news.) Give us daily bread. (I haven't starved yet.) Forgive my sins (mean thoughts about Janeway, Sage, so on). Forgive others. (Let go of it with Janeway, Sage, so on, also my mother, her mistakes.) Lead me not into temptation. (Don't overdrink.) Deliver us from evil (young men from the Aryan Nation and car crashes). God runs this show. So be it. Amen.

Driving home, Esme in the car-seat carrier, I felt like church had helped; the prayer took. I wasn't so worried about losing the apartment now, and Lupe going on all the time that a person with a job like mine could get a loan, and she'd help pay it back, and her cousin had rented a house, then bought it, and the house payment turned out to be less than rent. But I didn't have three thousand dollars. I also hadn't opened the credit union letter, knowing what I did about my mother's life in Cleveland—for instance, how her boyfriend had told the funeral director she didn't have money for her own funeral, and he, her boyfriend, sure enough did not. So he'd applied to the Health Department, Indigent Services, for a welfare-style funeral. All this before I got there. Didn't call me until Indigent Services had turned him down, said, no sir, we can't pay for this. My point is that this is how my mother, Hope Stoner, ran her life. And since I don't know anyone else in Cleveland, I didn't have a glad feeling about a letter addressed to Delia Frigein, which is, besides, a name only my mother would have thought was still mine. But I needed to face up. Wait until the baby was awake, drink a cup of coffee, open the envelope, read the letter, stuff it back inside the envelope while I absorbed changed facts. When you get a shock, it helps to go for a walk, which is why I'd wait until Esme woke—I couldn't go without her. God only knew, I thought, what sum I'd need to raise solving this new problem my mother had caused while dying.

So when Esme had eaten, slept, and woke up, I set her in her bouncy seat and opened the letter.

Dear Delia Frigein:
When Hope Stoner opened her accounts with this institution in 1984 she named you payee upon death. The fact that Hope Stoner is deceased came to our attention on Sept. 18. An individual attempted to utter a forged check against her account and we initiated fraud and forgery charges. In the process of their investigation the police determined she died on May 31. A sum of $379.83 remains in her checking account, $11.41 in her savings, and she kept a safe deposit box. In the event you are unaware you were named payee, we draw your attention to Hope Stoner's assets. Please call if we can be of further assistance.

Though it wasn't bad news—like she owed ten thousand dollars on a credit card, and they wanted me to shell out—I'd already set up the stroller, so I put Esme in it, thinking: payee. Also that I had $379.83 and $11.41 coming my way, and someone had tried to get it. Duster Dunlap, no doubt. In 1984, she wrote my name down. She was thirty-eight then—too pretty but not out of luck yet. I was nineteen at the time, working in an office, going to junior college, dating a guy who sold crank. All I knew about my mother was the photo of her my dad had, also the one time she came to see me. I can't imagine who decided we'd meet at my grandma's. I felt excited about this auburn-haired, fem-type—tiny waist, high-heeled boots—who'd come for me, maybe to beg me to live with her. I hadn't yet started asking the question: how could anyone have a baby and set it aside?

I wondered instead: would I go if she asked? My dad was a sad sack, but I was used to him. Yet I never got a minute alone with my mother, except when my grandma went to the bathroom and my dad got a beer from a cooler on the porch. She looked at me. "I hope you're a good girl." My grandma came back and said, "You don't have room to talk." So maybe ten years after that, my mother wrote me down as payee. Myself, I named my dad. You move to a town, stand in a bank lobby, they don't get down to business until you say who your next of kin is, also the address. She wouldn't have named my dad. She hadn't met Duster Dunlap yet—back then he probably wasn't old enough to shave, the creep. I was thinking this, walking around the block, and I looked at Esme—sweat streaming out of her hair, into her mouth, pooling on her chest. A baby dehydrates. I emphasize this in Expectant Mothers class. The street was deserted as midnight, I realized, this flood-lit Sunday, when anyone in her right mind was inside with the AC. I wheeled the stroller home, got Esme inside and two ounces of water in her fast.

I had trouble cooling down myself, my slow-boiling opinion of Duster Dunlap based on three days' acquaintance. I didn't have to include him in my forgiveness roster, big-love-for-the-human-race list. I'd go on hating him. Everyone has a vice. It wasn't that he tried to give my mother a cheap-ass funeral. He didn't think I was worth calling until he got stuck with this problem, a corpse, people pressuring him. He had no feeling left for her once she was gone, her wind, spirit, pumped away. Also I was thinking, fuming, if she had almost four hundred dollars in her bank accounts, then how come she didn't have a phone in her house, which was a trailer that didn't look run-down, though not clean maybe. She'd called me from her neighbor's, Harriet

Mosley. Later, Duster went there to call the police and say his girlfriend was dead. Like he didn't know, lying next to her all night. Unless he was fucked up too. He woke and his girlfriend, who was older than him, he said, depressed about her looks fading, he said, had been threatening suicide since he met her, so he didn't pay attention this particular night, but he woke and she was cold, not like in-the-refrigerator cold, but like a glass of a water you'd left on the porch all night. She took a whole bottle of Temazepam, which is like Valium. Nine or ten pills would have sufficed. It was Harriet Mosley's phone he used to call me, saying hey, help me figure out your mother's funeral.

Her dying came out of the blue. But not like I hadn't heard from her.

I'd heard from her two days earlier.

She got in touch like this:

Memorial Day weekend, I was on the couch, watching *Masterpiece Theater,* a mystery with women in long dresses and a villain with an accent. This is comforting, being able to spot a villain.

The phone rang.

"Delia, Delia. I got this number from your father."

Understand, I was waiting to adopt my baby. Every time the phone rang I'd think: Will it be him? Please, please let it be him. Like one of those sweet sixteen pop songs, except I was waiting for that guy with his stretched face and odd clothes to call me—adoption agency social worker.

"Who's this?" I said.

"Do you remember meeting me?"

"Who is this?"

"Your mother."

I thought, Well. Because never having had her, it was like a great aunt or my dad's cousin or some such person calling. Nice to hear from you. Haven't missed you since I don't know you.

"I'm at a point in time I need you. Please."

"We could arrange something," I said. You see it on those talk shows. It's not like you get your mother back. You couldn't. You're grown up. Not having a mother all those years, a real one with opinions and advice would drive you nuts. But the gap in the past might patch up a little.

"I can't come and see you. You come here. Your dad says you have a good job. Now, Delia. Because now is the only time I have. I want you to come right now. I won't see another year."

I thought she had cancer maybe.

Or felt morbid. Co-morbid, a term psychologists use. Cooperating with your oncoming demise.

"I might not live through the summer."

You know the argument. She was making a threat. It didn't matter if she meant it. It mattered she felt desperate enough to make it. That night I put a $579 plane ticket on my credit card—I hadn't spent money so sloppy since I was a kid, my first job. I drove over the bridge to Houston at 4 a.m. with second thoughts, third, fourth, fifth. Then calm flew down, a stupor. At the airport, I got paged. *Paged*. I'd flown once in my life. I'm thinking: what the hell is a white courtesy phone? I asked a man who didn't speak English. "No se." I asked a woman with blond-gray hair in a half-shiny dress—"matte," I think—who seemed aghast, like I had a disease. She pointed to a phone without a dial, which looks odd, like a clock without a face, a book without words. I picked it up. On the phone, a woman with a melodious voice said: "We have a message from your mother. Don't come. Stay where you are." I asked: "Did she say why?" "That's the message," the woman said. I hung up. I didn't know what to do with my ticket. I stood in line, told the guy who a minute earlier said I looked tired, try to catch forty winks: I need my money back. He explained he couldn't refund money, but he'd give me $579 toward a new ticket I'd have to book within a year. I ended up using the ticket two days later, to go to the funeral. But that night I thought: I'll visit my dad, whoopee, Idaho. She backed out, I thought. Figures.

But she was dying, which accounts for the groggy feeling that dropped down over me like a sheet of plastic, a tarp, so that all the time I was at the airport, getting the news from the white phone, standing in line waiting for my reprocessed ticket, I felt airless, stuck, sinking. I almost fell asleep, driving home. When I got there I couldn't stay awake. My mother was fading, and part of me was too. Another day passed and Duster Dunlap called from Harriet Mosley's. If he knew I existed, had my number—my mother had made a big deal out of writing it in her address book, he said—why didn't he call and say she was dead, before he said she was dead and by the way how did I want to pay for a funeral? I did by signing her trailer house over to the funeral home.

How had Duster ended up with her checkbook? Or who did? I decided to call Harriet Mosley. I got out the phone book for the area code, dialed Information. Esme hollered. I did a terrible thing. I put her in her crib, shut the door, then turned a fan on high so I couldn't hear her.

It was Sunday. Maybe hot in Cleveland and Harriet had to stay inside. She picked up.

"This is Delia Arco," I said. "We met when I came for my mother's funeral right after Memorial Day."

It took her a second. "Yes, honey. How are you?"

"I'm calling because my mother's bank wrote and said someone tried to cash a check on her account. I'm wondering what's going on next door. Maybe Duster got inside and took her checkbook?" I said. But if he did, it was strange he'd waited so long to go after her dab of money.

She said, "He's living there. He's driving that nice car."

I'd forgotten about the car—gold, 1970s model, a Cadillac. Or maybe a Lincoln? I don't know cars. "How?" I asked Harriet. "The funeral home was supposed to sell the trailer, or rent it."

She said, "I saw him carrying a TV out, and I know he wasn't taking it to be repaired."

"Maybe it was his TV to begin with," I said.

"I know for a fact it wasn't. You call the funeral home and get them moving. She kept that car nicer than her house. She would have wanted you to have that car at least. She always showed those pictures of you, black-and-white snaps. In one, you had little bangs and no front teeth."

School pictures from the 1970s. My dad must have sent them to her, I thought. By then Esme's hard-core crying had turned to steady, energy-conserving whimpers. If you didn't know it was a baby, you'd swear it was an engine with a bad intake valve. I had the sick insight she thought she'd gone back in time to her first two months of life, when no one held her. But I was also remembering the gold car Duster had come to the airport in to drive me back to the trailer park. I'd ended up sleeping on the couch at Harriet Mosley's. "I bet it feels spooky over there," she'd said, nodding toward my mother's. Maybe. I just wasn't sleeping in a trailer with Duster, who was my age, give or take a year. In the car he'd told me this was the second time he'd been involved with an older woman, though the last one broke up with him, which also left him high and dry, he said. Like my mother had dumped him, not offed herself. Besides, her trailer was dirty.

"You need to come up here and get this straight," Harriet said.

She'd kept her car nicer than her house. Of course. No one would see her in her house much. Her hair, her nails, her clothes, her car. High priority if you're auditioning for a better shake.

Harriet said, "She would have made a good wife for some nice man in business."

"She didn't have training for that," I blurted, no forethought. Like they had vo-tech classes in being a businessman's wife. You could pick up skills, though. But not in foster homes. One family my mother had stayed with, my dad said, kept her in the garage sometimes. Once she had to eat dog food. I told Harriet, "I don't know if I can come up there on the off-chance I'd find Duster and talk him into handing over the keys." I thought hard. "There probably needs to be some legal trick—title transfer maybe—before I could drive her car back here."

"You need a lawyer," Harriet said.

Like I need hives, I thought. "I've got to go." I hung up. I picked up Esme. There there, I said, holding her in the crook of my elbow against my ribs. I turned on the TV, but it was a documentary on Nazi death camps. Depending on how fast and deep impressions get made on you, you might need to study the Holocaust only once. I took a class about it in junior college. The teacher's relatives had been killed in Dachau. We watched film strips and movies. The book, illustrated third edition, had pictures. What did I learn? Evil walks up and introduces itself, some people don't notice. Why? Doesn't matter. And dead and stacked in a pile like hay or rubble, flesh crumbling, they're still human. By the eighth week, I just couldn't go. Took an F. Right now I switched channels to the regular news and learned two things. Hurricane season—heavy rain. And the Texas governor was running for president on a cut-back-spending-but-be-kind-to-the-poor-and-handicapped platform. I thought about it and decided kindness would take the form of thought: low-cost kind thought. And feeling bad about how I'd left Esme crying, I let her sleep in the swing, and I dozed on the couch. I dreamed about the presidential campaign, the governor having more money than other candidates, and I was standing in line to meet him and tell him about kids at Project Promotion, how smart they are, how we need to keep funding the place, the dorms, because some kids didn't have homes. He was saying churches needed to pay for that and parents needed to take care of their own. When I woke I had a fever blister.

I lay there in the dark, trying not to touch it, make it worse, and a phrase popped into my head. The policeman is our friend. I'd read this in a donated book at the reservation school where my dad taught. I went there until eighth grade. But we were in fifth grade when they gave us torn-up books with stains on them, someone else's old Spaghetti-Os, whatever. I'd sat in the room we used for the library and thought: *friend*. If my dad saw a cop, he almost fainted. He also hated the IRS and didn't file taxes. And kids on the reservation didn't think a white man in a uniform was a friend. Back then I mostly broke the law by not turning people in. My dad, for his plants. And the people I called friends then, small-time dealers. When I worked for Child Protective Services in Boise, my supervisor, the one who got me accredited though the apprenticeship program, said that's what he liked about me. Turning someone in didn't thrill me.

I stayed on the couch all night. If I can't sleep, I speak the same prayer over and over, like *bestow braveness when hardship rises,* but different thoughts for each round. At dawn, I got Esme and myself ready, then drove to Luann's. She seemed lonely. "Can't stay," I said, "I'm late."

At school, in the office, the first thing Sage said was: "What's wrong with your mouth?" Like she'd never seen a fever blister. My lip felt huge. I had these prickly spasms going between my jaw and eye. I said, "I had a dream about George W. Bush, and when I woke this had swelled up." I sank into work, worrying about Dannie. Having been female-gay up to now, did she know about using condoms? When I talked to her, I'd point out how she couldn't let personal impulses, which were her business, not mine, interfere with showing up for work, in this case taking Mason's class on a field trip to Exxon. Then Hector came to my office, leather vest taut, the ends of his fingers stuffed in his jeans pockets. He wears black pointed boots you know pinch his feet. He stared. I was thinking: say one word about the fever blister . . . He didn't. In some areas—emergencies mostly—he has good manners. Like his mother stressed the difference between concerned person and nosy buttinski. He said, "I want us to talk about your intern."

"Talk," I said.

"Why do you cut her slack?"

"I don't cut her any more than you would if she was Mexican-American." Low blow, also a weird comparison. Hector did favor students who were the same race. But how was I saying Dannie and I were similar? I mean, besides being Anglo? I looked to see if Hector was mad.

He said, "If you like her, help her by being tough. Don't let her get away with murder."

Maybe that was it. People who had a murder in the family—I tended to sympathize. Like this girl in my eighth grade, Liz Conroy, a half-breed everyone used to say then, like the Cher song. Her dad killed her mother and put her in a rock pile, had his kids stack the rocks. They didn't know she was under there. He told them she'd gone to Las Vegas. The police took forever coming. The dad was white. The mother was the Indian. Liz stayed in school a few more weeks. Kids stopped talking to her. I talked more, going out of my way. I didn't want her left alone with her scared ideas. Last I heard, Liz and her brothers got split up. Mother dead, father looking at life in prison. No one wanted all three kids. "Maybe you're right," I told Hector.

He said, "Figure out why you bother with her, and you'll be able to help her more."

He left, and I sat there thinking. Every day Dannie's black pickup pulled up in front of my duplex, dogs in back, snapping, howling. I'd answer the door like she'd come for an answer to a question. But she'd shift her weight from one foot to the other, tell me she'd messed up filing papers for graduation, or her phone was disconnected because she'd run up a six-hundred-dollar bill. I said, "If you've run up a six-hundred-dollar bill, it's a good thing they took the phone." She said, "Your input is so helpful." One night when I thought I'd gotten through the day without Dannie, Esme was asleep and I stood in the yard watering plants, the baby monitor clipped to my belt, and Dannie pulled up, got out, screamed at her dogs, "You shut your traps." She turned to me. "I tried to do laundry," she said, "and the dollar-changer took my money, and I don't get another check until Friday. How the hell am I supposed to have personal grooming?" She stared at me, gray-eyed, obsessive. "No more plate tectonics," she said. "I can't take these shocks." Something about her stance, hands on her hips, the angry slit of her mouth, but mostly her eyes—my boss in Boise said eyes aren't the window to the soul so much as an indicator of self-control, which is a word for sanity—scared me. Could she get as crazy as her cousin, could she kill someone? Water ran from my hose. "You matter most," she said. "You matter like my mother did. Once I had a dream you were wearing this white tablecloth on your head, like one of those saints in religious pictures."

Me like her mother or a saint?

Her cousin had killed her mother because he thought she and Dannie's dad were the opposite of saints. He thought they'd caused Dannie to be gay, a small-scale conspiracy theory, a crackpot version of right versus wrong, his own personal inside scoop, not much crazier than what passes for the regular view, from what Pat Buchanan thinks, for instance. Or me with my one-track idea that God likes poor people and former whores better than rich people praying in public. Her cousin's hate-trigger was gays. Mine was people with more license to belong. I had this lingering idea that if you didn't have a family like a fort or gang at the center of your life, a defense system to keep you warding off threats, you were disposable. You might not get exterminated, but it's not like people in charge would stop some other low-life from killing you either.

Why not cut her off? Why did I let her hang around? I'd studied that claptrap about codependency, that helpfulness is a racket with a payoff for the helpful one, who feels necessary while the other person stays a loser. That Mother Teresa has ulterior motives, for instance. That helping other people means you think you're high-tone, and bending over backward seems like durability, but isn't. On the other hand, I thought, what about feeding His sheep? How many people do you meet who are exactly where you are in solving a problem, not behind or ahead?

What people knew when they met her was the murder. Add to it that some people think gay is bad. Parents who could help her were dead. I moved my hose to a hanging basket of roses. I used to read in the paper about brothers killing brothers, husbands killing wives, and think: how could that person who's dead not have known the person they were close to had the urge? They did, I realized, and hoped for the best. I tried the feeling on: I was face to face with a killer. Dannie realized I wasn't a mother-saint and let me have it. Suddenly this tried-on feeling became true. I'd die. Just as quickly the idea left me, and I was only a woman watering flowers and Dannie's eyes didn't look crazy, just sad to be murder's leftover. Better than being a corpse, but still. Hector had said don't just put up with her—help her be something besides a freak.

I called her into my office. It was ninety-four outside, humid, and she had on a leather jacket with big zippers. I didn't waste time talking about clothes. "You're getting off on the wrong foot here."

She looked at the floor. "I know."

I started to say: don't tell people who assess you the worst things about yourself. But I didn't want to say that screwing three guys was the worst. It wasn't good, no. Still, you don't get past mistakes by posting labels on them: worst ever, can never be atoned for, the time I wrecked my life. I said, "You seem to be having a crisis or two. Maybe now isn't a good time to help the . . ." I started to say young people with worse problems. But as soon as I decided to help Dannie—or try to—a change passed through me, my nerve pathways overloaded. Thinking of all the people I was in charge of now and adding Dannie to the list, I felt something shocking and toxic had leapt from her bloodstream into mine, some foreign matter, but not foreign anymore, familiar, familiar, Dannie's past bleeding into mine. Maybe we were the same raw material?

"Am I fired?" she asked.

She brought it up first, so I wouldn't now. I'd have to rush in and disagree, comfort her. I wondered if she knew that. I said, "I'm giving you advice. At work—and away from work if you spend time with people who are coworkers—accentuate your positive traits. If you have to talk about a problem in the other part of your life, tell a friend or family member. Or a mental health professional who has training to help you." Though I felt like Miranda on the subject. A professional is someone who gets sixty bucks an hour if you keep coming, nothing if you get well.

And thinking about what I'd said—if something's wrong, tell a family member, and how not everyone has one—I remembered the first time I'd heard "the family" called "nuclear." I was in sixth grade and looking at a cow's backbone the teacher had bought from a butcher. She twisted it, splotchy with blood, to make the disks wriggle, and told us the spine is the regulator of impulse for the body, and the regulator of impulse in society was institutions, she said. The regulating institutions were schools and churches and the nuclear family. She pronounced the word like everyone did back then: *nuke-u-loor*. I understand now she meant central. But then I'd only heard the word used to describe bombs or power plants. When I first heard about nuclear families I got it confused with that talk about slip-shod construction, radioactive leakage. I got an idea that stays with me, that if a family malfunctions it's conspicuous, lethal: glow-in-the-dark.

Dannie said, "Damn. I grasp this. You are like family, my mother."

I scanned her expression for sarcasm. She was on the edge of her chair.

"I appreciate it." she said.

I said, "I'm not your mother." Why did I bother? Sage was right, Dannie should never have gotten past the out-of-bounds line. "But I do report to the people who let you graduate or not."

Dannie stood up. Along with the biker jacket, she had on items from her fieldhand getup, thick-soled boots, plaid shirt. She said, "When I first met you I got a buzzing sound in my head, and a lady who reads Tarot cards by the interstate told me that meant I was in exactly the right place, I was meant to meet you. But I've got to drive the little critters to the Cosmetology College."

"Fine," I said. "And don't talk to the kids about your problems. Or Sage. Or Hector."

She looked hurt. "You already said that."

After she left, I started worrying about other problems. And decided to call the funeral home. Which one? I called Harriet Mosley to ask if she remembered which funeral home we'd used.

"I can't think, honey. It was on that road to the fairgrounds."

I said, "Could you open the Yellow Pages and read off the names and numbers from the biggest ads?"

She gave me four names.

Pennington.

Still Rivers.

Eems.

Hafflefeinder.

Eems, I thought, as soon as she read it. I was right. I called and described my situation to the woman who answered the phone—secretary, receptionist, whatever. She said. "Let me transfer you to our funeral director." The minute the man got on the phone I knew his voice. I said, "Did you do a funeral in early June for Hope Stoner and instead of a fee we signed over her trailer?"

He said, "How can I help you?"

I said, "I talked to a neighbor who told me nothing's happening over there. In fact, someone's living there who shouldn't be. No telling what he's doing to the property." I started wondering why it mattered. Because of the credit union letter, I decided. I wanted Duster out fast.

"Are you the daughter?" he asked. "I just turned the whole thing over to a realtor."

So the funeral wasn't paid for yet. Duster, squatting. "Give me the realtor's number," I said.

And what did the realtor say? "I've been meaning to call you." He sounded fat. I heard him sift paper. "Mr. Eems jumped the gun a little. You need to file probate before you have a right to sign over the mobile home. I talked to the lawyer who does our title work, and he said to tell you to go ahead and file a petition to probate the estate and get yourself named personal representative."

Jargon. "What are you throwing at me?"

"You're the heir? No other survivors?"

My dad, I thought. But they were never married. Irrelevant. I didn't say this.

"So you're the heir. Go to your county court and ask for the probate clerk and look at a couple of files, decide which form you want to use. They'll have a couple different kinds. We'll get you a fax number for the probate court here. You might have to fly up and make a personal appearance before the judge. You'll be responsible for gathering assets, assessing debts, settling up."

My head hurt. Someone had loaded me up heavy, no warning. And mistook me for a person who had enough time and money to do this. "What if she had more debt than assets?" I asked.

"I'm not a lawyer. You might want to get one."

I hung up. I had night sweats, except it was day. I called my dad. Big phone bill this month, I thought, dialing. He answered. I explained what the realtor said. I was in charge of what she owed. "The sum total of what she owes is probably higher," I said. My dad said, "No way can they make you pay bills someone else ran up. If they try, go underground." Great, I thought. Great plan, Dad. She hadn't exactly run up this last bill; I'd signed the funeral contract. Then he started crying. It took me a minute to realize this. At first I thought he was wheezing, couldn't get his wind. "If I hadn't been authoritarian," he said, his voice ragged. "I was older than her."

Listening to him, I thought about the times I was little and I cried. He didn't hug me, but he didn't stop me either. "Crying is understandable," he said once, patting my arm. You could see crying freaked him out. He had to just sit there. But if I was happy, or scared, but not crying, he'd hold me. That's the tender thing I remember, his big hands, how they felt cupping my head. Lately I'd been mad at him about how my mother called him, got my number, and he'd never warned me she was getting in touch. When she died, and Duster said I needed to come to Cleveland, I'd called my dad then too, who wouldn't come. "I'm not going, no. No thank you." I went to Cleveland alone. I'd been thinking about chewing him out for that too. But couldn't remember a single other time he'd cried. "You did fine," I said. We hung up. I stood in my office thinking he hadn't asked about Esme. Sometimes he did. "How's the runt?" he'd say.

Sage walked in the room. "You look terrible."

I wanted to go home. I wanted to see Esme. I said, "Maybe I am coming down with something."

Hector stood in the doorway. "I knew this would happen. It's a lot of responsibility to have a baby and hold down a professional job, especially this." If it were another boss talking, I'd think I was out the door, that he was saying I couldn't do it, work and be a mother. But I've known him apart from the job. What he says, trying to be romantic. Or light-hearted, which for him is a stretch. I know what his bare feet look like, that he takes a shower first thing when he wakes, how he stays motionless and quiet when he comes, not a sigh. I know what he wants, which is to take care of someone and—but here's the catch—she'd take care of him back, only more.

Just then Creola walked in. Old home week. "That's the biggest load of horse crap," she told Hector. "People always trying to keep a working woman down. Delia here turns up with a twenty-four-hour bug. She who never takes a sick day. Go on home now, honey, put your feet up."

So I drove to Luann's. Her mother sat in the rocking chair; I couldn't tell if she was awake, alive even. I picked up Esme. Luann told me Esme's breathing did sound rough. I listened—it was worse. When Luann's kids were little she couldn't afford to cart them to doctors, so she bought a book. She handed it to me, *Mommy Cures*. How to put vinegar in a baby's ear, or a slice of cheese on a sore to draw out poison. "One time Sally had a cough," Luann said, "and her throat started to close. With croup, you get them in the bathroom, shut the door, raise steam. Otherwise they die." I thought: die? I'd look in my own book at home. Luann said, "Don't you feel good either?" Funny, if people say you look bad, you feel bad. "You must be starting," she said. She meant my period. "I'm done with mine," she said. She helped me get Esme in my car. I drove home, the AC huffing. When I got there I saw the FOR SALE sign.

It shouldn't have been a surprise. But I didn't dance a jig.

I went into the house, spread a blanket on the floor. With a baby, you don't get sustained sleep. But you make a plan to have as little out-going energy as possible and as much in-go and recharge as you can. What was on PBS? Some blond woman in Minnesota, printing her kid's T-shirts with raw potatoes she carved designs in and dipped in paint. She dipped a raw fish in paint too and flattened it on a shirt, which turned out nice. But really. She needs a job, I thought. Esme and I dozed. In dreams sometimes, I mislay Esme. A book I read on how to be a mother said that when you first have a kid, dreams like these are normal, anxiety draining off. Once I dreamed I put her on a shelf and she rolled off; I couldn't catch her. That afternoon I dreamed I was at T.J.Maxx, looking for her under piles of discount clothes, saying: she has to be here.

Around 5:30 Mike Cleary knocked on the door. I answered it, groggy. He was on his way out of town. He'd come to say good-bye. I would have been pissed off if he hadn't maybe. This turned into a reason for Lupe to drop in. "Hi," she waved at Mike. "Nice surprise to see you again."

And she was off and running about the FOR SALE sign. How she and Arturo had looked at a house in a *colonia* where her sister's son-in-law lived. But the problem with *colonias* was sewage. "They think we live like it's Mexico City right here," she told Mike, "but we are American."

Mike Cleary's entree. He loves sewage. He pointed out once that the word *septic* means poison. This makes sense: *anti*septic, the cure. Right now he told Lupe, "If *colonias* were anywhere but a few hundred miles from the border, the EPA would be on them like white on rice."

Lupe said, "We lifted a sewer lid and saw all kinds of trash down there, if you believe it. *Tripas.*"

Treepahs.

I didn't know this word. I said so out loud.

Mike said, "Animal guts. Tripe."

Which got me thinking. *Tripas, treepahs. Greepay.* Maybe *greepay* was "grippe," a word my grandma used? I considered what Luann said about croup. Then I noticed Dannie coming up the sidewalk. What on earth now? I opened the door. "We're leaving," I told her, a lie.

She said, "I won't stay long. I have a date with my boyfriend."

Boyfriend?

Then it was silent. I wondered how far out of her way she drove to act this out—that we were so close we dropped in on each other. I watched her. She had on more makeup than usual. Red lipstick, which made her eye shadow seem brighter, the color of pool cue chalk. I said, "You know Lupe." Dannie held out her hand, but Lupe kept hers tucked under her arms. "This is Mike."

Mike shook Dannie's hand. He gestured at her jacket. "Aren't you hot?"

She gave him a big, fake smile, like someone had yelled: Cheese. She said, "I don't wear hairpins or high heels. Now if you ask me, *they* look un-comfortable. Say, I like your McCloud mustache."

Lupe straightened up, huffy. "What is McCloud?"

"A TV show, fifteen or twenty years old by now," Mike said, "the first urban cowboy." He looked at Dannie. "Thanks—not having much hair on my head, I'm a little vain about my mustache."

He was? He never said so. I didn't mind his looks though.

Dannie turned and lowered her voice. "I've been worrying about you, Little Hoover. It's the way Hector stares at you—here one night, then at work. He's sexual harassment waiting to happen."

I thought she'd made this up as a way to worry about me as a payback for me worrying about her, not to be indebted. Or to indebt me further, make us equals who worried about each other always. Mike glanced at me, curious. Lupe narrowed her eyes and stared at Dannie's head. I said, "You don't have the whole story. You don't know Hector like I do." Then Lupe gave me a look: I told you so. Whether she meant she'd told me about Hector or Dannie, I couldn't say. "Next time you have a work-related comment," I told Dannie, "wait until the morning."

Dannie looked crushed—her frame, shoulders, her spine.

"Stop it," I said. "Stop acting like you're in a bad movie."

She stared at me. "What movie?"

Before I could answer—that I meant bad acting, her responses exceeded prompts—she slipped out of eye contact and listened to a joke Mike was telling. When he got to the end, Lupe laughed. Dannie laughed, but her face looked flat as cardboard. I wondered if she was taking those—what-do-you-call-them?—psychotropic drugs. I looked down at Esme, and she opened her mouth and laughed with Dannie, Mike, and Lupe. The first time. Ha ha, an emission. Four months old, and she was pretending to laugh to fit in. Then she coughed, and I remembered to get my book off the living room shelf and look up croup. I found the book, the entry. True, babies could die from croup, and you did steam them in the bathroom. You knew it was croup because of "the distinctive cough," the book said, "not unlike the bark of a baby seal." I also looked up grippe, *greepay*, but they didn't have that. I went back to the kitchen and said, "Does anyone think Esme's cough sounds like a seal barking?" They all looked at me like I was crazy. Well, the only variable for anyone is how much and on what day. Sage Hearttsock once said her mental state was like a magnetic strip on a credit card that got demagnetized until she got Elavil to reorganize highs and lows. Me, I want to feel good and don't mind a trade-off, being sad now and then. Happiness is fly-by-night, and when you get it and for how long is God's business. Your part is the little fix-ups, which is the point of my job, helping kids decide what to save, what to scrap. Dannie was dropping hints about her bits of the undigested past mixing together like waste—reactive, festering. What could I do? Ignore it, I decided, and take Esme to the doctor.

F I V E

I called for an appointment, and the receptionist gave the phone to a nurse who said: "Is this an emergency?" Not exactly, I said. "Is the baby running a fever?" No. "Refusing food or liquids, turning blue or gasping?" No, she made a thick sound when she breathed. "Probably a virus," the nurse said. "The first nonemergency appointment we have is October 31." Weeks away— I said so. The nurse seemed to hold her breath. Then she barked, short yaps: "That's the best I can do." I pictured her on the other end, a Weimaraner on hind legs, wearing a white dress and starched cap. I'd been watching *Sesame Street.* I must have stayed too silent, thinking, because when she spoke, she said, "I'm sorry. But we're overrun because of HMOs." I said, "Really?" I had an HMO, ten bucks for the doctor, thirty for prescription. She said, "People with time on their hands think to themselves it's only ten dollars to come in, and the child isn't sick enough." So doctors' offices were filling up with people with too much leisure—this was the national health care crisis. I remembered a mother I'd met at Port Town High, waving her hands, saying her son's teacher didn't like his ideas, squelched his creativity. The mother needed intervention, I thought as I listened to her, not the son. Then she apologized for taking up time, saying she'd been tense lately because her youngest child was having his stools tested. This seemed vaguely interesting. What for? I asked. He's constipated, she said, and told me about collecting his shit in a cup, icing it down in a cooler, driving across town. I thought, Why not try prunes?

I told the nurse now, "I don't have spare time. Esme's not dying, but her breathing isn't normal."

The nurse said, "Those are my instructions. Call if there's a change in her symptoms."

The only change was her new habit—belly-laughing when I came near, flapping her arms and legs in a stationary fit that communicated: happy to see you. And she made noise when she slept, *poof-click*, the *click* like a trap door with a rubber gasket slapping shut. On October 31, I dropped her at Luann's and said I'd be back at 1:00 to take her to the doctor. Her breathing seemed so clear I wondered if we needed to go. Yes, I decided, thinking three weeks to get an appointment.

And when I got to Project Promotion, Creola had on a clown costume, red nose and wig, dotted pajama suit. Sage wore those black plastic glasses with a nose and mustache attached, but took them off as soon as she sat down. "We didn't dress for Halloween last year," I said. "Did we?"

Creola said, "Get yourself a straw hat, Delia, and you can be a scarecrow."

She always tells me I've lost weight. She can see it in my face, she says. I tell her I'm thirty-four now and the skin on my face is thinner. My bones stick out. But this doesn't cut it with Creola, who's twenty years older than me, sturdy and plump. And on my way to pick up grade sheets, I passed Hector. He wasn't in costume, not quite. He had on a T-shirt with a clenched fist and slogan: La Raza. Probably not a shirt he'd wear on a no-costume day because we discourage group-think based on race identity here, gangs. He also needed a haircut, like weeks ago.

"Can I talk to you away from work?" he said.

"About what?"

He shook his head no. "No." And walked away.

I gave this zero consideration. Because when I got back to my desk, the ex-stepfather of a girl named Veronica called and said he wasn't married to Veronica's mother now, and though they had kids in common Veronica wasn't one of them, and he had kids with a new wife so he couldn't help Veronica. But having raised her for years it concerned him she was running with a grown man and covered with hickeys. "Her mother don't give a shit," he said, "excuse my French." Poor Veronica, I thought. Makeup and short skirts, her silver jacket that says Sal's Saloon. Her IQ was high but her performance consistently low. Dyslexia test: negative. My theory is that she has a learning disability no scientist has named yet. Not to mention a longing-for-father complex, which translates to boy-craziness. I went to the class she was supposed to be in. She wasn't there. I asked if anyone in the room had seen her in the dorm or cafeteria the last few days. They hadn't. I got her mother's number from the office. The secretary said I could call Veronica's mother, but I couldn't give the number to Veronica. I asked, "What do you mean don't give Veronica her mother's phone number?" The secretary shrugged. "Her mother said not to."

I called her mother. Veronica wasn't there, she said. She herself couldn't come to Project Promotion to meet with me because she didn't have a car. She used her boyfriend's just to buy groceries. "I've been out of work," she told me. Obviously. "Veronica came home for a while and I'd lock her in, but she leaves out the window. I called Rafe's mother and told her I could have him arrested for statutory rape, so she needs to stop the *pinche* fucking going on over there."

While I was on the phone, Dannie walked in and sat in the chair across from my desk.

Veronica's mother sounded hoarse, like she'd been yelling. I said, "When you talk to a family member over and over about the same problem, you can get in a rut. You sound tired." Sympathy. Most parents try hard. "I don't have no more inner resources," Veronica's mother said, crying.

It must be easier to cry on the phone than in person, I thought, remembering my dad. I looked at Dannie.

"I tried to find someone to, you know, talk with her," Veronica's mother said.

Dannie was cracking her knuckles. I said, "You did? That's so smart."

"I called the police," Veronica's mother said. "I said, talk. She didn't break no law, so they couldn't arrest her. The policeman, he said, 'Lady, I feel sorry for you. You want to borrow my belt?'"

This was going nowhere. I decided to track down Veronica through her friend who's named Betty. Neither of them thinks this is funny—they've never heard of Archie Comics. And I gave Veronica's mother two phone numbers. Free family counseling at one place. Or twelve dollars a session at the other if you prove that's all you can afford by bringing in last year's tax return. "Go on. Make an appointment," I told her. She said, "Fine." But she didn't say: wait, let me get a pen.

I hung up.

Dannie said, "Little Hoover, I came to say I'm going to be moving because I have a watcha-ma-jig detector from the Radio Shack. My daddy used to own bad old apartment buildings, and sometimes he'd let my sister live in one if she collected rents, and he bought her a detector. I never go anywhere without my mine, and it went off, and the gas company came and said the whole place could blow if the gas line doesn't get fixed, and my landlady's doubling the rent."

It takes skill to find a new place and correlate the day you move into it with the day you leave the old place, not to mention paying a new deposit before you get the old one back. I'd be doing it soon myself. I wondered how Dannie would manage. And who'd rent to her and her dogs?

"The good news," she said, "is I found a place three blocks from you."

It crossed my mind to say, No, don't move so close. Of course I didn't. "Where?" I said.

She said, "It's next to the used car lot. My boyfriend has a duplex like yours, Siamese twin apartments joined down the middle. He lives on the other side. He's going to charge me two hundred and fifty dollars."

"This is the one you hit?" I asked.

She looked puzzled.

"Your boyfriend?" I said. "The one you hit? Or is this the one who was your friend?"

"The other one," she said. "The third one."

I thought about how she was trying to be heterosexual now, and I wondered if it was because of the murder, publicity like Janeway's true-crime book, everyone talking about Dannie's sex life and her cousin's take on it. Then something immediate crossed my mind: what happens if Dannie goes back to being gay, and the new boyfriend doesn't handle the news, and now he's her landlord, not to mention neighbor? I didn't say this. Was it my business? I needed to find Veronica. Go to Port Town High. Take Esme to the doctor. I said, "So what do you need?"

"Nothing," she said. "Bye now. I've got to help in TV and VCR Repair."

So I went to find Veronica's friend Betty, who was in Child Care Accreditation doing CPR on a pink rubber mannequin. I pulled her aside. "How long since Veronica hasn't been in the dorm?" Betty said, "Miss, she's staying with her boyfriend's parents. She eats there. She likes her boyfriend's mother." Maybe this was good, I thought. Three squares a day, a clean bed. For a while, she'd slept on the couch at some kid's house whose dad let runaway girls stay there. Strays. I said to Betty, "Maybe she's looking for a substitute family." This is an idea from social work books. Betty frowned. "They're using her for free babysitting, Miss. All the boys in that family got at least one girl pregnant before they turned eighteen. It's not a good family." I trusted Betty. I said, "If you talk to her, tell her I want to see her to make sure she's okay."

On the way out, I asked the teacher, "How's my intern, Dannie Lampass, working out?"

"Fine," the teacher said, "real bubbly. The students love her."

I popped into Mason Pratt's classroom, which was empty. He was grading tests. I asked, "How's my intern working out in here?" He's bald and skinny, close to retirement. He wears those royal blue zipped-up jumpsuits all old men in Texas wear. He looked thoughtful. "She has winning qualities, no doubt. She's smart about people. A natural-born psychologist," he said. He frowned. "Or salesman." All this in a tired, wary voice. He paused—like it was my turn to talk.

"What else?" I said.

He shook his head. "These kids make my heart hurt. I've done this kind of work for years."

I felt depressed. Given our student-teacher ratio, we didn't have heart-hurt to spare on the staff. I wondered how long we'd last, spread so thin. And in the back of my mind, a nagging reminder, a cinder-block outline: Port Town High. It's a new building—they hired an architect who specializes in prisons. They needed four social workers over there, not one, part-time. I thanked Mason and went to my office to call Caroline Blakely at Lee College. I wanted to ask about Dannie. I couldn't see how she'd ever made it to class, understood what pages to study, like that.

Her secretary connected me. "Hello, Delia," Caroline said. "How can I help you?"

If someone asks that as soon as they pick up—count on it—help is not free-flowing. I said, "I'm calling to see what you can tell me about Dannie. Her performance has been a little sketchy."

Caroline said, "Delia, be specific."

I said, "She didn't show up one day."

"Treat her like any employee. Give her a warning."

"She's seems unstable."

Caroline paused a long time. Then her accent—some old childhood part of herself—came on thick. Not a Texas accent, more like Scarlett O'Hara. "I know you're referring to the fact she's homosexual, Delia, and I'm person-ally quite clear on what the Bible says. But in this day and age we can't fire her for that." I was reeling from the idea she thought I wanted to fire Dannie for being gay, and I didn't get a chance to say: don't you paraphrase to me, the Gospel according to Caroline Blakely. She said, "None of us are without sin, and if she acts homosexual the best thing to do is act feminine yourself and be the positive role model she obviously grew up without."

So sane people thought this bullshit too. I collected my wits. I said, "Homosexuality is not a side-effect of a bad childhood." I'd read this in a book. "People who are gay have different genes." This wasn't exactly what the book said, but close. "In Indian culture, in every tribe except for Comanche, gays were considered sacred for being halfway between male and female."

Caroline said, "It seems like you get along with Dannie just fine."

I said, "But she seems messed up. She's starved for attention."

Caroline said, "Don't you think that comes with the territory?"

"Her parents' murder?"

Caroline paused. "I mean social work. People go into it because they've had social work themselves. They had a good experience with their social worker, and now they look up to the profession."

"That is the lamest thing I ever heard," I said, "but thanks for your input." I hung up before I could find out if I'd offended her. I sat there thinking I couldn't believe how mad she'd made me. Why? Maybe I liked my job, I thought, and didn't like her saying it made up for my lack.

I got into my car and drove to Port Town High. On the way, I remembered Dannie had a sister in Atlanta. This cheered me up because it meant if I did drag Dannie kicking and screaming through the school year and she graduated, or didn't, or got a job she wasn't ready for and screwed up, she wasn't my responsibility; I wouldn't have to answer for her. I couldn't tell if this was wise, paying attention to the boundary lines, like Sage says, or just passing the buck, ignoring the fact that, like my preacher says, referring to Matthew 13, useful seeds get mixed with weeds, and do-gooders ask if they should rip out the weeds, and Jesus tells them: are you crazy? you'll rip out the whole crop. For example, you put a zinnia in the ground and a nettle pokes up, you can't pull out the nettle without ruining the zinnia, which is to say we're tangled up in ways we can't see even if, above-ground, we do separate into categories, the helpful and useful versus the pesky and beside-the-point. It goes to show that being a Christian is like doing the Jane Fonda Workout with Yoga when she says to push your back to the floor and your hips toward the ceiling, a contortion, because you're always getting told to do unto others but also to take care of yourself with the self-help and boundaries, so you stretch the other way. And cramp up.

Also, I thought, getting out of my car—weaving my way through extra police cars in the parking lot on account of Halloween, which people think is a big gang day—there had to be standards. If Dannie wasn't qualified, why hadn't someone at Lee College failed her? How could I be the person not to rubber-stamp her and pass her on to a new level, another worried overseer?

Me, who hadn't even finished college.

When I got inside and went to my office, I found Miranda sitting in the dark. Probably her mother was still crying, her dad working long days. I turned on the lights. "Are you skipping?"

"Yes.

"I can write you a pass to get back into class."

"Don't," she said. "I want it on my record. What do I have to do to go to your other school?"

I said, "You'd need to get suspended, then expelled. Or drop out. Why?"

"I think I'd like to go there."

I said, "Miranda, you don't. It's not the school for you. A diploma from there is better than no diploma, but you'll have more options if you graduate from here. Why are you saying this?"

She said, "It's big and lonely here. It's smaller over there, right? You, you're there more."

"You can do some work over there for me for an hour or two a day—you can help in my office. I can get you credit for it starting next quarter. But I won't let you go to school over there."

"For pay?" she asked.

"No pay," I said. "You'd do it instead of a class."

She said, "Miss, when can I start?"

"As soon as we get the paperwork filed. Your mom or dad will have to sign on. But now you need to go back to—what? Biology class. And if you get a grade lower than a B, the deal's off."

She went back to class and I opened my box, three notes. One from a boy named Asa, asking to be moved out of Miss Winnicott's class because she never got him a textbook and how could he study? He'd flunked a test. Miss Winnicott does this every so often—overtaxed, I guess.

I had two notes from Sean.

The first, or I assumed it was the first: *Are you brave enough? I presume people care even if they don't give public demonstrations of concern.*

The second: *Are you afraid to meet me?*

I had an aide look him up on the computer. He was in physics. I told the aide to bring him to me. I thought about my own experience with physics. I never had good math at the reservation, not a drawback until I took algebra at the real school in Stites. That was the end of my career in the scientific and technical fields. I looked up Sean's grades. Four As, and a C+ in phys ed.

He stood in my door. "You want to see me?"

I said, "I wanted to see you last week, but I couldn't find you."

He shrugged. "I go to class maybe once a week, but I'm still on honor roll."

He was in the hardest classes we had here. Smart kids drop out because they're bored and then don't last at the manual jobs they qualify for, which is bad. People need work, not just for money. Being idle makes you pick your brain like a scab. When I lived in Idaho, I had to go to the prison to talk to a man about his son's custody, and I got dazed, staring at his face through Plexiglas, thinking I knew him, his expression. A week later eating lunch at the zoo, I realized he looked like a lion—too big for his cage, so bored he'd turned mean. I looked at Sean. Blond hair, tumbly curls, face as pretty as a woman's. I said, "What do you do all day if you're not in class?"

"Go home, watch TV, surf the Net."

"Your mom's not there?"

He nodded.

"What sites do you log onto?" I wasn't sure this was the lingo. I'd used the Internet just once.

He laughed, a fenced-in laugh. "You wouldn't want to know."

"Try me."

"Pussy dot com."

"Anything else?" I said. "Seems like you'd get a little bored looking at one site."

"Good answer." He laughed again. "I happen to think pussy's fairly interesting, but I see your point. You look at it all day, it can cause . . ." he paused, ". . . lethargy. I do have other interests."

"What?" I was thinking: what are they? Build on that.

"Jews."

The history of Jews? "What?"

He shook his head. "And I don't like blacks, or people who are friends with them."

It took me a minute to register this. He couldn't mean Esme, I thought. Who could hate a baby? But he might. Mention Mormons, I thought, and he'd hate everything having to do with me.

"I also don't have much to do with Mexicans."

Not me, I thought. I've fucked one.

I was scared, maybe.

Or burned out. I said, "We need to channel this interest in computers." Maybe he could take a class at Lee College, I thought. But there were problems that hobbies and classes couldn't fix. And counseling—no one ever went. Seemed like it would have to be your own idea anyway, if it would work. Maybe he needed to be around a man more—absent father-figure, hypermasculinity issues, that sort of thing. I'd read a book chapter about this. But I wasn't sure I believed it. I mean, I had an absent mother, but no one would call me hyperfeminine, would they? I remembered the first note Sean sent. I said, "Do you find other students hard to get to know?"

He stayed slumped in his chair.

"Because I can help you come up with strategies for making friends."

He rolled his eyes.

"You make a plan. Talk to two new people each day. Walk up, say one sentence that comes to mind. Like, that test wasn't so bad. Or, I see you got your hair cut." I'd read this in a book when I was fourteen and starting out at Stites High. I'd gone to the library and looked up shyness. After a week, people started making comments back. I've taught it to kids since. It helped Betty, and a girl named Shawna, and a big overweight kid, Maxwell. "If it seems hard at first," I said, "take a minute to think of a comment and jot it down. After a while people start talking to you and it comes natural. Every-one hangs back," I said. "They need permission to be friendly."

"I suppose you want us to role play now."

"If you want," I said. "It's good practice."

He said, "You look like a Goth wearing black clothes all the time. You need a face lift."

I thought for a minute before I answered. "You're going to have to bone up," I said. "This is one subject you're not good at." I'm not saying I didn't feel ugly. But it's not like he meant just me. He thought the world was ugly. I said, "We're going to meet next week, and meantime I'll nail you if you miss any more class. You're too smart to sit around the house all day."

He stood up. "Fair warning."

I said, "I'm not the enemy."

"And you want me to have a positive educational experience," he said.

"I'll walk you back to class."

Then I drove to Luann's to get Esme—across town, clipped lawns, spot-less driveways, to the edge of town, clapboard shanties. I thought that if you told people in nice houses with two cars, two parents and two kids inside, about these stray kids who decided that what they got from history class was an impulse to side with losers—Robert E. Lee and Adolf Hitler—they'd be offended I'd focused on the nonoptimistic side of public education. Or say,

Right, I saw something about neo-Nazis on Dan Rather, and get excited in the way Janeway Regan gets about true crime. Or a woman I met through my job in Boise who had a Ph.D. in neuropsychiatry. Every time she made small talk, she'd describe the plot of a made-for-TV movie about a killer. Maybe she needed to brush up against death to remind her she could die, and therefore feel thrilled to be alive. Not me. I'm thrilled as is. It's a statistical fact poor people die earlier, more accidents, more murder. Kids at Project Promotion say, Miss, I was gone because I went to my cousin's funeral, or my sister's boyfriend's. And bring me a funeral program with a kid's name on it.

I got to Luann's house, a white stucco bungalow she bought for four thousand dollars twenty years ago. I parked my car and went inside. I found myself telling her about Sean. She said, "It's a cry for help."

"Right," I said, "an ugly one." Ugly, I thought. I looked in the mirror above Luann's couch.

"Tell me," she said. "I raised three kids."

Her mother was sitting in the rocking chair. She lifted her arm like a TV Indian. "How."

Luann said, "She wants to know how you are."

"Fine," I said. And Esme and I left for the doctor's.

I sat forty minutes in the waiting room—my right ankle on my left knee to make a hammock-shape for Esme. I ran my fingers over her forehead to relax her. If her breathing had seemed better, it was worse now. A woman near me, holding a boy, asked, "Has she rolled over yet?"

I said, "By herself?" Dumb-sounding, I realized. "No."

"How old is she?"

"Almost five months."

"She should be rolling over." The woman sounded alarmed. "Do you put her on her stomach?"

Esme was a spitting-up baby. The book said some babies didn't spit up, and some did and outgrew it. I didn't put her on her stomach because it made her spit up more often and lay her face in it.

"You should," the woman said, "because she'll have underdeveloped muscles on one side and she'll never learn to roll over." She stared at me. "Aren't you worried she hasn't rolled over yet?"

I said, "I'm sure she will by the time she goes to prom." I didn't look at this woman again.

A nurse called out, "Tandela." She meant us. "I call her Esme," I said, as we hustled into the examining room.

We took her temperature, her heartbeat. "Her airways don't sound good," the nurse said.

I said, "What do you mean?" And before I realized it: "She might die?"

The nurse glanced at me. "No. But it needs to be cleared up."

When the doctor came in, he said, "I always say young mothers don't know enough and overlook potentially severe problems, and mothers in their thirties know too much and convince themselves the baby has every rare disease and get mad if I disagree. I'm surprised here. This is abnormal."

I didn't know if he meant my lack of astuteness or Esme's breathing.

He said, "It's a precursor to asthma. She'll probably outgrow it. But right now she needs treatment." He flipped through her chart. "She should have been in for a checkup once a month."

"What do you mean?" I was feeling like I wasn't my age yet—thirtyish and projecting hypochondria.

"We like to see newborns every month," he said, "until they're six months old."

My book hadn't said so. Maybe the doctor who delivered the baby was supposed to tell me. I said, "I didn't get her until she was two months old, and we came in then. We came when she was three months old, for more shots." So we'd missed the four-month appointment, I thought, big deal, and the nurse had put me off when I tried to make this appointment. But I felt guilty.

He called in a prescription for a machine with a mask I'd hold over Esme's face a few times a day. "Don't be alarmed if her heart seems to almost jump out of her chest, because that's how we get the mucous out. The medical supply company will deliver the machine and teach you."

I said, "I'm a quick learner." And left. I was upset at the doctor, at myself for not bringing Esme in sooner. As for watching her heart jump out of her rib cage—I'd have to wait and see.

On the way home I stopped by the courthouse, parked the car, unstrapped Esme's car-seat carrier, brought her inside, and asked the guard by the door where the probate clerk was. He called someone on his walkie-talkie. Turned out I was in the wrong building. I was supposed to be in the courthouse annex, down the street next to Pep Boys Auto Supply. I put Esme back into the car. She fussed. "Hush up," I said, not in my calmest voice, and I drove down the street, parked, got her out again. I found the probate clerk, a dark-haired woman with a big bust. I said, "I need to look at probate forms. I have to file a petition to probate an estate in Ohio, but they said I could use your forms." She said, "We don't have forms. You need to go to the library and check out a book about doing probate, and they have the forms in it— you Xerox them."

Esme was screaming. A person standing in line behind me said, not to me particularly, maybe to someone else, to the air, the universe: "Shut that baby up." And Esme cried in the car on the way to the library and inside the library. I checked out two books. *How To Live and Die with Probate. How to Probate an Estate with Forms and Checklists*. I drove home. I didn't get a chance to study the books right away, because as soon as I got inside the phone rang. The man who was going to deliver Esme's breathing machine wanted to set up a time. I'd just hung up when the phone rang again. "Chuck Hayden here." Landlord. "I wonder if I could show the house."

It was his house. "Why ask me?" I said. "Whenever you like."

"Right now? We're around the corner in my car. I'm calling from my cell phone."

Waiting for Chuck to get there and show the house, I fed Esme strained peas, which not only improved her shit but she didn't spit them up. I spooned them in, thinking of a nursery rhyme: pease porridge nine days old. Easy to picture if you've seen split-pea soup that's set too long.

Maybe because I was thinking about pease porridge and looking across the street at Janeway's big house with its window grilles, a fortress, I remembered a history class I'd had, how I'd liked the Middle Ages best. I identified with serfs. The textbook said, what experts overlook is that most people didn't own land and spent all their time worrying about getting enough to eat, grain and peas, meaning there wasn't time for deep thought. Since then I've read more books about the Middle Ages. I even had a dream. This was after I'd watched the *Jim Lehrer Newshour,* a man talking about millennial beliefs and that sect in California where everyone wore turtlenecks and Nikes and offed themselves so they could meet up with a comet. In my dream we were waiting for the end because life was hard. I was gleaning, which is picking up wheat that rich people's serfs drop—old maids and widows get to. Then I watched a boy getting his head hit with a stick because he dropped too much, and I had an idea that anyone who'd had his head hit much would naturally believe the end was near, the heavens collapsing, because that's how his brain felt. But after I woke and thought about it, it didn't seem brilliant, this idea that anyone who believed in Armageddon was a person who'd had his head stove in, though I did read once that researchers found a link between sick people and a tendency to believe in civilization's decline. People's bodies fall apart. They think the world is falling apart too.

I'd finished wiping peas off Esme's chin when these people wandered through, Chuck and a middle-aged couple. I turned on the TV and sat on the couch with Esme. The woman—blue suit, purse as big as a suitcase—stopped in her tracks, held her hand on her breast. "What a picture you make, like a special madonna." She meant like classical art, not the pop star Madonna, though she does have a dark-skinned kid. I don't love the word *special* either. Special Olympics, I think. Then she said, "I admire you." A lady in my church says this too. Some people want to keep the races separate. Others don't, but go around telling me I'm brave to break the rules and raise a black baby. To them, I say: it's braver just being black. I told this woman now, "I did it for selfish reasons." Before she could stop looking confused and ask me to explain—tell her I didn't get it how people could wait five years and spend tons more money to make sure the baby they got was white—I jarred Esme to make her fuss so I could focus on Esme and ignore this woman, who was admiring my furniture now, which I buy at yard sales mostly. "I love collectibles," she said. Maybe she was friendly, but what I saw was someone who could smooth her way out of trouble. Yet I didn't want to piss her off because if she bought the house and I could stay, and she didn't raise the rent, I would. I wanted Arturo and Lupe to stay.

She said, "Our son is moving to town to do public relations for Exxon."

They need it, I thought.

"We decided we'd put a down-payment on a house for him to live in. A duplex seemed like a good idea, because the money the other unit generates will help recuperate the remodeling costs."

"If you keep a renter," the landlord told her, "keep Delia. She's the best renter I ever had."

What did I think? Arturo and Lupe, good-bye.

S I X

"I cooked fish and didn't flush the toilet," Lupe said, "to make the toilet look broke." She did this yesterday to unnerve another set of buyers the landlord brought by. I read in a magazine that if you want to sell a house you should bake cookies with vanilla extract and keep your bathroom clean, so it makes sense, this opposite strategy: fish and pee. Myself, I'd sat on the couch and blocked out people traipsing past, saying I don't like that closet, this room would look better with drapes. Right now, 7:30 a.m., I stuffed Pampers into a suitcase. I'd already packed jars of baby food, spare bottles, a brush for washing bottles, a carton of wipes. I was thinking about where to put the breathing machine—nebulizer, the guy from the medical supply company called it. You plugged it in, put a mask on Esme, poured a vial of albuterol, which is like speed, into a whirlpool that spun drops toward the mask. When Esme finished inhaling, I'd put my hand on her chest and her heart raced. The idea was for her to get rid of old phlegm. And she had new formula, twenty bucks a can, to keep her from getting new phlegm. I needed to run the machine three times a day, which would be impossible tonight when we'd be in the sky, flying.

Esme lay on the bed. I combed my hair. Lupe sat next to Esme. "What is this trip to Chicago for?"

"Cleveland," I said, "my mother died. I have to decide what to do with her things, her money."

"Money?"

"Probably not enough to pay her bills," I said.

"We have that in common then."

Money situations going from bad to worse, she meant. Esme was eating solids now, strained yams, peas, pears, apples, which meant, thank God, she drank less formula. But I was putting this plane ticket on a credit card and hadn't paid off the last one. I'd get to Cleveland after midnight and take a cab to Harriet Mosley's—forty bucks, the cab company I'd called had quoted me. Hopefully, as the lawyer, Mr. Johns from Brask & Greenstein, had said, this would be my last trip, because I'd filed the order authorizing letters of administration, which, once I went to the hearing and the judge signed on, would free me to sell my mother's trailer. I'd also filed a form for appointment of resident agent, which meant the lawyer could go to court instead of me when we filed the next forms: the list of claims and affidavit regarding debts. I had to buy an ad in the Cleveland paper saying if my mother owed anyone they'd better let us know, and I was required by law to buy insurance for the amount my mother's stuff is worth in case I'd abscond. I'd borrowed from Food/Miscellaneous for months into the future. And knew I'd waste money traveling—eating, running to 7-Eleven for aspirin, those pricey minibottles on the plane.

Lupe said, "Should I water your flowers?"

After Lupe got home from her job at Furr's Cafeteria, she was going to drive me to the airport. Dannie had asked if she could house-sit. I didn't want her inside. I told Lupe, "Dannie will water my plants."

Lupe said, "The *lesbiana* who begs for food."

Dannie did sometimes show up when I was cooking and say, "My God, that looks good," and let on she hadn't eaten in thirty-six hours and when she did it was a cheese sandwich from the gas station.

"Why can't Mike?" Lupe asked.

I was putting a jacket on Esme. "He doesn't live here."

Lupe looked puzzled.

"He lives in Lake Charles, Louisiana," I said.

She still looked puzzled. "Why?"

"I don't know. He grew up there. He has a kid there."

She gasped, like we were in a soap opera. "*Dios mio!*"

"What?"

"Married," she said.

"Divorced," I said. "It's a grown kid. He doesn't like little kids, avoids them like the plague." But I was thinking about what she said. What if he was married in Lake Charles, and I was R & R on the side? I hadn't thought of it before. Lie to me about this, I'd tell him, and I'll kill you.

"He likes *la bebita*," Lupe said. "So lucky. Nice man. Divorced. That's good." Then she said, "Delia, when Esme walks I could babysit. You could work, and when Esme wants me to hold her I can sit and she can get in my lap and my knees won't ache. You pay me cash, no checks."

A nice idea, but who knew where we'd be? Still, if Lupe lived close maybe she could be my sitter. Then I wouldn't have to drive to Luann's and back, morning and night, forty-five miles a day. I didn't like leaving town and being swallowed up by trees—cemetery-type trees, cypress, something to do with Jerusalem—that people planted here a hundred years ago to block the everlasting wind. A mile from Luann's is a plank house behind rows and rows of these trees, and a stockade fence posted BEWARE MEAN DOG, a Confederate flag flying, which might signify school spirit, because a town nearby, Clute, has a football team, the Clute Rebels, who use it for a logo. Or it might stand for the Holy Knights of Midnight Scare Tactics, like that. A few years ago, Luann said, she went up and down the road ripping down KKK posters from electrical poles. She's a good babysitter except for her sadness about those years raising kids without a dad or money, and now she has her mother's money but her mother is the opposite of a kid—growing backward in time, more frail and grouchy, harder to take care of as each week passes.

I packed up Esme and headed out that way.

When I got there Luann asked, "Do you want me to bathe the baby before you pick her up?"

"I can do that tonight," I said. We had a few spare hours after school, and I'd planned to wash her and put her in the plush fuchsia sleeper Sage had bought. It was bound to be cold on the plane, not to mention in Cleveland in the middle of the night. Also, I'd read in the Lifestyle section of the newspaper, advice to new moms heading out on vacation, dads too, that the cuter your baby looks on the airplane, the fewer annoyed glances other passengers give you if she cries when her ears hurt. This was no vacation, but I was nervous. About motion sickness too. Once, when I was getting a muffler put on at a place called Auto Depot and sitting in the waiting room, the owner—tall, loud, he does his own TV commercials, shouting prices—came over to look at Esme. "Cool baby," he'd said. "Let me hold her." What could I say? Everyone stared. He jiggled her up, down, up, like for an ad: here at Auto Depot where kids matter. Esme spit up on him.

"If you have travel tips," I told Luann now, "pass them on."

She said. "Sing songs to her the whole way."

Her mother started singing, low and croaky, something la la la weeping willow.

I left for work. Project Promotion, first stop. Inside, Hector, Sage, and Creola were clustered in the mail room. They stopped talking when I walked in. Clearly I'd been the topic. You might say they'd been discussing me with loving concern. If so, why clam up and stare into space?

Sage said, "I love these cool, gray mornings."

I went along with the weather talk. "I like sunlight." True. I never got warm until I left Idaho.

"But we need rain," Sage said, "though a hurricane would be too much."

"Enough," Creola said. "Delia, are you taking the baby?"

"Yes."

Sage said, "We didn't know your mother died, you see. We would have sent flowers."

She meant to the funeral, I suppose. Six people there, total. Me, Harriet, Duster, the minister, and he'd asked his secretary to sit in a pew. The minister didn't know my mother. It was Harriet's church and she'd asked him to preach. There's no rule against it—like for a wedding where you have to belong or at least go to a marriage class first. The other person was a guy Duster invited, who wore a black T-shirt and jeans—dirty, ripped, but probably the only outfit he had. Who was he? Duster's friend. He'd never met my mother. I should talk. I'd met her once. Duster wore a Hawaiian shirt. Me, a black dress. "It wasn't that kind of funeral," I said.

Hector was watching me. "Can I drive you to the airport?"

"I've got it covered."

"Pick you up?"

"My neighbors Lupe and Arturo are."

Sage frowned. She was lagging behind in the conversation. "I didn't realize you had to take the baby."

"I couldn't afford not to. Babies fly free. I don't want to leave her."

Sage said, "You're so hard-boiled. I mean this as a compliment."

Hector turned to go to his office. Before he shut the door, he said, "The student you were looking for, Veronica Chavez—her boyfriend's parents said she and her boyfriend's brother ran away."

I tried to read his mood. "Do they know where they went?"

"They seem to think Salt Lake City."

"Maybe they know someone there." I was thinking: north, cold. Imagining what Veronica would do if she got scared. Not prostitution exactly. But she'd be so relieved to eat and get in out of the wind, she'd donate herself. Women all over the world do this when plans fail and fail.

Creola walked me to my office. "It's good you're bringing the baby with you. Take it one task at a time."

"You mean when I get to Cleveland?"

She said, "It's sad, and it's work—wrapping up someone's business."

I said, "I don't know how sad it'll be. I didn't know my mother."

"A lifetime of sadness boiled down to a dry pot then," Creola said, "boiled down to a weekend packing up rummage for Goodwill. What'll hit you is that there aren't any second chances."

I was curious where this advice came from. "Are your parents living?"

"Nope. It took me years to pay off my daddy's funeral," she said. "I signed on for the cheapest one—nice, but the economy version. The Holy Ghost doesn't care what you spend on a coffin."

My interest picked up. "How much did the funeral cost?"

"Twenty-four hundred. Had to sign a lien on my car."

"When did you do this?"

"1991."

"Have funerals gone up?"

She looked confused. "I don't know."

"I appreciate your help," I said. I buckled down to work then, changing the shift schedule. I arranged to have Dannie assist in classes where teachers knew her. She'd help drive Mason's kids to Port Town High so they could use the shop tools. I scheduled her for Child Care Accreditation. I canceled my Expectant Mothers class, also Anger Management, which Dannie had been slated to teach solo. I called her—her new number. "You have fewer hours next week."

She said, "Are you going to be home later? I have a going-away present."

Her mother's rosary. I didn't know this at the time, though. I said, "I'll be gone just a few days."

"But among Yankees."

A Texas phobia—fear of people from the Northeast. "I'll be fine." I hung up. I'd forgotten to ask about her new apartment, I realized. Maybe she was on an even keel. If she did drop by, I decided, I'd compliment her on seeming calm. Seeming calm, as opposed to being calm, is a first step. I learned this when I left home. People rented apartments, I knew, but how did they get money for them? How would I find pots, pans, a bed, a dresser? The woman from the county who helped me fill out Pell Grant forms—she had black hair and a wispy trace of mustache—gave me the want ads from the newspaper. A few weeks later, when we were done filling out grant forms, she gave me a present, a record by Holly Near. I'd never heard of Holly Near, but she has red hair and sings songs that, as the album cover said, life-affirm. Later I got a record player from a pawn shop and listened and waited for the songs to take. I also tried to pray. But then I'd stop praying because I wanted clear answers. I wanted God to move a tree branch or knock a picture off a wall. I still don't like Holly Near. You'd never catch yourself humming to that music. But I see you could get improved thoughts from happy music if you could stand it. Or by getting on your knees and making contact with the will-not-freak-out forces, which might be external—I mean, God—or internal and just not activated yet. I'm saying that how you act turns into how you are. Act useless, and you turn into a place where bad ideas land.

I thought this as I pulled up at Port Town High, where I had an appointment with Sean's mother. But when I got to my office, Miranda was there. I said, "Why are you skipping class again?"

"I messed up," she said. "I went ahead and had sex."

I set my purse down. "With who?"

"Esteban."

"How old is he?"

"Sixteen."

"Is he in school? Does he have good grades?"

She said, "He's a junior. He was on honor roll last year."

"It would have been better to wait," I said, "but the important thing now is condoms."

"That's just it."

A woman with platinum hair stood in my doorway. She smiled. "I'm Sean's mother."

"I'll be with you in a minute." I shut the door. I said, "Miranda, I can't say anything else about birth control. It's against the law. I could lose my job. But you need to research this subject."

She looked scared. "Could you talk to me after school, Miss, over the phone?"

"You mean call you from my home phone? I think it's still illegal."

"Please, I can't ask my mother."

"I'll call you about five and we'll have a vague discussion."

She frowned and left.

I let Sean's mother in. "Call me JBD, everyone does," she said. "I'm glad Sean is self-sufficient, because I travel for my job." Her job was pep-talking teams of people who sold computer packaging, she said. "His sister is self-sufficient too. It never bothers either one of them that I'm not home. Their grades have actually improved. Of course we moved here, and the curriculum's not hard. But it's better for them to be home alone at night here, rather than in Houston."

I said, "Have you met your daughter's boyfriend?"

She smiled. "She's very pretty. Naturally, men notice."

I said, "She wants to be a nurse."

Sean's mother said, "I try to discourage that—the hours, the pay."

"But you work long hours."

"I'm surrounded by fun people."

I was in over my head, I thought. I was a good social worker for Project Promotion, but Port Town High needed a different social worker for kids who don't have all the outward signs they're messed up. But what are the outward signs? JBD sat across from me in a red dress with brass buttons. She'd had her hair done at a good place, streaks and highlights. I'd lost track of why I'd even asked her to come. I took a deep breath and remembered. "Sean is skipping classes."

She said, "He had all As last term."

"Except for phys ed." I stared at her eye shadow, taupe shading into fawn.

She said, "If he skips, why doesn't he get penalized?"

We do have an attendance policy. But it hardly affected a kid like Sean, who never missed days, just hours now and then. I said, "He needs challenges. He's understimulated at this school."

She said, "That's your problem."

"Maybe he should be in private school."

She raised her eyebrows. "They pay you to say that?"

I said, "Do you even care? Have you asked him what he's looking at on the computer always?"

She said, "You have a fear of technology."

I said, "Let's call Sean in here."

We waited a few minutes while an aide hunted him down. I was thinking how to tell her what he'd said about Jews, blacks, Mexican-Americans, pussy. All healthy boys are interested in pussy, she might say. Then Coach walked in. I'd hung up the sign: Conference In Session. But I guess he thought we were killing time, coffee klatch. He told us about his football team—he'd lost two senior starters and was struggling on with greenhorns. JBD smiled. Coach loves to talk. I tune him out. JBD interjected her cope-with-it clichés. "The only constant is change," she said.

"There's some diversity of opinion on that subject," Coach said. Me, Delia Arco from Idaho, I'm not pro-Yankee or anti-southerner. But I do get bored with how slow some people talk down here, how long it takes to say something that's not even interesting. "Take the minorities," he said, "we have to get used to the idea of them filling niches. The Spanish are like hackberries."

He meant Mexican-Americans. We don't have students from Spain.

He said, "Oak trees are sturdy and will grow, one here, another over there. There aren't many oaks but they're big. Hackberries reproduce fast. They don't get big but there are more of them."

You could see where he was going with this. I wondered what he thought blacks were—sumacs?

Then Sean showed up. Coach left. Sean sat down.

"Hi, honey," his mother said.

He looked at her. "I thought you had to be in Seattle."

She glanced at her watch. "I do have to leave pretty soon."

I said, "Sean, tell your mom what you do when you skip."

He said, "I wanted to tell you I took your advice. It was corny, but I thought, what the hell."

"Sean, your language." His mother.

He ignored her. "I picked out kids like you said, went up to them and made comments. The first day people acted like—whoa, the geek, he's talking. But after a few days some of them said hi back. With girls I notice it's important to remember their names and remark on it if they've changed their hairstyle or something. I finally made a best friend and we're exactly alike."

"So you have helped him after all," JBD said, standing. "It's time for me to go."

After she left, I said to Sean, "Tell me about your new friend."

"His name is Conrad Okuda. He moved here from San Francisco. His dad is Japanese. His mother is originally from Texas—Tyler or somewhere—and divorced. That's how we're alike."

I took this as a good sign, because lately there'd been Asian-bashing, Vietnamese-bashing especially.

He said, "We don't look alike, but inside but we're the same."

Not exactly, I thought, no one is. But he did seem better. "Right," I said.

And I left work that day thinking I was good at my job.

I stopped by the post office. I had a card from Mike saying he'd be here on the 10th. CALL IF THIS IS NOT OK. And his phone number. In terms of the is-he-or-isn't-he question—married—supplying his phone number was a good sign, unless it was for a mobile phone he used only in his truck. I also had a letter from Dad. A clipping about a school banning books by Maya Angelou. His note: "Delia, planning a trip to see you. Sorry U have to do your mother's business alone." It struck me odd he was planning a trip. He's not a tight-wad, but a question that embarrasses him is what his job is. He used to teach at the reservation school. He works for loggers. He buys and repairs used Airstreams but never has much luck reselling them. He's a hunting guide. My point is, he doesn't have a steady income—I've never known him to travel.

I drove to Luann's and got Esme.

When I got home, I gave her a bath. She's so good-looking. When I first got her—when the social worker handed her to me—I unwrapped the blan-ket and stared at her. *Magnificent.* That was the word that popped into my head. I held her in a towel in my lap as I dialed Mike's number.

When he picked up, I said, "This is Delia. Are you in the same time zone?"

"Hey," he said, "you got my postcard."

"Are you at work?" I thought I heard the sound of a beer opening, pop. I wondered if drinking would be it, his flaw.

"I'm balancing my books but watching a TV show too. I did bid on a job today."

"You work out of your house?"

"I couldn't hope to keep both a house and an office clean," he said.

So now it seemed rude to blurt: better not be married, you son of a bitch. "I'll be gone on the 10th."

He didn't answer.

"Out of town, Ohio. I have business."

"Something to do with work?"

"Legalities. My mother died without a will."

"I'm sorry," he said. "When did she die?"

"Months ago. Memorial Day weekend."

He said, "That was right after I met you—you never said a word. You don't talk about her."

"I'm talking now," I said. "I didn't know you that well then."

He said, "Could we get together in a week or so? There's something I want to ask you."

I wondered, what? Something kinky maybe, like he'd read in *Penthouse*?

I almost said so. Then reconsidered. It's like *I* had a dirty mind. Or too much contact with the not-so-sunny side.

"Are you flying?" he asked. "I love to fly. What about the baby?"

Why did people keep asking this? I gritted my teeth. "I'm taking her."

"Is someone going along to help you?"

"Who would pay for the ticket?" I said. "Who would go?"

"I might have gone, if you'd asked. What about your friend the dyke?"

"You're not supposed to say 'dyke,'" I said, "unless you are one."

"I know that." He sounded like he had hurt feelings now. "I'll see you in a week or so."

I said, "All right already." I'm not a phone person. Not a talker period.

Which might be why my conversation with Miranda turned glitchy. "Is this a good time for our discussion?" I asked. Her mom wasn't home but she was babysitting her cousins, Lidia and Angelica. She didn't know how to operate the phone. "Miss," she said, "do you know how to turn the speaker on a speaker phone off?" I didn't. I didn't stay vague either. She'd shoo Lidia and Angelica out the door, and I'd get to the point fast. How close to your period was this? Was Esteban a virgin too? One of you needs to got get tested for STDs then. Having sex is an adult decision, and that's why you have to act like an adult. In the future, his penis shouldn't be anywhere near you unless it's covered in rubber. She said, "Miss, wait, I think Lidia is inside listening."

I hung up, feeling bad. Miranda needed to go to a clinic, to get a checkup and patient-education pamphlets. Also, I'd broken the law now. Not only am I not supposed to discuss sex, even when I teach expectant mothers, I'm required to notify parents if kids tell me they've had sex.

I was still worrying about this, on the back burner I mean, when Dannie came by to give me her mother's rosary. "To keep you safe on your trip, Little Hoover. I know how it is to lose a parent."

She'd lost both. I just shuddered. I thought about her cousin. "Were your parents close to your cousin?" I asked. "Did he grow up spending time at your house? Do you hear from him now?"

"You've been reading up on me," she said, eyes narrowed. "Curiosity."

"It killed the cat," I said, casual. I did wonder what her cousin had been like, what premeditating led to that irreversible minute. Yet if I thought too long I kept coming back to one idea: wanting details was wanting gossip. Policemen, people on the jury, they had to know. I didn't. Besides, if I got the inside view of a murderer, maybe a *People* profile on the life and times of Jeffrey Dahmer, I thought: okay, those people exist, but no point in obsessing, since you may as well enjoy living, try not to be too scared until your last choked-off breath. I held Esme close.

Dannie said, "I'm not in contact with my cousin. I couldn't be."

He'd ruined her life, so she hated him. Or he brought back memories. Sad? Vile?

Her face crumpled to a frown. "Call me when you get there. You and Esme, you're everything to me." She set the rosary on my table. At the time I thought: not there, not where we eat.

I wrapped it up, put it in a drawer, then reconsidered and hauled it to the shed. I wasn't thinking about it by the time I headed for the airport, Lupe behind the wheel, Arturo and Esme in back. And when we passed the intersection to Highway 45, Lupe started saying how fifteen to thirty women, depending on who's counting, had turned up dead or missing along this highway. They're not looking for one guy. The police ran a computer search for registered sex offenders in the area and turned up eighty names. There's prisons nearby, see. I got to the airport and hopped out with my suitcase and Esme in her car-seat carrier and waved good-bye. Then I had to take Esme out of the car seat, and she cried as I carried her through metal detectors and sent her car seat through the x-ray. I was trying to block the idea of fifteen to thirty women, gone, missing, mutilated, a grave site Lupe had described, fresh dirt, fake flowers, someone's underpants on top. Then I sat and coddled Esme back to sleep, and waiting to board, I read the *Port Town Sun,* Janeway's editorial about deadbeat dads, inspired, she wrote, by a report about a hospital orderly who'd scratched his son with an HIV-contaminated needle to avoid paying child support. She should move to Hollywood with Marla, I thought, hire out as a source of ideas for bad TV.

Once we were in the sky without the umbrella of clouds, slipping through the on-and-on of nighttime, Esme woke and started vomiting, calmly, politely. Understand, baby spit-up doesn't smell like much besides what the baby ate, in this case pears. But most people don't know that. So it seemed kind when, out of the dark, from the seat beside me, a voice said, "I have a six month-old at home." He was an architect, he said. When Esme fell asleep, he bought us drinks.

I never did see his face.

He asked where I worked. Had Esme rolled over yet? A nick of worry opened up. No, I said. What nicknames do I call her? Little Sister, I said, also Pea Pod and Missy Moo. He told me he called his daughter Pigley, and his wife who'd quit being a lawyer to stay home with the baby told him not to or she'd grow up anorexic. He paused and said, "I saw you boarding with the baby and wondered . . ."

I was finishing my second drink. "Wondered what?"

"Never mind."

"Go ahead and ask." This is unlike me. Must have been drunk.

"She's an adopted baby, right. Why adopt? I work with this woman who adopted a Chinese baby, and I wondered then. If you're female and want a baby, why not just go get pregnant?"

"There's many ways to look at that question," I said, chatty, expansive, like Coach. "But what it boils down to is, I didn't trust having another parent in the picture—unknown factor, wild card."

"I'll be damned," he said.

First time I'd put it like that. Soon as I said it, I knew it was true. Then Esme woke and—remembering Luann's advice, but I'm no singer—I prayed in her ear, low, rhythmic. I wanted a semblance of lullaby. I prayed quietly because I didn't want to flip out the guy next to me, make him think I was a cult member. But on a never-see-the-light-of-day level, I was scared how to get around in Cleveland, if my showdown with Duster would turn nasty, what it all might cost in the end. I made up peaceful thoughts, people saying hello, good-bye. If someone isn't glad to see someone, they don't let on in an airport. Warm display required: happy to see you come, grieve to see you go. Even if this isn't so. What prayer did I hum? Thank you that we go on living, surviving, among people who come, go, arrive, leave, our lives among people coming and people leaving, I meant to say, but I was tired. Came out wrong. Among people's leavings. Amen.

SEVEN

When people leave a plane they follow arrows to baggage claim. But how they know which conveyor belt to stand near, beats me. I stopped and read a TV screen filled with white code. ATLA 351 2:51. NWK 113 4:15. Nothing about suitcases. So I followed a woman wearing a black dress with scraps of red fringe stuck all over it at odd angles—like a kid with a glue gun had been in charge of decorating. I'd seen her in first class, those soft, wide seats. She'd know where to go, I thought. She got to Baggage Claim and stopped. I stopped too—hoped to recognize a few more people from our plane. But we'd traveled in darkness. Then beep-beep, and suitcases tumbled out a chute. The lady in the fringed dress picked up her tapestry-weave bag. I saw my suitcase roll by, cream-colored with steel corners that my dad bought when he got out of the army in 1964, also the portable baby bed Lupe's niece loaned me and, before I could grab it, Esme's car seat rolled by, also my canvas bag dripping shampoo; I could smell it. And, I don't understand, one of my shoes I'd polished to wear to court had fallen out of the bag and spun alone on the belt. I picked it up, repacked it. Then a man grabbed my suitcase, said he owned a car and would take me anywhere. This might be a legit business—with permits, a license. But it sounded expensive. You'd get in and he'd charge blackmail to let you out again. "Shove off," I told him. I rented a cart for two dollars, jiggled Esme, and waited outside for a taxi.

This would be the second time I'd ridden in a taxi. The first time, twelve years ago, I let some Good Samaritan who had plenty of cash at a bar shove me into one and pay the driver to take me home. I was too drunk to wander around. I was careless back then, but lucky. Now someone butted ahead of me, a woman in a trench coat yelling, "Taxi." An airport guard sent her to the back of the line. She'd seen too many movies maybe—planes, fog, rushing into crowded streets. But real life won't speed up for you even if you are in trouble. Finally I was in a taxi, telling the driver, "Take Clark Avenue to West 130th." I didn't know these roads, but Harriet Mosley had told me to say this—give the impression I was from here and no wild goose chase around the back of the airport. The driver was a newcomer to Cleveland too. He wore a turban. "Wattage?" I shook my head like I do in Texas when people talk Spanish fast. He pointed over the seat. "Wattage?" Suddenly it came in clear. "She'll be six months on January fifth."

He talked more and I nodded. Janeway Regan once told me she can't stand it when she travels and people strike up conversation. "I frost them," she said, sitting on my porch. I got the picture—someone asked a leading question, and she answered a degree or two too cold, and that person never snapped back. I do minimize talking, but not rudely, having once or twice made an offhand comment myself, and to a person who stared at me as if my lack of good sense was catching, the way poison ivy is, for instance, if you stand close to someone who has it. But I had to strain to understand this guy. I needed to save myself for the night ahead, cleaning up Esme and putting her to sleep. Also, in the morning, court. A low-energy plan, I decided, was to say "yes," also "I agree" for variety's sake. Right now, he said my baby was attractive. "I agree," I said.

"Most American babies are not," he said. "Light skin and no hair, those blue veins on their heads."

I nodded. "Yes, this is true."

The meter was going up—forty-three dollars by the time we got to the trailer park entrance. Inside, I tried to direct him. I was looking for two trailers, Harriet's with a white lattice porch, next to my mother's with no porch, just steps. I looked for the gold car. I couldn't remember what Harriet drove. Then I realized I was looking out the wrong window. We'd run up four dollars driving past Harriet's maybe ten times, but with my head pointed the wrong way. Her porch glowed like a lit-up bird cage. "Here," I said. The driver helped me unload. I gave him two twenties and two tens. "Give me back five," I said, "and keep the rest." This would have been a good tip. He put all the money in his pocket. "No. I keep it. You had many baggage." I hoped Harriet would drive me back to the airport, and I'd pay her a set amount, no last-minute shakedown.

Harriet opened the door. "I couldn't get down to serious sleep until I knew you were in." She had on a pink robe that zipped up the front. Her face is broad, not pretty, but calm. Almost happy.

I said, like I did on the phone, "Are you sure you want us to stay here?"

She repeated herself, "Honey, you can't sleep over there."

We set up the baby bed. Lupe's niece had demonstrated how. "Turn while I crank," I said.

Harriet frowned. "I had no idea she was black."

I looked at her. "The baby? Is this a problem?"

Harriet paused. "No. She's cute enough."

If she wasn't, I wondered, would we have to leave? Still, it wasn't a planned speech Harriet had made, more like blurting. She'd been asleep, and now near-strangers, an Okie and an Okie's baby, were setting up furniture in her living room. I said, "Tomorrow we'll go next door."

She said, "Honey, you have to get rid of Duster first. He's in and out all the time. I do have a spare bedroom, but since my son's been up in Lansing I use it for my crafts. I moved the bed out."

"I'm fine on the couch." Harriet had put a fitted sheet over the cushions, draped a top sheet and blanket across the back. She set an afghan on a chair. "More covers if you want." When I'd come for the funeral last spring, I'd told Harriet I was waiting for a baby, waiting to adopt, and she said she hoped I'd get a girl. She'd wanted one, she told me, always wished her son was one. "It was hard teaching him to tee-tee," she said. "Can you imagine what I said when it came time for the birds and bees?" At the time I liked her mother-advice, even if it was the depressing hindsight kind, like Luann's: looking back now, I see I made mistakes. But being in her house felt nice, all the world's mess outside and, inside, neatness and hygiene. A misty deer-in-the-forest scene over the couch. Love My Carpet potpourri-scent wafting with other smells, coffee, bacon. But it being late, and me, tired, paranoid, and Harriet having said what a surprise Esme is black but she's cute, I worried. Maybe we wouldn't be able stay here? If it came to that, I thought, my house in Texas was cozy too, even if it was for sale, and it wouldn't kill Esme and me to go to my mother's as soon as we could and spend a night or two somewhere dingy.

I peeled off Esme's sleeper, stuffed it into a bag. I ran warm water in the kitchen sink, propped her up, sponged her. I'm supposed to put Vaseline on her every time she bathes—Esme's birth mother had told me so, dry skin. I didn't put any on her tonight. I would in the morning. All night long I heard noises, walls settling, furnace clicking on. A car door slammed. I got out of bed to see if someone was going in my mother's trailer. It looked locked up. A pot with a dead plant on the front step. One curtain hanging from a broken rod. When I can't sleep, I pray. Yet I was prayed out. I shouldn't have had those drinks on the plane. I thought about what Creola said—the Holy Ghost doesn't care what you spend on coffins—and I remembered that part in Matthew where it says blasphemy is forgiven if you curse the Son of Man but never curse the Holy Ghost. I tried praying to the Holy Ghost then, saying bring peace over here and sleep.

Esme woke, crying. She wanted a bottle, I thought. I fixed one. She didn't want it. I tried to hold her on my chest. Then she messed her diaper. I got off the couch in the half-dark—mercury vapor lights shining through windows—held her in one arm, squatted, reached into the suitcase. I made contact with Pampers right off but slammed my head on a table, the corner mashing into my eye socket. If pain takes you over, accept it. Remember: pain, thank you, is a timely reminder you're hurt. And next, get in a comfortable spot and don't drop the baby. I held Esme, covered my sore eye with one hand, stared at the clock, 3:00. I changed her and we fell asleep.

I had a dream about school.

A kid, Marvin, needed to see a pediatric neurologist. I'd once read an article saying a pediatric neurologist detects adolescent mental illness using a CAT scan, which costs a grand. Most students at Project Promotion don't have health insurance. I'm telling this to a man wearing a blue suit and a red-patterned tie, diplomas on the wall behind him. I'm holding Esme and my eye hurts. What he says next sounds lawyerlike: "About the matter of how you intend to pay, I'll need a retainer." I think of Tupperware. Container. "We have to petition," he says. "It'll be months before judgment." These are church words. Petition. Judgment. One question that nags me is how we answer for mistakes we don't know we're making. Suppose you hone in on your best impulses for the well-being of others and, in the course of doing so, feed your own selfishness but don't even know it. You congratulate yourself for sacrificing things that, even if you don't know, go straight to your own gain, your pride. In the Catholic Church they mention this. Forgive the sins we don't know. This seems lax, because if you can be across-the-board forgiven for mistakes you haven't noticed, you wouldn't spend much time on the specifics of right or wrong. But if you get too afraid of your own motives, you'd give up on helpfulness altogether.

I woke with Harriet tiptoeing around the kitchen. "Go crawl into my bed," she said, "sleep in."

"I can't." I shifted Esme and sat up. "I'm wide awake."

Harriet stared at me, an empty coffee cup dangling from one hand. "You have pink eye."

Pink eye is contagious. If someone comes to school with it, we send them home. My eye did hurt. "I bumped it in the night." I looked in the mirror—it wasn't black, just swollen, the white part all pulpy red. I fed Esme fine-ground oatmeal with apples and held her as I drank coffee from a pink plastic cup. My grandma had these same cups but didn't drink coffee, Mormon taboo. She drank cocoa. I asked Harriet, "Do you know the way to the courthouse?" She did. I said, "Is there a bus? Should I get a cab? I could pay you twenty dollars for the use of your car and buy some gas. I see I should have rented a car." Fakery, a lie. Like when Dannie says she hasn't realized how hungry she is until I start cooking. The idea was for Harriet to say: I wouldn't dream of you renting a car, honey. I don't like dropping hints about my dearth of funds and swear I won't always be so broke, but a rented car costs forty dollars a day. By taking the cab last night, if I didn't take another, paying Harriet and getting my mother's car, I'd save a bundle.

Harriet said, "A man your mother used to know way back when—he had money, maybe a wife too—he gave that car to your mom, brand new. She was real proud. It might need a repair or two, but it's not broke down. Go ahead and use my car today. You can pay me a little something."

I watched the clock. I was supposed to meet the lawyer outside the courtroom. He'd know me because I had a baby, we'd agreed. "Can you make me a map?" I asked Harriet. She was using a piece of notebook paper to draw major intersections when we heard car wheels on gravel. An engine shutting off. A door slamming. I didn't pay attention. I already had my ride arranged. Besides, last night I'd imagined I heard cars. But Harriet, attuned to her neighborhood noise, adjusted this ruffled curler cap she had on and said, "It's him." She seemed to like the drama. "Boys like Duster got my Ray offtrack," she said. "Go on, borrow my shoes. I'll hold the baby."

I put her shoes on. I felt tired. I was wearing my bathrobe. I opened Harriet's door.

Duster glanced up at me

I said, "Thanks for tending to my mother's business." He narrowed his eyes. "But I need to take back the house and car now." Like it had all been agreed on—Duster, professional house sitter. "You give me the keys. Then go on inside and gather up your belongings. You'll also want to use the telephone and call a friend to pick you up and give you a ride to some place else."

"There is no phone."

I'd forgotten. "Right." But if I took the car, I wondered, and I wasn't letting him get back in if I could stop him, how would he leave? And how did I intend to keep him from getting into it?

He said, "If your mother was here, she'd give me the car and maybe the house too."

You can speculate about my long-term motherlessness coming to a head. Or me resenting time spent straightening out her snafus when she'd never bothered with me. But I don't give a rat's ass about the past. Or what I've stifled. Repression is good. You couldn't get by without it. That said, nothing has ever pissed me off as much as Duster in his green sweatsuit, greasy face, scruffy beard, gray eyes shamming he's the sympathetic kind. I wanted him to hate himself. This is pointless because some people don't have what you and I call a conscience. Like this guy back in Idaho I one time agreed to go out with, to a movie. We never got to the movie. The decision to have sex wasn't mutual. I did hit him. He hit me harder, which is often the case. Men have upper-body strength. When he put his pants back on, he said, "I'll call you." I screamed at him. Not during, you see. After. Remembering this—thinking why wait and yell afterward—I said: "Idiot. If she was here, she wouldn't be dead and wouldn't give anything away."

He made a sudden jerk forward—to fake me out. I did flinch, because I was tired. I said, "Harriet's by the phone, ready to dial 911." Not true. Also wrong-headed, dragging Harriet in.

He said, "I used to wonder if you were her daughter, but I see you're a raving scum-cunt too."

My anger-surge left. I said, "Fine. And I'll help you find a ride later. I'll even drive you."

"I put up with a lot with your mother, which is more than you did. I helped her."

I wondered how much. Like she talked suicide and he said: Seems like a good idea to me, honey.

He said, "I paid the electric bills."

I told him, "You pawned the TV and lived here for months, free. You don't have a legal pot to piss in. Now give me the keys or I'll call the police. They're looking for you anyway." I'd just remembered. "It's an all-time new low, I bet—writing checks on your dead girlfriend's account."

In the middle of his beard, his mouth clamped down. He threw the keys in my face. They glanced off into the snow. He said, "Your mom liked cops too, but they got sick of coming here."

So he'd hit her. And stood here telling me. I said, "I'll give you a ride when I leave to go to court."

He raised his eyebrows. "Court?"

"Someone dies without a will, you have to," I said. Like I'd known all along.

He nodded.

I picked up the keys and went back in.

Harriet was holding Esme. "What did he say? He's going inside. What's he going inside for?"

Esme cried. I took her. "I told him to pack up. I'm giving him a ride to town."

"What if he tries to carjack the car?" Harriet said.

I thought about it. "Duster doesn't have that much get up and go."

What he did have, I came to see, was tone-deafness to the situation—Esme sitting in back, batting at toys attached to her car seat. People who hang around while you lug your baby all over and don't notice, don't say I see you have a baby there, act instead like your baby is a box or suitcase, I don't like. This might rule out a lot of people, but so what? At any rate, at a big intersection waiting for lights to change, protected left turn on all sides, semi-trucks idling like big beasts, Duster reached across the seat, put his hand on my neck, and said in a well-oiled voice he must save for fine occasions, "I find I'm attracted to you." I started laughing. For some reason, I thought how Dannie Lampass would think this was funny too. I said, "Get your hand off me."

He left it there a minute and said, "You think you are, but you're not better than me."

I dropped him off at an IHOP. I wondered if what he said was true, that on some level we were the same—did the same things, were the same kind of loser. I drove the rest of the way to the courthouse, just a little lost at the end on a one-way street, trying to find the parking garage entrance. Inside the courthouse, on the third floor, where the lawyer had said to wait, I looked for someone who might be him. Maybe this thin man in a wrinkly suit, carrying a briefcase with an American flag on it, wearing lizard skin boots. Well-situated people can dress this way, a wild touch here and there, saying: I'm playful. I must have stared too long, wondering if he was my lawyer, because he winked. Next I looked at a rotund man with a good mustache. Men look better rotund than women. It never bothered me about Hector. First time he put his arms around me, I thought: arms like tree trunks, shelter. It didn't matter whose body the arms were attached to and where he worked and that—chances were—we wouldn't fall in love, get hitched, and have social

84

work as a source of marital inspiration and focus, no. Most people who get together don't stay together, so you better not fuck at work. A man leaned over and said, "Miss Arco? Ready to go in?"

We went into the courtroom and waited our turn. A family, a mother and four grown children, stood at the bench. The mother, the widow I suppose, cried the whole time. Missed her husband. Either that, or the judge was giving the money to someone else. The next people who went up were an old fat woman and a young woman with teased hair and red pants. The old woman's son was dead, shot—how or why, no one said. The young woman had been planning to divorce him at the time he died and thought she deserved money from the insurance because the old woman, her mother-in-law, never told her her almost-ex-husband was dead. "So I wasn't able to get to the funeral," she said. The judge asked, "How much time passed before you knew?" The young woman said, "What?" The judge said, "When did you first notice he was dead?"

I didn't get to listen any longer because I was reaching into the bag to get Esme's bottle, pop it into her mouth the minute she made those hungry, mewly sounds, but I couldn't locate it before she'd heard me rustling around and understood the getting-fed phase was coming on and lost her patience and squalled. The courtroom guard with his double-knit uniform and holster tapped me. "You have to take the baby outside." The lawyer nodded and whispered, "I'll come and get you when it's time." I stood up, dropping the blanket, making a snap decision to leave the car-seat carrier behind. Esme was screaming now. The judge banged his gavel. He said, "Miss."

"Yes, Your Honor."

"Sit down."

I did.

He said, "This is a family courtroom. Feed the baby here."

A non-cricket, I thought.

Esme had finished eating and felt drowsy-happy by the time we stood in front of the judge for two minutes, the lawyer handing over the death certificate, my birth certificate he'd asked me to bring, also an application to sell my mother's trailer. The judge said, "Any other heirs?"

"Not to my knowledge." With my mother's bad taste in men, this was a scary idea.

"Do you understand what comes next? Gather assets and determine claims."

I must have looked confused because the lawyer jumped in. "We're putting a notice to creditors in the newspaper, Your Honor, but it looks like the only Class A claim is the funeral home."

The judge looked at me. "I'm setting the bond at eighteen thousand dollars. I'll see you in six months."

The lawyer stepped forward in that suck-up way I guess is required, shuffled through the papers he'd laid in front of the judge. "You'll see that when we filed for permission to probate, I also filed a paper for the appointment of resident agent. Miss Arco can't afford to make the trip again."

The judge glanced at the paper, banged his hammer. "Next."

Outside the courtroom, the lawyer said, "Join me for lunch?"

So we were in a posh place across the street—he picked the restaurant, I thought, he better get the tab—when I saw these fake parchments on the wall behind him, the fake Gettysburg Address, fake Declaration of Independence. The lawyer was wearing his blue suit. He said, "About my retainer." I thought container, Tupperware. Except I didn't think this. I'd thought it the night before. I almost said so—that I dreamed this whole scene. But decided not to. Didn't want him making a note: client is a nut. Besides, since having the dream, I'd thought his question through. "You decide how much interest," I said, "and when this business is settled, I'll pay."

He had smooth skin, like he used cold cream. "It's customary for a client to pay a retainer."

I said, "Have the realtor pay you, and they can make it up when the trailer sells."

He said, "Technically, I'm not working for them. Technically, I work for you."

That's a lot of technicallys, I thought. I told him, "I'm a good risk. Run a credit check if you want." This started me thinking about my landlord, Chuck, how he always told people I was reliable. I squirted ketchup on my hamburger. "How much do you figure my mother's trailer is worth?"

He was twirling long noodles on a fork. "I have no idea."

"Ballpark."

He shrugged. "Ten thousand, or more."

"The funeral home tried to service me," I said.

"Pardon me."

"When a farmer hires a bull," I said, "he wants the bull to service the cow. The funeral home director tried to get me to sign over the trailer house. My mother's funeral wasn't ultrafancy."

He nodded. "You think you were overcharged. We need to get them to make up an official bill."

"There's bound to be money left over."

"The realtor gets fifteen percent. Other creditors could file."

"After we put the ad in the paper, you mean?" Those ads had always seemed pointless to me—as if businesses hire someone to go through the newspaper looking for dead people who owe.

He said, "Don't forget you have to pay me."

I'd spilled ketchup on my dress, pale yellow with a collar and cuffs. I wasn't fazed yet. I said, "I've been thinking about my mother's car." Its odometer read 34,000—could be 134,000, but I didn't think so. When my dad knew her, my mother was afraid of traffic, drove on back streets, access roads, sometimes through parking lots, to avoid it. The odometer on my car said 95,000. Maybe I'd turned greedy, deciding a beat-up compact wasn't good enough for Esme, who looked high-up and royal in this car. I pictured myself driving us around Port Town, and I wasn't wearing a stained dress either, no swelled-up eye. My mother had put my name on her bank accounts, right? Esme was her grandchild. Details fit in fast—this is a sign you have a vested, too-personal slant. "If I want to take ownership," I asked, cool as a cucumber, "when can I?"

He said, "You can drive the car now but don't cross the state line."

"I'm leaving in two days anyway," I said, "by plane."

EIGHT

Two days later in the cushy interior of the gold car packed to the hilt—Esme above it in the center in back, Dannie Lampass in the passenger seat beside me saying, "Mind if I smoke?"—I crossed the state line but didn't get that King of the Road freedom-jolt because we were conspicuous, I worried, a probable cause to pull over with our junk, our baby who didn't look related to us, Dannie in her John Deere cap and sheepskin vest, wearing pink lipstick, and me with a black eye and my mother's gaudy clothes. I drove under the speed limit. I'd gone to a gas station and had the attendant check other reasons for getting stopped: headlights, taillights. The nuts and bolts of how to leave town had first crossed my mind that day I got back from court and sat at Harriet's looking at my return ticket and making one of those stripped-down deals with myself—short route to peace of mind—I think of as moral turpentine because I once handed in a school paper copied straight from a book and meant to write *turpitude* but got it wrong. As I sat on Harriet's couch, my options turned simple. If I left my mom's car, the belts and hoses would stiffen. Someone would scratch it. Duster might steal it. Besides, I'd never come back. Harriet said, "You could pay to put it in storage and later sell it." And I'd been thinking of the four hundred dollars in my mother's bank accounts the lawyer never mentioned—for gas, motels. I looked up Cuyahoga Credit Union in Harriet's phone book. "I have a letter saying my mother who died named me payee on death," I told the lady who answered. "How do I close her accounts and get the money?" Two forms of picture ID, she told me. I hung up and told Harriet, "I'll drive the car home."

She was making a pie crust Kathie Lee Gifford had talked about; you add a dab of Miracle Whip. She said, "I thought you weren't supposed to. Besides, you can't go alone with a baby."

"When she gets hungry," I said, "I'll pull over and feed her." Still, she'd cry and fuss. I'd need to stop and run the nebulizer, which I'd been scanting on and already her lungs sounded thick.

Harriet said, "You could make the trip with a friend. Do you have a close girlfriend?"

I thought of Sage. Once we went out to lunch and she ate garbanzo beans and said, "I think friendship is worth working on." At the time I thought: work is worth working on. The worst that could happen, I decided, would be that Esme would cry and I'd have to pull over and we'd make slow time—I'd phone Hector and ask for a few more days. As for the trailer, I'd sell it furnished. The realtor had said to get rid of her clothes, also food in the fridge. Soon as he said so, I'd gone to the kitchen, opened the blinds. I read somewhere that dust swirling is 80 percent sloughed-off dead skin and it creeped me out, breathing my mom's dead skin and anybody's who'd lived there. I tossed out a bottle of mustard, a jar of Coffeemate, a bunch of soy sauce packets, a bag of onions. How much cleaning was my decision, the realtor said. "But it does have a psychological effect on the buyer." I planned to go back tonight, once Esme fell asleep, throw my mother's clothes into her car, drop them at a thrift store in the morning, carry beer bottles to the trash, and vacuum. When I was done cleaning, I'd decide whether I had the gumption to drive across seven states with a baby. "Do you have an atlas?" I asked Harriet. She didn't. I put Esme in my mother's car, went to the store and got one, also Fantastic and Soft Scrub.

And cleaning my mother's trailer that night, I thought: no phone. That I could go back to Harriet's and tell her that if she looked out and the place seemed too empty, and I wasn't walking toward her, to call the police. But I'd sound spooked. The trailer was quiet except for the refrigerator humming. I unplugged it, propped it open. A dog barked. I heard traffic on West 130th. Next, a car pulling up. I looked out the window. Nothing. I heard another car and looked again. This time one of those little pickups—black with flaming orange stripes, a plywood topper—pulled up under the light. The passenger door opened and Duster got out. The guy who'd come to my mother's funeral in dirty jeans got out on the driver's side. He had on a fur-edged parka, and his hair was longer now, puffed out around his head like a dad on a 1970s sitcom, but not stylish, just long. I went outside. Duster's friend acted like we'd met at some party. "How have you been keeping?" I ignored him. I asked Duster, "What are you doing back here?"

"I forgot something." He went in and came out a minute later with a sleeping bag.

They drove off.

The city looked faraway, skeletal. The temperature had dropped. I thought about the times my dad used to take me tavern to tavern on the back of his snowmobile. He'd play pool while I sat on a barstool and ate Cheetos and read anything I could find, for instance, moldy novels from boxes my dad sometimes bid on at estate sales. Once I read *The Autobiography of Malcolm X*—I don't know how this ended up at our house. We also got Reader's Digest Condensed Books when my grandma was done with them. When day turned to night, we'd go back outside and ride the snowmobile into the woods and build a fire to cook sausage and beans. Smoke rose like a column in the black sky, the stars sharp as ice. When it's cold, smoke doesn't spread out—it huddles close to itself, its own kind. Me, I like Port Town, Texas, even if we do sweat and have what you call palmetto bugs, cockroaches. I went back inside and finished tidying.

Then I locked up and went to Harriet's. She was watching *Wheel of Fortune.* I thought about my trip, how Esme would cry and I'd get tired. But nobody dies of tiredness. I felt reckless, also afraid how far recklessness could take me. When I was younger, I had spur-of-the-moment impulses, for instance, once I ate hash. I'd heard of smoking it, but here I was at a party and people said eat it. That particular decision turned bad—mucked up my thinking for days. But even good impulses scare me. Every step of the way adopting Esme, I'd think: I've never done this before, it's too hard. But I filled out papers, went through interviews. And one night came home with a kid. On Harriet's TV, *Wheel of Fortune* had turned to news, Connie Chung talking about a kid two guys beat and left for dead on a fence. "Bad old news," Harriet said.

I used my phone card to call Information for Dannie's number. I wanted her to stop by Arturo and Lupe's and tell them not to meet me at the airport. The phone rang about eight times before she picked up and said: "Shut your fat traps right now." In the background, her two dogs yelped.

I said, "This is Delia."

"Delia, I can't believe you had to go all the way up there," she said, outraged and perky, like a disc jockey, I thought, exaggerated fluctuations of tone. "I miss you. How's little Doo-doo?"

I said, "I've decided to drive back. I inherited a car." Almost true. "I'll call Hector and tell him I need a few more days off work, but I want you to tell Lupe not to pick me up at the airport. She doesn't have a phone. Drive over and tell Lupe, not Arturo. Arturo doesn't speak English."

Dannie got quiet. "Alone? Just you and the baby? What if this car breaks down?"

I'd thought of this. I had credit left on my Visa.

"How many miles is it?"

"Two thousand." Actually a little more.

"Jesus Christ."

"I can do it in four days," I said.

"You'll kill yourself trying."

For the first time, Dannie sounded like a social worker with real promise. I said, "But I want this car." Like some nights I want liquor, I thought. Like in the morning I always want coffee. I buy good coffee and parcel it out, one cup per day. Mike Cleary said I'd feel the same way about good vodka if I ever tasted it. "I'd better not then," I'd said. My old car? I hated it already.

Dannie said, "Look. I'll fly up tomorrow and we'll drive back together."

I said, "A ticket like that costs a fortune. You can't even afford groceries."

"That's just bad planning," she said. "I have my sister's credit card for emergencies."

I said, "She won't think this is an emergency."

"I've charged weirder things. I charged a dog once. Besides, you hardly put me on the schedule."

I said, "I'll fly back after all. Never mind about Lupe." I hung up.

An hour later Esme started coughing.

I got the nebulizer. I put a blanket on the floor and lay Esme down, fitted the mask over her, emptied a vial in the canister, hit ON. She shook her fists and thrashed. Every time I ran the nebulizer I'd think I couldn't stand to, which is why I didn't as often as the doctor had said. "Hush, little baby," I told her. Harriet turned off the TV, pulled her La-Z-Boy upright and gave me a look, her eyebrows raised, nose wrinkled. "I can't believe she stands for that itty-bitty gas mask."

I said, "She doesn't, really. It's not a gas mask." The doctor had said to expect the crying, also her heart flailing inside her ribs like a trapped bird. Blue in the face, she coughed. Eyes glassy, arms and legs spastic like her nervous system was broken, she stopped coughing and spit.

Harriet said, "I saw this on 60 Minutes."

Esme was crying. "What?"

Harriet said, "She has AIDS."

"She does not," I said. Like Harriet had said something harmless and half-funny. A few weeks earlier a man at Randall's had looked at Esme in her car-seat carrier and said, "Is that a crack baby?" I'd looked at Esme and wondered: why on earth did he think that about a fat baby? He couldn't see why a white woman toted around a black baby unless she got paid to, I decided. Thought I was a Florence Nightingale-type. As for Harriet, she probably never had much contact with black people, only heard about them on TV. Later on, I worked up snappy comebacks, but back then these comments from people who'd lived entire lives in the same town as black people but never saw blacks and whites mix and now walked up to me like a state-funded exhibit, all you wanted to know but were afraid to ask, were too new; I didn't have answers. I looked nervous, not mean. Strangers all the time fingered Esme's hair and skin. Maybe they'd wanted to touch a black person for a long time and her being little and me being white gave them a chance. At Wal-Mart one day, a woman said, "What is she?" Nationality, she meant. I told Creola Wheat once, "I've heard it all." She shook her head. "That's just it. You haven't."

Harriet stood three feet away. Thinking about rubber gloves and disinfectants.

I said, "She doesn't have AIDS. She has reactive airways disease."

"That's good," Harriet said.

Esme eyes rolled around in her head. I could hardly stand to hold her, her heart thumping rapid and unreliable, her skin hot. Maybe she had a fever? "She gets build-up in her lungs," I explained.

Harriet said, "Contagious?"

I said, "It's like asthma, not contagious."

Harriet nodded. "You be careful about putting your hands near your sore eye."

One piece of advice I give people about bad environments is that just because you know you need to leave doesn't mean you leave without a plan. I left without a plan. Fuming, holding Esme while carrying suitcases to my mother's, which took a long time, one suitcase at a time, I made a point of not speaking. Harriet looked worried. "Can I help?" Freaking out she'd held Esme yesterday, I thought. "No thanks," I said, "and if she did have AIDS, you wouldn't catch it from her skin." Wrong approach, I realized. Like Esme did have AIDS, and I was holding out. When I worked in Idaho I met people all the time whose son or brother was dying of it, and they called it colitis or ulcers. Also—this happens when I let my rude thoughts out, don't hold them in—I felt guilty for making Harriet squirm. She couldn't help being ignorant, ignoring facts. She'd been nice to me before, letting me stay. By the time I came back in to take down the baby bed, she helped me, hangdog but distant, hands fidgety. I thought about her Renuzit and Ty-D-Bowl. My ex used to tell me I'm so clean I'm weird. But not because of germs. To me, a mess is a bad surprise. "Thanks for your hospitality," I said, after we carried the baby bed across the yard.

Harriet looked around. "That's fine, honey. You'll be fine here. You did a good job cleaning."

I hadn't, though. I'd vacuumed the middle of rooms, wiped surfaces. I'd also turned the thermostat down. I hiked it back up. Esme lay on the couch, limp, dazed. I hadn't packed a thermometer. I did have Infant Tylenol. After Harriet left, I measured some out, squirted it into Esme's mouth. I tried to set up the baby bed myself, but couldn't. I walked back across the yard. Harriet answered her door, wiping her hands on a towel. "I was heating you some food," she said. Hamburger and noodles and tomato paste on a paper plate. I carried it back to my mother's, where Harriet and I set up Esme's bed. She said, "It'll be real quiet tonight without a TV."

She left.

I looked at the food. I opened a drawer, found a fork—clean, no doubt. I washed it anyway. I thought about when I'd first started working at Child Protective Services as a secretary and needed outfits, and my grandma gave me a dress that belonged to a woman who'd died. It buttoned up the front with a wide skirt. "It's a Towncraft," my grandma had said, "top of the line." I told her, "But the person who wore it is dead." My grandma said, "Well, she wasn't when she had it on." I sat on my mother's couch, using her fork to eat Harriet's clammy noodles.

Esme slept. Heat blasted out of the vents. I stared at my suitcases heaped like rubble in the center of my mother's living room. Harriet hadn't exactly shoved me out the door, I thought. Or begged me to stay. Maybe she never wanted Esme there in the first place? Or didn't understand why I'd left? Last spring, the night after the funeral, I'd tossed a long time on Harriet's couch, thinking about my mother's face, which looked like mine—but also like that country singer's, Naomi Judd's, who I'd seen in magazines, at any rate more than I'd seen my mother's face, real or photographed—and which, I thought while lying in the dark, was sealed in a coffin they planned to cover with dirt. Harriet, wearing fuzzy slippers, had clopped out of her bedroom, handed me a paperback, and said, "Turn on the light, honey, and read. Relax." Since Esme maybe looked so different from Harriet, I speculated, so not-related, this made Harriet think Esme's illness was unusual too. She wouldn't think a white baby who coughed had AIDS, would she? Hector once said that people who aren't the same race don't dwell on it until they argue about something else—time, money, where to eat lunch. Then all differences seem like race differences. I was inches away from a mood I sometimes get, thinking I don't fit, no clan or clique. I do fit with Esme, I thought, also with my dad, who all the same acts like I cause trouble, even if—like *this,* my mother's loose-end way of dying—he'd helped cause it.

My plane ticket was for the morning. Twelve hours, I told myself.

I'd tidied up the bed earlier—ripped off the sheets, threw them away, lay the bedspread over the mattress. Duster had slept on that mattress, probably had sex with my mother there. I decided to sleep on the couch. I looked for a blanket in the closet. I found bikini-line bleach, Bioré pads, a compact with eye shadows. Also a box of photos. I looked at a few. My mom with a 1980s hairdo—spiky, greased—and holding a Coors. My mom's car piled high with snow. My mom and a clean-cut man sitting by a lake. A group of people, young and old, standing in rows, my mother, blond by then, in the center. I thought how she'd been alive all the time she'd been in these photos, even if I hadn't known her. You make a family, I saw, from the pieces you get handed, the good bits, complete wreckage too. Now there'd be no going back, like Creola had said, no chance to learn right or wrong as I patched together a way to be Esme's mother.

I found a blanket wadded on the floor and decided to wash it in the double-decker washer-dryer combo. But the washer wouldn't drain. I found out later lots of washers do this, kink in the hose. You unkink it. I didn't know that then. I left the blanket sitting in soapy water, got the bedspread off the bed. No telling who'd done what on the bedspread either, I thought. So I kept my clothes on when I wrapped up in it on the couch. I tucked it under my arms so it wouldn't touch my face. I thought about my own bed at home. Also Esme's white crib and ruffled curtains. Harriet's house, its bric-a-brac and fresh smell. Esme woke and I ran the nebulizer again, then stood over her, saying: Sleep, come. When I wait for sleep, I think of it as a helpful man in a lab coat, a doctor or scientist. But sometimes he's a punk, showing up late, withholding.

I fell half-asleep and had a half-dream: I dreamed I was on a couch in a trailer, wrapped in a bedspread, and someone came near. When Esme was older I'd get the same sense in the night, that I wasn't alone, and she'd reach through the dark and touch me; I'd throw out my hand and help her into bed. But that night someone leaned over, put their arms around my neck. I said: You're going to choke me? I didn't get an answer, just this writhing body weighing the same as mine. I told myself: this is a dream, not a good one. That skinny body twisted like a flag in wind and I was the pole. I tried to shake it off. Then I sat up, turned on the light. Or dreamed I did, because I looked across the room and Esme was sleeping in fog in a ditch, and I walked over, adjusted her blanket, and pushed the weeds away so she could breathe. Then I went back to the couch, turned the light off, and that skinny broad pawed me again. I said: I can't help you. You're over there now. We're still here. On another brain level, I was listening for Duster, scratching to come in. I'd scared him off before, I reminded myself, and could again. The body hung on tight. Scram, I said. I woke all the way up. I got a radio from the bedroom and tuned it to an all-night show, oldies, shrieky music from when I was young, Meat Loaf, AC/DC, Alice Cooper.

Someone once told me you can't keep a baby awake who wants sleep, but I tried.

I sang and tickled Esme. She struggled and pushed me away.

I put her back to bed.

My whole life, when I get scared—that hooing midnight sound I suppose is owls, the rustling of twigs or whatever else outside the pane of window over my bed—I calm myself by pretending I'm one-half of holy matrimony, a wife, sheltered, respectable. This doesn't make sense by daylight. Marriage itself won't save you. But in the middle of the night I move to one side of the bed, wedge a pillow next to me, hug it, and say, Good night, my prince. Or Good night, Mannix. Whatever name I like. In this case, I said, Good night, Mike Cleary, which didn't work. So a minute later I said, Good night, Hector. Because he's big like a wall, a barrier. In the morning I'm always fine again being me, Delia alone. But I watched this morning arrive—the sky turning the color of indoor light, gray-gold. Then ice-white. Cold blue. Esme was burning up.

I dressed her and got us in the car and drove around looking for an Eckerd's or Wal-Mart to buy a thermometer. I was also thinking about finding some kind of emergency room or whatever, and would my insurance cover it. As I drove around, Esme slept, and I took the car seat carrier inside like a big bucket thumping against my leg as I went up and down aisles, trying to find thermometers, and she never woke, not at the checkout either, where the clerk—a black woman with her name, LaKeesha, embroidered on her smock—glanced at Esme and then me, a glance like we were poor, homeless, pathetic, sinking down deep, and said, "That baby is sick."

And me with no sleep, buzzed, wired.

Sleep is for losers, I decided. People who can't stand being awake.

A brain with sleep has cobwebs on it.

Outside, I covered Esme with a blanket because the wind was cold and wild, rearing up. My dad calls it combat adrenaline when your body goes to Emergency-Alert. "The jitters," he said, "saved my life." In Vietnam, he meant. I thought about my mother's trailer. I didn't want to go back there. I found a pay phone. The wind huffed and puffed, and a man walking down the sidewalk tripped over Esme's car-seat carrier and almost fell. I moved her close to the wall and looked in my checkbook, where I'd written down Dannie's phone number. I meant to call her and ask her to tell Lupe not to meet me at the airport after all—this time because Esme was sick and we couldn't fly today. We'd fly back later. But standing there listening to Dannie's phone ring and ring, I felt like I could run a hundred miles. I could lift a car. I wanted to hit someone. Or go back inside and tell that woman who said Esme was sick, like I was too dumb to notice, to fuck off, fuck herself. I could drive for two days, I thought, and cure this speeded-up feeling, shocks tremoring through me, a voice in my head: faster, faster. When Dannie answered the phone, I said, "Tell Lupe not to pick me up because I'm getting in the car and heading out. I'm wide awake and Esme's fever would make a plane ride a bad, bad idea, since it would rule out running the breathing machine, no electrical outlet. And the dirt and clutter here, you have no idea."

I heard muffled sounds—Dannie with her hand over the receiver, mumbling.

"Who's there with you?"

She said, "Delia. I talked you out of this yesterday."

"I could stay awake for a few days' driving," I said, "and then be real tired when I stopped."

Dannie didn't answer. It was 7:00 a.m. at her house, I realized.

She said, "What happened last night? Where are you?"

"At a pay phone." I hadn't realized you could tell from someone's voice they'd had a bad night. You can, I saw suddenly. I remembered how Dannie was always buying melatonin or Excedrin PM or kava kava. The sound of no-sleep is the sound of Dannie Lampass, extra-lively like Jiminy Cricket or Newt Gingrich. "Just because you know you're paranoid doesn't mean you're not going down the tubes," my ex-husband used to say, a piece of life-advice that never made sense until now, broad daylight but my mind skittery like at midnight. "It turned out bad with the lady whose house I was at," I said, "so I went to my mother's and something groped me."

Dannie said, "Delia, listen. Go to a motel. Super 8 is good. Anything Best Western. Find a drugstore and buy some Sominex. Go to sleep, let the baby sleep. When you wake up, call me. If I'm not here, I'll leave a message on my machine telling you what time to pick me up."

"Where?" I asked.

"The airport," she said, "Cleveland." She hung up.

I tried to picture Dannie buying a ticket, driving her truck to Houston, parking it, boarding a plane. Lots of potential snafus, I thought. But I liked her idea about the motel—I could watch TV. I went back inside and asked the clerk, LaKeesha, how to get to Bagley Road. She looked at me. "Is that your baby?" she asked. I kept my head down so she wouldn't stare at my sore eye. I said, "Yes." She said, "I thought I'd ask because sometimes, you know, you think you're talking to the baby's mother but, no, it's the baby's grandmother." The baby's grandmother? I thought. "Take Porter Road to 10," she said, "then watch for the exit." But when I found Bagley Road, Cuyahoga Credit Union wasn't open yet, too early. I waited in the parking lot until a man unlocked the doors. We went inside and Esme cried. I had on the same makeup as yesterday, same dress with ketchup, but I've learned not to blurt my worries, like: sorry I'm dirty. "Don't volunteer information," my dad says. Of course he's ducking the IRS. The guy at the counter, polished and angular, checked my picture ID against my face, then looked away. I signed a form, took the cash, left. I checked into the first motel I found, Comfort Inn.

Once we were in the room, I took Esme's temperature, 103. I dosed her up with Tylenol. Got her to drink some water. Then I turned on the TV and watched *Biography*, the life of Don Johnson.

When I woke it was after 4:00, dingy-dark. I touched Esme, who opened her eyes, slow, dull. I'd left her breathing machine at my mother's, also my luggage. I'd left so fast I hadn't locked up. I remembered LaKeesha the drug-store clerk staring at us like we were vagabonds. The man at the credit union, glancing away. Standing at the pay phone listening to Dannie say she'd fly here—this didn't seem like a memory now, just some last-ditch escape-dream. Still, here I was at a motel, Dannie's idea. I got out my phone card and called her. Her voice on her answering machine said, "If this is Delia, pick me up at 7:00 outside Baggage Claim. I don't want to wander around Cleveland. I'll kill you if you don't show up." One of her mock-ultimatums. A kid at Project Promotion once complained: "Why does she say she'll kill us always?"

I looked at the clock. She could have missed the plane, I thought. Dannie had two ways of operating. If someone seemed helpless, she was competent. Otherwise she made a big show of messing up. Just like when a small dog meets a big dog, it squirms, defers—a way of kowtowing, avoiding getting damaged, a sign of brains. Or the opposite is true. You turn smart from using your brains so much to avoid pain. We'll see if she gets here, I thought. I gave Esme a bath, then realized I didn't have clean clothes for her. Or me. So before I showered, I went out to the car, opened the trunk, dug around in tumble-down stacks of my mother's clothes. When I was a kid, all I had was used clothes. I picked out a lime-green shiny velvet pantsuit because it looked new.

I had it on when I pulled up at Baggage Claim and spotted Dannie in her Marlboro Man outfit—carrying a red and blue satchel with a white Lone Star on it. I pulled up, opened my door, flagged her down. She grinned and hurried over. By then, Esme's temperature was coming down, 101. I'd eaten a bowl of soup at a restaurant. I'd dumped the rest of my mother's clothes at a drive-up bin outside the Four Square Gospel Thrift. I told this to Dannie as I pulled away from the curb. Sometimes when Stephen Arco had temp jobs—construction, spare shifts at UPS during Christmas—I'd chatter like this. He'd come home tired and want to doze and I'd tell him what I ate for breakfast, what I thought at noon, how sunset had struck me. "The baby seemed sick-est about ten this morning," I told Dannie as we drove off, "but in the after-noon she slept."

"Did you keep anything back?" Dannie asked.

"I am talking too much."

"I didn't mean that," she said. "Hoover, you'll want to keep something of your mother's."

"Well, this pantsuit was hers." I pointed at my leg.

She started laughing. "I wondered—it's real bright for you. And what happened to your eye?"

I said, "I bumped into a table changing Esme's diaper." And I thought for a minute about how Dannie was sometimes too confused to get to work, or so flat broke she couldn't do laundry. And yet she got to Cleveland over-night, presto-chango. I said, "I still can't believe you came up here."

She nodded. Then she shrugged. "I'm good in an emergency, Little Hoover. I excel at emergencies. It's ordinary stuff that floors me." She pointed at the passing skyline. "Where we headed?"

"To my mother's, to pick up my luggage."

When we got there, a minivan was parked under the yard light, also that black and orange truck. Duster's friend was nowhere in sight, but Duster stood in the yard arguing with a man in a down vest.

Dannie got out of the car. I got out, unhooked Esme from her car seat and held her.

98 |

Dannie said, "Look at this freaking snow the Yankees have to live in."

Duster said, "The microwave is mine. I paid for it."

The guy in the down vest looked at me. "Are you the seller? They said the seller was a woman."

Duster stared at Dannie, then at me holding Esme. "They let the two of you adopt a baby?"

The real estate guy looked at Dannie. "Who are you?"

Duster said, "The head of household, I suppose."

So Duster thought I was a lesbian, a submissive one at that. The lady at the drugstore had thought I was a grandmother. I looked at Harriet's trailer—she thought Esme and I were sick, contagious.

Duster said, "So that's why you don't have any interest in men."

In him, he meant. "That's assuming you are one."

He shook his head, got in the truck, started it. It shuddered, jerked forward and died.

Dannie yelled, "Take the parking brake off, Einstein."

He flipped her off and drove away.

The real estate guy said, "All right already. I need to put the lock-box on."

So I went inside and got my suitcase, but first I put the box of photos in it. Also a doily my dad later told me my mother crocheted right after I was born when my grandma had tried to teach her wife skills. I also took a lamp, a picture of a bird made of feathers pressed under glass, and an embroidered bag I didn't look in that day but it turned out to have stones inside. I later showed them to Sage Hearttsock, who explained they were runes—tools from some old Viking religion obsessed with how brief life is, full of chill and hardship. After thinking about it, I also unplugged the microwave and took it. I ran through the right versus wrong. Whose stuff was this? The car, cash from the bank I'd started to spend, knickknacks, gimcracks, the microwave Duster maybe did buy. Not mine, yet. *I deserve something,* another voice said. I recognized it. People talk this way when they've been busted. Guilty, yes. Repentant? Hardly. Full of alibis and no pity. I've always known I have potential to be bad, that I need precaution. But standing in my mother's trailer, I wondered if being good was easy, the coward's way. Maybe—for people who don't have steel nerves—being bad was too hard? I closed my suitcase and walked through the trailer one more time. When I opened the bedroom door, someone lurched. I lurched too, then staggered. The other person staggered. It was me, I realized, my eyes beady and alien in my washed-out face. It was the lime green outfit; I looked strange. I didn't blend anymore. Dannie came in the door. "I'm so tired I didn't recognize myself in the mirror," I told her.

Outside, the real estate man shook Dannie's hand. "We'll keep your property secure."

People treated us like that all the way home—like we were married.

We didn't pull over except to buy gas, big towns like Cincinnati, Nashville flying past, also long stretches of emptiness and silos. We weren't supposed to have this car. We needed to get back to our jobs. Dannie and I took turns—whoever wasn't driving turning around to shake toys for Esme, or me riding in the back, taking Esme out of her car seat, which is also illegal, but I thought how cramped she must be, and besides she was crying. What were the chances, I thought, that we three, who'd put up with so much, would get pulled over, or the car would crash. Rules are not for us, not now, I thought. I told Dannie to drive careful, watch for cops. That's how we rode into Beulah, Arkansas, where we stopped the car in the parking lot of the Pine Tree Inn.

It was cinder-block, one-story. The front office was a living room with olive drab carpet and drapes, except the door was locked and you were supposed to communicate through a Plexiglas window. The sign said Vacancy. The man behind the Plexiglas stared. His two kids stood behind him, also staring—a boy and girl, school-age. I gave him thirty-nine dollars for a room with two beds.

Then all of a sudden Dannie popped out of nowhere and stood behind me, holding Esme. She waved at the man in the window and said, "You all have a cute motel. Did you fix it up yourselves? This here is our baby. I call her little Doo-doo. She's been riding in a car for three days."

The man turned to his kids. "Go on. Get back inside."

They disappeared behind a door.

He said, "I'm out of double rooms."

"What?"

"I don't have room for two more." He pointed at Dannie and Esme.

I said, "You just sold me a room with two beds."

He paused. "I told you the wrong price then. It's seventy dollars. And the towels you find, that's all you get."

I gave him more money.

We walked back to the car.

I was thinking how he'd rented me the room, then saw Dannie and Esme and changed his mind. Maybe he thought I wanted a room with two beds for myself, and the price for two people and a baby was higher. Or he didn't like Esme? He objected to mixed-race families? Or the whole package—two women, one dressed like a man and holding a baby of a different color? He had to draw the line somewhere, he might have thought. I puzzled this through as Dannie and Esme and I crossed the road, traffic whizzing by, people staring. It was a small town. People do stare. But all my life I've been under-the-radar. I'm white and straight-looking—fem, not butch, I mean—and though I'm poor and have low confidence, or self-esteem like they say, that makes me the opposite of special. In a few days I'd go back to being without Dannie, but I'd never be without Esme again, and what I'd lost, I saw, was cover. My inconspicuousness was over.

We went to a restaurant called the Imperial Dragon with a banner over the door. MOM'S NIGHT OUT, DON'T COOK ON THURSDAY. FREE PARTY FAVOR FOR MOM! The hostess looked at us and smiled. "Nice to see you." She gave us each a bar of jasmine soap.

We sat down. Dannie sniffed the soap. "Damn friendly, if you ask me." She ordered a pot of sake, then a second pot. Esme, who'd been gnawing on an egg roll, grabbed at a plastic palm tree and tipped it over, which knocked a room divider into the water fountain. "Hells bells," Dannie said. She jumped up, pulled the room divider out of the water fountain and set it back up. "No harm done," she said. She looked around the room. "Go on back to your meals, people."

We finished eating and headed back to the motel. Dannie started jogging back and forth. "I need," she yelled, loping past me, "more to drink tonight. Don't you? Anyone in this situation would." She ran toward a 7-Eleven. I waited for her, but a truck slowed and two guys stared, like: why was I standing in the road with a baby? I went back to the motel and got Esme ready for bed. When Dannie banged on the door I let her in, and she popped open a quart-sized bottle of Zima, got into bed with her clothes on, picked up the remote and said, "Monday Night Football."

No point in telling a drunk person much. The alcohol content of Zima, for example. Or that it's Thursday, not Monday. The less you argue, the sooner they sleep. I sat on my bed. Esme lay four feet away. Dannie on the other side of the room smelled like sweat and Chinese cooking. What was on TV? The ten o'clock news, sports. A pro-football player had been arrested for cocaine possession. This confused Dannie. "Enough yapping, start the game," she said.

I felt sorry for the football player, Dion Somebody. A job is hard when you worry all the time you're not good enough—all push-push, keeping your eyes peeled, and at first your boss mistakes this tension for passion. Then you get tired and stop complimenting everyone and checking your back always. Your trouble-spot detector stops going off. Or, if you had a subnormal start in life, you never had a trouble-spot detector to begin with. My point is that everybody needs all-purpose fear. My ex used to say I'm paranoid, but fear, you see, keeps you from demoting yourself, one preferred spot giving way to a less-preferred spot, a string of bright spots blinking out. Then you're like my dad, who'd dropped into a dark place and probably wanted somewhere better. Or my mom, who once got fired from a drugstore for taking ten bucks out of the till, my dad said, and spent the rest her life trying to get a hand back up but mostly met people with the same dim options. I wondered if she'd felt a twinge the minute her direction shifted, like the room she was in all at once felt windy-cold, unprotected, a wayside on the trip down.

"That tight end, count on it, has enough money to solve his legal problems," Dannie said. "You can't imagine my fines from the night I punched the cop who said I'd been breaking and entering."

Breaking and entering?

"I can't pay them and take care of my girlfriend, who my landlord hates."

I said, "You have a girlfriend?"

"I met her at the grocery store. She needed a place to stay."

"But you were involved with your landlord," I said, "right?"

Dannie had fallen asleep. I walked over to the bed and stared at her, her cap tipped onto the pillow, her face dusty, smudged. She had on the same clothes as when she got off the plane, except her shirt—she'd carried her satchel into a gas station bathroom yesterday and came out wearing a fresh shirt. Me, I still had on the lime-green. How had Dannie gotten in so close? I looked out the window at the front office with its lopsided drapes. I had to protect myself and my baby, I told myself. I couldn't afford hangers-on, attention-attraction. But Dannie had helped me, and I didn't want to be like Harriet, who'd liked me fine up to a point, or Janeway, who lets you know the minute you say or think something she wouldn't. Or the man in the front office, who thought, first impression, I was okay, and then didn't anymore. Someone to cling to or cast off, I never could tell the difference. How does anyone? And if your hopes aren't high in the first place, is it a guarantee you'll never get laid low? In the past, I would have prayed these questions, but I sat still, hands folded, a feeling like a shut lid. I put a blanket over Dannie and locked the door. Then I turned the TV, the desk lamp, the bulb over the mirror, the ceiling light, off.

NINE

I got home and had what?

Phone messages, *Mike Cleary here, call me, hope you're fine, Mike again, call me*. At the post office, a letter from the lawyer in Cleveland. Bad news? I didn't open it right away. And a note from my dad saying he was coming but he didn't know when: "Stand by. Clue U in later." Also Dannie a few blocks away in a duplex with her landlord, who was jealous of her girlfriend she'd met at the grocery store, and I had more trouble than ever keeping Dannie away, keeping her at bay, because, face it, I'd let her in when I shared food with her, motels, two thousand miles of road. And every time I looked out the window I saw my bad-luck charm, the ill-gotten car, my mother's big-finned car that had taken her uptown, downtown, but nowhere happy or safe. Yet it was better for Esme in case of an accident, I told myself, also convenient, four doors, getting her in and out, strapping and unstrapping. When I first got Esme, I'd asked Creola Wheat for the best advice she had. I was thinking which car seat to buy, how to test bath water or sterilize bottles, clip her tiny nails. Protect me from misjudgment, I meant. Creola looked at me. "Enjoy her," she said. This takes time. First thing I carved out of my schedule, church.

I know the idea that faith is like a mustard seed that can take root anywhere, on a sandy rock maybe, but is also hard to hold on to, not drop. Still, I'd pray at home, I decided, Do-It-Yourself.

I started thinking what to get rid of, because I was remembering my dad in wintertime with five, six, seven holes in the ice, a tip-up in each, which is a rig that lets you ice-fish from far off, a flag popping up if you have a bite. He'd get his tip-ups going and lose one fish heading out to check bait somewhere else. He ran his life like that, wood-chopping, fiddling with Airstreams, teaching at the reservation, guiding hunters. I couldn't recognize anything big or total in my life either. I was seeing my obligations in a one-speck-at-a-time way; I'd lost my place.

Each of us is here to fill a gap. If you start thinking otherwise, remember Satan is a big, fat liar. A lady at my church says so. I don't go for blame-it-on-Satan talk, but I do think it's best to get on the side of something good. After I put Esme to sleep one night, I got on my knees and asked: What am I meant to do? The answer seemed obvious, raise Esme. But she's not a room to clean, a term at school, one task done, another to move on to. With a kid you can't see where you've been. Or if you do, it's bad news; you've left your mark, too late. Or you don't notice you're a bad parent, can't see it. Like on Thanksgiving I gave Esme Gerber sweet potatoes and myself a TV dinner. I'd cook next year. But this Thanksgiving, our first, I didn't. I worried our family life—which should be like a boat that stays put when the wind shifts—had drifted.

Besides, at night, in bed, lights out, my mind reeled. Check on Miranda's sex life, I'd think. Tell Luann not to feed Esme spongy bread, choking hazard. Run the breathing machine. Track down family of girl who ran away. Break up with Mike Cleary or move on to being a real girlfriend. My mind spun, and my body revved, legs twitchy, pressure building in my head. Forget it, I'd say. I can't fix jackshit. But the list rolled on, new worries arriving, such as where would I live. We had a yard here, a quiet street, good neighbors, Lupe and Janeway. When I first moved to Port Town and called an ad for a place to live, a realtor had told me there weren't typical rentals in Port Town because of the oil bust ten years ago, which coincided with a population spurt, and no speculator had stayed solvent enough to build apartment complexes, and maybe I'd be interested in a vacant Taco Bell. "To live in?" I'd said. We did look at it, the drive-up window you could maybe fill with plants, black-top for a yard. I told the realtor I had another place to see, and she asked where. I told her. She said, "That's Pesquera, honey. You can't live there."

But I could. I could afford it.

The night I remembered this—third in a row I lay in bed, not sleeping—I decided to get up and open the letter from the lawyer in Cleveland because darkness, I saw, is like the future. A word Sage uses is *immaterial.* "That's immaterial," she'll say. Darkness is immaterial, all guesswork until you're in it and walking into walls. Daytime, on the other hand, is not, and neither is the past. I'm not afraid of things I've seen and can troubleshoot. But not knowing the near or far future, a stockpile of accidents, a sum total of good and bad, scares me. I figure there are two categories of people: those who follow a usual pattern or plan, and the rest of us bumping around taking chances no one else wants. I slit the envelope open. I was picturing my lawyer. I pictured all lawyers I'd seen that day at the courtroom, showing up with clients to settle scores. Being in the category of person that has to make her own way, no blueprint, I've mostly felt it was best to shun others—co-workers, neighbors, boyfriends—have don't-extend-myself contact and survive alone by my own wits. Because people never do keep to themselves, quarantined. They affect and derange you. You could predict how if you knew their pasts, but how can you know all of someone's past? For instance, I could never catalogue each mistake my mother made, every unreliable type she'd hung with, still alive and making trouble. I read the letter.

This letter confirms my fee as fifteen percent of the estate.

How much gain was likely? Would I end up in red ink? The phone rang. I kept reading.

I've asked the realtor for an appraisal and the funeral home to submit a bill.

Keep faith in the dark, I thought. Be impromptu with shifting plans.
The phone rang again. I picked it up.
Mike Cleary said, "You're back." Not happy-sounding. "I left you messages."
I said, "It took longer than I realized."
"To call?"
I thought how to answer him. I'd been home two weeks, seemed like days. I could tell him about my trip—spending the night with a dead woman who pawed me, driving a car some people might say is stolen through parts of the country, Tennessee, Arkansas, as bad as Idaho, bad as certain parts here if you turn up abnormal by the local standard, and I did it with a person who has no clue about how to lay low or play safe. I went through hell, I'd say, I drove through it, and the food and lodging were lousy. What I did say I didn't think through. "Why are you calling so late?" Then I glanced at the clock, 9:30. Like I mentioned, I'd been going to bed early.
He said, "If you don't want me around, just say the word."
"I've been in bed," I said. Did I want him around? "I've had a hard time getting in the swing."
"Why not say what's wrong? What do you want?"
I heard knocking at the door. What I don't want, I thought, is for him to cost me any money. Or be crazy or even detectable in front of Esme. I wanted someone not bad-looking, holding down a job you can point to as taking

brain-power, and I wanted him to want me. Not that I felt bad without it, just bored with sameness. Or lonely. I wanted him on his own side—side of the room, state line, whatever—and crossing over. Was this too little? I remembered telling Hector once: No, I don't want to meet your mother. I want to keep it simple. He'd scowled and said, "A person is not simple. Two people combined, especially if they've taken their clothes off, are not simple. You want pleasure without responsibility." The knocking got louder.

Pleasure without responsibility, no. Nearness with limits. "Are you there?" I asked.

I heard that sound again, pop-a-top a beer. "Yes," he said.

"Someone's at the door. Let me answer it."

I looked out. Janeway in one of those golf outfits, navy blue stripes. I unlocked the door, waved her in. "I'm on the phone." I picked back up and said, "It's not that I don't like your visits."

Mike said, "Who's there?"

"My neighbor." I looked at Janeway, who looked distracted on purpose, like she didn't want to seem to eavesdrop. She stared at the pictures and plaques on my walls, which are from second-hand stores. I like my walls to look normal, regular, Bless This House, that sort of thing.

I told Mike, "I appreciate our . . ." I couldn't think of the word, or words. Arrangement? Relationship? "Being with you," I said. "People tell me I seem standoffish but it's more that I'm . . ."

The phone line whistled, like he was on a mobile. "Scared," he said.

Of what?

"We all get scared if our, ah, heart . . ." He stopped. "Feelings," he said, "if our feelings are extended. For me, it's been years. I'm going to be in Port Town, and I have something to ask you in person. If you need to say no because you're too busy, okay. But it's yours I want, TLC."

TLC used to be stenciled on donated tables at the reservation school. Trinity Lutheran Church.

"Tender loving care," he said.

I don't have it to spare, I thought. I have enough for Esme. We said good-bye and hung up.

Janeway smiled. "Didn't mean to intrude. I came to invite you to Christmas dinner. It'll be all women. I'm thinking of putting together an empowerment group. I'm making Yorkshire pudding."

I didn't know what Yorkshire pudding was. Was it was helpful for empowerment? "Can I bring Esme?"

Janeway said, "It's one of the things I admire about you, how you took on the social taboos."

I tried to think of an answer.

"And doing it alone, single," she said.

So Christmas dinner was going to be motivational.

She said, "Don't you worry about Esme's birth mother?"

This question. "What?"

"What was wrong with her, how it'll show up in Esme."

Who had time for that? I had hope. It's not like *I* came from a stellar gene pool. "No," I said, "I don't."

"And bring Dannie."

To Janeway's? I said, "I'm sure she has plans. She has a new girlfriend." Also boyfriend, I thought. Charges pending for breaking and entering. I wondered why—I'd meant to ask.

Janeway said, "Was that her on the phone just now? I couldn't help overhearing your quarrel."

I thought about this. "Dannie and I aren't a couple." I'd said this before.

"Not officially, no. But all kinds of ties bind," Janeway said. "Jealousy is a primordial emotion."

Soup, I was thinking. Only way I'd heard the word used before.

Janeway said, "It's as if we try to fit our relationships into some centuries-old model of heterosexual marriage—when we should accept that ours are different. But a little jealousy is natural."

So Janeway was gay—and in an open relationship, maybe? And thought I was, that my heart was broken over Dannie. I guess if you don't fit the mold of what people expect, they try to match your ideas and feelings with their own, or someone's they've already met. If you don't fit, they get nervous. This is a crossing-the-boundary problem, like Sage says, except Sage thought I didn't have boundaries, when actually I'm sitting on one, between one category of familiar person and another, so only half-crazy people, daredevils, misfits, people on the fence too, don't get scared off by me. All my friends end up being untypical and pushy, because everyone who's normal gets confused or jumpy and moves on. "I'm not gay and never have been," I told Janeway. Too blunt. "I don't mind you are, though. I respect your lifestyle." I sounded like Sage. "Friendship is worth working on," I added, I'm not sure why, fancy last touch.

"I'm glad you feel that way." Janeway smiled. "Then you're coming to dinner, good."

I didn't say no. I wanted to go to bed. I had plans to get up early, scope out places to live.

Flawed plans, I realized as I packed Esme into her car seat, also a diaper bag, fresh bottles in a cooler, and Lupe came outside and asked where I was going. I said house-hunting, thinking this would please her, since she told me yesterday I was in denial. Those weren't her words. "The future is coming," she'd said in the testy voice she saved for Arturo. "Do a favor, and pay attention." I was paying attention. The house hadn't sold, and when it did I'd have a chance to stay on because if anyone moved in they'd need only one half, and the landlord had recommended me as the tenant to keep. And we all might keep living here if a rental tycoon who didn't need a place to live himself bought it. Either way, my chances were better than Lupe's. But I didn't say so. She got in the passenger seat and said, "Arturo no va ir. He won't go looking. I'll go with you."

I'd made appointments to look at a small turquoise house in Pesquera, also an apartment in a two-story house on the highway next to a pawn shop. We went to the turquoise house first. The landlords were two sisters—their mother lived here until last week. One room, tilting into the mud, was added on last, they said, on beams that weren't anchored. I walked down the sloping floor—plywood covered with indoor/outdoor carpet—and stared through a rotten board at dirt below. The rest of the house, kitchen, bathroom, living room, bedroom, was level. One sister fussed over Esme, *mija,* so cute. The other said she liked my fancy car, and where did I work? I said the public school, also Project Promotion. "Oh, the reform school," she said, "our nephew went there." Lupe volunteered that she worked at Furr's Cafeteria and her husband at Butch's Auto. The other sister said, "We can't afford to fix anything, but you could board up the bad room and live on one side." This rubbed me wrong—rent a house and watch part of it sink. And did they think we could we sleep three adults and a baby in one bedroom? Not that I wanted to. "We don't live together," I told the landlords. "We're not a family." Lupe glanced at me, sniffed. "I wouldn't live here anyway." We went to look at the other place, and as soon as we got there Lupe said something about Arturo, and the landlord—a short man in those snug, double-knit shorts gym teachers wear—said, "I'm not renting to two people and come to find out you've got fifteen relatives stacked on top of each other. Fire hazard, not to mention wear and tear."

Driving home, I tried to tell Lupe we had to house-hunt separately. But I understood she hadn't looked for a place to live for twenty-odd years, whereas

I'd looked just a few years ago. She was afraid. Arturo, more afraid. I thought about overseeing Lupe's house-hunting and finding my own place later. But I didn't have time. I drove through town in the big, gold car, air-conditioning pumping primo-cold air, Esme happy and bossy in back, gurgling at trees and utility poles. Lupe said she had a newspaper at home, ads circled. "It's not practical to look together," I said as we parked. Lupe interrupted. "The *lesbiana* is here," she said, "and someone else."

Dannie was in the chair Arturo usually sits in. A girl with brown hair and tilted-up eyes sat on my porch swing. A pretty girl with slanted eyes like I always wanted, Dannie once said about someone somewhere, maybe in a dream. This is the girl she met at the grocery store, I thought. She looked like a kid from Project Promotion—but a few years down the road and her options still dicey. I thought of Veronica, who'd run away. I pictured her under a viaduct, hands in her pockets.

Dannie said, "This is my friend, Tawny."

It took me a minute. I shifted Esme to my other arm. I said, "You're Tawny." She gave me a look like kiss off, like I was making a joke she was soft brown-colored or something. Or I didn't like her. I didn't *not* like her, but I didn't want Esme's life full of strangers. And besides, her name—she'd made it up to sound sexy. Or her mother did. I was also thinking she didn't look gay. Not that you can tell by looking. But sometimes. Maybe she wasn't. Just hungry enough, and tired. I didn't want her inside, though. I said, "We can't stay. We just stopped to get the newspaper. We're house-hunting." Later I'd be firm with Lupe about going alone.

Dannie jumped up. "We need to find a new house too," she said. "Our landlord fell through the ceiling. He cut a tunnel through the crawl space, and he fell down through it three feet from our bed. He was spying on us. He watches us with binoculars every time we leave the house."

What could I say? No one spoke. I looked at the sky. Saturday, December 18. Humidity thick. Tree branches sagging. I was standing on my sidewalk, thinking, if landlords didn't want to rent to me and Lupe and Esme, we sure as hell better not house-hunt with Dannie and Tawny. Also that a landlord crawling through an attic to spy on a tenant was wrong, crazy, but he'd rented to Dannie when he was sleeping with her and maybe she owed him, and nobody likes to be jilted and have the new one turn up living next door and, in this case, be female too, a fact some men might find ultra-insulting. Had Dannie even told him she was gay, mostly? And I was thinking about the breaking and entering. It was bad timing—Lupe, and Dannie's girlfriend right there, listening—but I asked, "How did you get arrested for breaking and entering?"

Arturo opened the door and walked out.

Dannie looked startled. Maybe she couldn't remember she'd told me. She said, "I was coming out of this bar in Houston, and I couldn't find my truck. People like me should never drink, which is what the officer said. And I saw the Ima Hogg House. Do you know what that is?"

I'd heard of Ima Hogg, a dead governor's dead daughter—famous for antiques. "Sort of."

Dannie said, "Well, it looked pretty with the glowing lights, the little rugs and chairs. I tripped the alarm going through the window."

"Why were you going through the window?"

Tawny glanced up, barely interested.

Dannie said, "I thought it looked homey." She thought about this for a minute. "I thought it looked like my home. It looked like a home, and I wanted to go inside and go to sleep."

That's the way Dannie was, forlorn and tricky. Not forlorn *or* tricky, if you see my point. I don't know if she broke into the Ima Hogg House, a museum with oil lamps and carved highboys, because she was on a rampage, or if this orphan-explanation, this offered-up delusion—my childhood has been obliterated and I was trying to get back to it—was real. Or the delusion itself was long-lasting enough to explain how, drunk or not but bleary-eyed and looking through a window at a mirage of her lost home, she'd blinked and the mirage didn't vanish as she meantime located a crowbar, jammed it under a window, crawled in, all before realizing Ima Hogg's house wasn't hers, or anyone's, and wouldn't help her back to the past, which had been wiped away like a chalk drawing on a blackboard. It bothered me she could be smart about reasons but helpless in the face of them. She'd had a bad life and had learned to milk it, I'm saying.

"You were charged with breaking and entering?"

"And assaulting a police officer, but they might drop that. I was asleep when I swung at him."

"You did go to sleep?" Or passed out, I thought.

"On the floor," she said, "on a braided rug. But I'd better scoot. I just wanted you to meet Tawny. If you can't find us, you know to tell the police our landlord did it—hacked us to pieces."

I had a feeling like bugs crawling on my arms and legs. *Habitually abnormal stress reactors,* a phrase I'd read somewhere. Dannie looked calm, though. "Do you think it's a possibility?" I asked. I meant being hacked to pieces. I was also thinking that talking about murder as a change of plans—we're not sure we'll be able to attend because someone could kill us—might be a survivor tic. And that Winston Churchill said never to react at once to a crisis but go use a different part of your brain and return to the crisis later. Tawny trailed after Dannie on the way to the truck, like a dog. This made me think of Dannie's dogs. I said, "How are your dogs?"

She turned. "They're in the pink. They're home, watching TV." And drove away.

I looked up, and Janeway was coming outside with a box. She set it next to her fence and started stringing up fir branches with red plastic ribbons. I happen to think piney Christmas decorations look strange next to yuccas and palm trees and, besides, the air was muggy-hot, a rumbling, gray-yellow sky. Arturo went inside. Lupe followed him, slammed her windows shut, turned the AC on. It roared so loud I couldn't hear as Janeway yelled something to me. I crossed the street, "What?" "A front," she said, "a change in the weather." As soon as she said this, fat raindrops fell. Thunder cracked. She scrambled in, and I ran back across the street with Esme.

It rained and blew for three days.

First day, I mostly looked out the window at Janeway's branches half-attached to the fence, drenched, swinging. I waxed the floors, cleaned a closet, also under the stove burners, lined the drip pans with foil, gave Esme a bath and washed her hair, which, unlike hair I'm used to, isn't supposed to be washed but once every ten days, good thing, since it takes a half-hour to comb again. Next I sat on my couch, sick of PBS—over and over I'd seen this show about Douglas MacArthur, another about teenagers in Florida who'd had a lot of sex. I switched to the regular station to check the weather, Port Town's county a lopsided square a little below and to the left of Houston. Even when the weather bulletins ended and *Friends* and *Seinfeld* and *M.A.S.H.* came back on, a map in the corner flashed green for heavy rain, purple for floods, a whirling yellow smudge in the Gulf a hurricane named Melissa. A town on an island nearby, Port Aransas—unlike our town, it really has a port—had been evacuated, cars bumpered up in a ten-mile chain. All night I got up to turn the TV on and keep an eye on Port Town, the flashing green.

Second day, Sunday, I dragged Esme and me to church. I didn't hunger for the Word exactly, but I didn't want to be stuck home. Where else could I go? It wasn't a good outing, soaking wet in a pew while that man with the necklace read from Acts about a woman, Lydia, who sold purple cloth and ran into the disciples and was happy to be converted. Somehow this led the preacher to say that we have to love bad weather along with the good. I'm sure there was a connection between Lydia of the purple cloth and bad weather, but I missed it. And during the part where everyone talks—most people ask for prayers for the sick—an old man stood up and said he wanted to read something he wrote. He pulled a piece of paper out of his pocket. He coughed. "In 1963 at 2 a.m. I leapt from bed, jerked up the window shade and beheld a clear, moonlit night. I'd sensed . . ." He coughed again. ". . . a tornado." He stopped to wipe his head. "The next day I found out a tornado had come close to my house, lifted up, then sat back down behind it. In 1949, a tornado blew my truck 360 degrees. I've seen four more tornadoes at a distance." Jiggling Esme and waiting for him to wrap this up, I wondered what his point was. Had a tornado been spotted? "In conclusion," he said, "no one needs to be hurt, because God can forewarn them." Loose talk, this, I thought, bundling up Esme. And too bad for the people God apparently didn't warn. This guy hadn't been warned anyway—he woke up, looked out a window, and the tornado had already passed. I got ready to dash out into the rain, and a family—a father, mother, son, daughter who are always there, lighting candles or handing out church pamphlets—stood in the doorway. "Good to see you here again," the father said. "We missed you."

"Same feeling back at you." Not the right tone, I know.

When I got home I had a phone message from Creola Wheat, saying she'd heard on the radio Port Town High had a foot of water in it. "Schools, city offices, all of it," she said, "closed Monday."

By then—thirty-six hours of rain—a leak was running from the seam between the living room wall and ceiling, down the wall, so I couldn't catch it in a bucket, just a towel on the baseboard. It rained heavy, pounding, and I'd get used to that, then it'd go lighter, then louder. Kept me jumpy. Another day, I thought, stuck in my half-house, half-duplex, and even this not mine for long or for sure. And what was that feeling I'd had about how nice the cream-colored paint and pale green window trim had made the bedrooms look? The way I'd gone around tweaking, polishing, adding a pink vase here, thinking it mattered? I couldn't look for new places to live in the rain and besides hadn't figured out how, what with the house for sale but not sold and a new landlord looming, an unknown who'd weigh in with his opinion: Stay, Go. Then someone knocked. I barely heard because of the rain, but a yellow plastic poncho blocked the gray light coming in the porch window.

I opened the door. "I knew you were here with the baby," Janeway said. "I brought you homemade soup. She held a ceramic pot shaped like a chicken.

I was a little surprised. "Do you want to come in and sit down?"

She handed me a brown paper bag too. Inside was some bread, a bottle of wine.

"What's this?"

She said, "I shop like a mad woman. You'd think a famine was coming. I must shop because I'm bored. I always have enough food in the house to last through Armageddon. I was going stir-crazy so I started cooking and sipping wine, and I thought of you inside all weekend with the baby. Think of it as a care package—what I'd want someone to bring me if I were stranded."

I said, "Do you want to stay and eat?" Though I'd vowed not to let anyone get close until I got my business settled—I mean, my mother's money problems, also a semi-permanent place to live.

"I already did eat," she said. And was out the door and across the street.

I felt half-relieved she'd brought the soup, but I couldn't eat much, with its floating green grass that tasted like lemon, also okra, which is south-ern, and white crunchy stick-like vegetables. As for the wine, I didn't have a corkscrew, but one of my old boyfriends once taught me to take the business end of a screwdriver and push the cork on through, the downside being that the cork stays inside, floating, so you have to drink all the wine, though I suppose you could cover it with Saran Wrap. Back in Stites, when they say wine they mean Lancer's, which comes in a brown bottle. Once I left Stites for Boise, I tried to order Lancer's in a bar, but people acted like they'd never heard of it, or had and wouldn't touch it. So I switched to vodka, always available and no one looks amazed you drink it. Janeway's wine was red, no fizz, and tasted almost not there, like air on your tongue, but warm and wet. Pleasant, I thought. I could get used to it. Ever since I heard alcoholism is hereditary, I've wondered if my mother had it. I've seen my dad drunk maybe six times total—real drunk, staggering. But six times in twenty years, not bad. I've noticed, though, I do once in a while crave alcohol. A lady at my church once said she craves it at Christmas. "Why Christmas?" I'd asked. "I have no idea," she said, "but I never give in to it. Never."

When the phone rang I was wandering around the house, thinking the wine also tasted like moss, I'm not sure why, but meant this as a compliment. The leak in the roof had stopped, and I'd wrung out the towel and hung it over the shower rod. The muted sound of Lupe and Arturo's TV—rapid Spanish, a steady laugh track—seemed homey, familiar. And the drumming rain I liked.

It was Hector on the phone—hadn't called me at home in maybe five years. I should have felt surprised, but I felt social. He said, "We don't have to go to work tomorrow." I told him I knew, Creola had called. "I was going to the store and thought I'd see if you needed Pampers or something. I know you don't want to get the baby out in the rain because of her bad lungs."

"Her lungs are fine," I said. Lately, they had been. "And I'm all set for Pampers." Then I was telling him about the soup with grass in it. "And this special wine," I said, "which would remind you of moss." I looked at the bottle. "See if you can get more wine." Though I still had a half-bottle left. I spelled out the name. "It's made in Portugal," I said. "And we can have a drink."

When he knocked on my door a half-hour later, I opened it and he held up a bottle. "It's not what you wanted. I went to the corner liquor store, and they'd never heard of what you asked for."

"Figures," I said. "My neighbor brought me the other bottle. She goes to Los Angeles."

"Oh, Los Angeles, I see." He smiled. He does this while looking out the corner of his eye.

And I remembered what we'd liked about each other, or found easy. He'd grown up in a town called Pharr. When I asked once where he was from, he'd said, "Pharr." At the time, newly arrived from Idaho and not having heard of Pharr, I thought he meant far away. But he'd never been far from Pharr either, which was four hours south on Highway 77. "Sit down and taste this wine," I said, "and we'll try your new wine and compare." And he poured himself a glass, and I switched the TV back to PBS, and he said he liked the concert that was on, a singing group famous in the 1970s, and his favorite song was about not wanting to know if your lover is cheating. I started thinking about him being from Pharr, and I said, "I never thought of you listening to this, Stevie Nicks. I guess I pictured you listening to that polka music with brass horns."

"Mariachi?" He was skeptical.

"They call it something else now."

"You mean conjunto. I should like it, but I don't."

He meant he should like it because he worked hard at being in touch with his roots.

"If I were consistent I would, but I'm not consistent. It's also strange not being Catholic. My mother raised me Baptist, because when she was growing up in Mexico City she learned to hate the Catholic Church—she was illegitimate, and the Catholic Church had a problem with that."

I'd met his mother when she came to visit. Hector brought her to my desk at noon and said we were going to lunch. She smiled and bobbed. I couldn't think of saying no, how to say no. I could tell by her questions—was I married? had I been? was I sure I was divorced?—she thought I was Hector's girlfriend. What I *was* was unclear even to me. In the restaurant she had us hold hands around the table. *"Señor,"* she said, which is how you pray in Spanish, *Señor en el cielo.* Hector squirmed and sighed, embarrassed to be praying in the Sirloin Stockade. For a few days back then, I thought I might be with him in a wide-awake, unbroken way—not just in the dark once in a while with my body, my gut instincts. In particular I remember a day with leaves on trees turning orange, the air cool like we never get in Port Town, Indian Summer, and I was standing next to my car wearing a blue plaid skirt and sky-blue turtleneck. I don't know what possessed me. I buy outfits like this and wear them maybe once. Hector said, "Look at you, you're all blue today." As romance goes, this isn't a great line. But I felt blood rushing to my face, took a deep breath, and he kissed me outside Project Promotion at 4:00 in the afternoon. What happened? A few weeks later he called on a night I was tired, close to crying about how hard work was. I needed to go to bed. He said, Right, I'll be right over. I said: alone. He hung up and called me back, hung up and called me back again, again, and said we needed to work it out.

I didn't want to. Work it out. Work.

And now I had Esme.

I looked at him. He was holding her under the arms, dangling her over a basket with folded laundry in it. *"Cuidado!"* he said. Like she could hurt herself on the edge of a plastic basket. A few minutes later she fell asleep. He said, "Take her, I worry I could accidentally hurt her." In the transfer—a sleeping baby passing from him to me—our arms locked up, Esme weighing on them, and we pried ourselves loose, but not before I got the close-up smell, not shampoo or aftershave but more specific, skin, blood. Someone told me once—a girl I sat next to one semester in a community college—that if you have that feeling about a man, your pulse picking up, your eyes stuck on him, it's a sure bet he's having it too, a quick, over-before-you-know-it signal of the nerves: his to yours, yours to his. Then one of those spells of hard rain came, water hitting roofs and streets outside like waves breaking, or a fire hose turned up high. He stood. "I don't want to get rained in here. Take care of yourself. This weather could get worse."

How? That's the good news about being a town without a port—it might be stagnant or boring, yet you're safe from obvious catastrophes. Hector is a worrier, though. When I stumbled into bed with him the first time, which was also in a December, the holidays ahead like a blank to be filled, he kept talking about how cold it got here compared to Pharr and gave me a space heater. Now we stood on the porch a few minutes, rain rolling over the eaves. Then Lupe pulled her curtains back to look out. Hector jingled his keys, hurried down the sidewalk to his truck.

I didn't see him again until the sky had cleared, crystal blue, a cold snap, and we were back to work, the last day before offices and classes closed for Christmas and New Year's. That morning I'd gotten Esme dressed, and I drove her to Luann's, where Luann's mother sat at the table eating tofu mashed with Miracle Whip and onions, spread on saltines, because any other protein source, Luann said, she couldn't chew. "Luann," her mother said, except she said it her way, Lew-un. "Could you buy me some oranges? Because I haven't had any in so long I just can't remember."

"That's the God's truth, Mama," Luann said. "You had some for breakfast."

Her mother said, "Impertinent."

Luann told me how she'd taken her mother to the doctor, and the doctor had asked, "Do you live with your daughter?" And her mother answered, "Well, I see her some." And she'd stopped wearing her Depends and had peed everywhere. "So I bought these pads at the thrift store," Luann said. She pointed at white absorbent mats lying on the couch, the living room chairs. "That's where I met such an interesting man," she said. "He shops there because of his job."

"The thrift store?"

Luann said, "He collects scrap—doors, mantels, windows. Sells it to people trying to build a home."

"You have a lot in common," I said. Because Luann had gotten her kitchen cupboards from someone who was remodeling, and once traded babysitting for a used bathroom vanity and commode.

She said, "That's a good point you've made."

At work, Creola had brought platters of cookies, also paper plates so we could take the cookies to our desks. People stood around, talking. Creola said she was leaving for Beaumont to be with her grandkids. Mason Pratt was staying in the dorms with the students who didn't have anywhere to go, and his wife would bring the ham dinner there. I'd stayed in the dorms last Christmas, and the Christmas before, before Esme. One reason I'd wanted to be a mother was not to be alone. Now I felt different from lonely—sorry I didn't have relatives, someone to sit with while Esme lunged at wrapping paper and boxes and we'd say: how cute. Dannie stared out the window. I wondered where she was going and would have asked, but Hector walked in, tight-toed boots clattering, hands full of file folders. Caught us loafing. Sage picked up her plate like she was on the verge of getting back to work, and said, "Hector, I suppose you'll go to the Valley."

He looked around. Paused. Looked at me. "Does everyone have somewhere to be?"

I said, "I was just headed to my desk."

"I meant on Christmas Day."

Sage said, "I'm going to Fort Worth, thank God."

I said, "I'm going to my neighbor's for dinner."

Hector nodded and left.

Dannie said, "My sister, who's also lesbian, is coming. She's the one who's in charge of my money."

Mason sat quiet. Creola didn't talk either. It's hard to say what they thought. A lot of people still think being gay is something you decide on—that it's trendy, a bad habit, like shoplifting. At a church I went to before I found mine, the preacher said: God didn't make homosexuals. TV shows make homosexuals. All the same, even with straight people you don't remark on it: my sister who's straight is coming for Christmas. You don't mention someone's sex life.

Sage was still talking. "When I took this job, I figured I was forty miles from Houston, and so I'd have access to that. Even now if I tell my dad how I can't stand it here, he says to get to Houston and try to make friends my own age. I go every weekend. But you're not going to date someone you meet at the store or standing in line to go to a movie. That's why I took the classes."

"What classes?" Creola said.

Sage said, "Creative Writing. I'm just now finishing up World Religions."

Creola rolled her eyes. "You may as well take some useful class. Might meet a useful man."

Sage said, "I wouldn't say World Religions wasn't useful."

Dannie said, "Damn right. It's important to know everyone believes in afterlife, not just Americans. Makes you feel like heaven might be there, and you will run across people you care about."

Sage said, "I'd like to meet someone with a spiritual side."

Creola said, "There's no fence around this place. What was it made you decide to come here anyway?"

"I had this idea I'd be needed," Sage said. "I'd be needed more here. Maybe it was my self-assigned penance." She was blushing. Penance? I thought. She said, "Delia, how about you?"

I said, "It doesn't seem that different—just warmer. And I like the plants."

"Exxon?" Sage said.

"I mean flowers and trees."

Still thinking this—that I like what you'd call native plants—I stopped at a Christmas tree lot on the way home and bought a Christmas cactus, thornless but spiny and long-limbed with mauve flowers; I'd set it on a table and put Esme's present underneath. When I was growing up the only indoor Christmas tree I had was when one blew off someone's truck and my dad found it. The rest of the time he said he wasn't going to chop down a living tree or pay cash, though we did sometimes hang popcorn and paper chains on a blue spruce outside. I was making a space for the cactus on the front seat of my mother's car when someone said, "Miss, I got my period."

I turned around. Miranda.

"And Esteban," she said. "He went to the county clinic like you said. He doesn't have diseases."

"That's great," I said. "Now have him buy condoms. But don't tell anyone I said this."

"I promise. I won't." She laughed and pointed across the lot. "That's my dad, buying a tree."

I looked at a sad, handsome man in coveralls, counting out money.

"Merry Christmas, Miss," she said. "My mother is having another baby."

Christmas at my house, I could smell Lupe's cooking through the walls. I heard her cupboard doors open and shut, her voice raised at Arturo. And they headed out in thick coats, hats, gloves, carrying disposable aluminum pans. Tamales, I thought, watching through the window, a draft whistling in around the edges. On cold days here, houses feel worse than most Idaho houses on bone-cold days—thirty below zero—because even old houses in Idaho have cellars and double-windows. I put Esme in the plush sleeper Sage had bought and gave her present to her, a cloth doll that cost only four dollars, but it had a chocolate brown face and twisty black hair, and for all the black people who do live here, and Mexican-American, it was hard finding dolls that weren't rubbery pink with corn-silk ponytails. Esme focused on the doll's face. She looked confused, moving her eyes around fast—like she was rearranging her brain. Then she lurched, grabbed it, more with her wrists than hands, because she was still developing basic motor skills. And hugged it. This thrilled me because, even with my little bit of training, one technique I know is that if you need to see if a baby has bonding issues, has been so neglected it doesn't understand loving contact, you hold up a doll. If the baby acts blasé you call your supervisor, make follow-up visits, study the situation. A baby who laughs and leaps to hug is fine. I ran the nebulizer next, patted her to loosen the mucous, like the man who delivered the machine said. Sitting on the floor, my hand on her back, I felt like we were enough, a colony of two, one-and-a-fraction. And ready to go to Janeway's and pass muster with the empowered women.

I was carrying Esme under one arm, the football hold, and she had her doll, and I was also carrying a pan of green bean casserole and fiddling with my keys, and I saw a man in the yard—looking at the For Sale sign, I figured. But on Christmas Day? I saw long gray hair, a black and blue plaid jacket. He was holding a slip of paper. That, and he'd set a duffel bag on the sidewalk.

I opened the door. He looked up, ashen-faced and puffy under the eyes.

I barely recognized him.

"I like your weather," he said. "It's balmy."

T E N

"And that must be the runt."

He was smiling, prominent teeth. He once told me that when he was in the army someone had said he looked like Ernest Hemingway but with buck teeth. My arm ached because Esme was facedown, chest balanced on my wrist. I said, "I didn't know you were coming."

"Came by bus," he said. "I had trouble finding one that went through here. Had to switch off in Houston to one of those big coaches headed for Mexico. Dropped me off out on the highway."

I set the casserole down. "How long did this take?"

"From Idaho?" He considered. "Little over six days."

That explained how pale he looked.

"I was trying to get here for Christmas."

A car pulled up in front of Janeway's, and two women got out and clicked up the sidewalk, fancy shoes. Janeway opened the door. I noticed this with the edge of my attention. They gestured, a hug, a handshake. "Delia," Janeway called across the street, "I hope you're ravenous."

My dad said, "I'll go in and have a nap and we'll catch up later."

I opened the door wide for him. "Let me drop this food off, and I'll come right back."

He said, "I don't want to be in your way. Just work around me in the corner."

An odd thing to say, I thought, crossing the street. It reminded me of something else someone once said—a professor at the junior college I'd gone to see about a test I'd missed, and he started talking about himself and how hard he'd tried to fit in in Idaho. "I find I've developed a marmoreal anonymity," he said. At the time I had to go home and look up both words. He meant he was like marble, also nameless. I pictured my dad in my living room, a statue made of pale rock, limestone. I was explaining the suddenness of his visit to Janeway. "He mentioned he might come," I told her on her front steps, handing over the casserole. "But it sounded like talk."

"Ask him to eat with us," Janeway said.

"He needs a nap. Besides—it's all women."

She shook her head. "We're not exclusive."

So my dad went with me and I felt edgy, waiting for his blunders. It was like being married to Stephen Arco if I took him someplace where I cared what people thought, for instance, to dinner with my boss from Child Protective Services, who'd been my guru, starting me as file clerk and moving me to better jobs. We went to a restaurant, and Stephen told my boss about his friend who had a broken satellite dish and had advertised in the back of *National Enquirer* that he could beam up prayers, seventy-five bucks a pop, and every day or so money orders arrived. "If He didn't want them shorn, He wouldn't have made them sheep," Stephen said. He had a grin that made his eyeteeth stick out in a devil-seeming way, like he'd been interfered with long ago, in the cradle. My boss was noncommittal. He said, "It's odd how religious desires attach themselves to the major technology of an age." But with my dad at Janeway's, it wasn't only what he said but also that he needed a bath, not that he was dirty, just an overwhelming smell of hair. He also had a white plastic bottle in his pocket he'd take out once in a while and sip from. I looked to see if other guests caught this, but they were passing food. One woman, Karen, was a physician's assistant, which is like a doctor, only a doctor supervises her when she works. Janeway was handing out Yorkshire pudding. This is like stuffing, just thicker. Another woman, Sharon, taught art at Lee College. The other, Martha, taught at Lee College too. I asked what, and she said, "Parks and rec." She was gay, I was pretty sure—spiky hair, one ear pierced three times, unisex-type sweatsuit made of gray velour. I asked if she knew Caroline Blakely. "What's her title?" I had no idea. Lee College is small. They might know Dannie, I thought. Esme was in my lap, reaching for water, food, the salt, silverware.

And Janeway, letting fly with perfect-looking pieces of beef, pale pink in the center, said to my dad, "So you surprised Delia for Christmas. Is this the first time you've seen your little granddaughter?"

He looked confused. I realized he hadn't yet thought of Esme as his granddaughter. "Yes, ma'am," he said. "Seems like a top-notch baby. She's given Delia a new lease, a reason to live."

Everyone listened. Extreme talk, like I'd been suicidal and getting a kid saved me. Still, I knew what he meant—I needed someone to care about. But he doesn't talk much. When he does it comes way out of his past, from his mother, also movies and TV he saw before he was a hermit.

Janeway said, "She's natural and easy with the baby, the way she handles her."

I hadn't thought of this. Made me glad. My dad, staring, gave me a half-vacant smile. He said, "I had a dog once, good hunter. But I bred her and she didn't know squat about caring for pups."

A quiet minute here, the sound of people eating.

Then the Lee College women asked Janeway about the *Port Town Sun*, how was business? She said, "I could care less. But how can I sell it, when my father sent me to journalism school and talked about me running it since I was little? One year I went away on vacation to Florida and didn't come back. He drove there to bring me home. I cried the whole way."

"Poor thing," Sharon or Karen said this.

"I wanted to work in a dress shop or be a secretary. But finally you're what your parents want."

"Yes and no," Martha said, gruff. "It's our birthright not to be miserable."

My dad said, "Damn right, Martha." But he'd forgotten her name. He said: "Damn right, Myrna." He put his balled fist on the table. "I'm the bastard offspring of a Jewish shepherd and a Mormon nut. I'm still getting over the brainwashing." He blushed red, his cheekbones and forehead.

Martha didn't seem to mind being called Myrna. She clinked her glass with his. "It's almost a gift to have to break so completely. You discover who you are and what your strong suit is."

He lifted his glass to drink. "Speaking of breaking completely, have you visited Belize?"

No one had.

"It's in Central America," he said, "but they speak English. The English settled it."

Everyone nodded. They knew that part.

Dad took out his white bottle, nipped at it, and this time left it on the table. Imodium, I saw. I figured he was sick from traveling. But why set it on the table? Kind of unappetizing. I wondered if anyone else thought so. But only the doctor-helper seemed worried, her eyebrows pursed.

"I want to live on the beach in one of those houses on stilts. You don't use electricity. You can fish—for your three squares a day. I've heard where a fellow can live for sixty dollars a month."

"Are these your retirement plans?" Martha said. "Marvelous. People have dreams, but you're going to live yours."

This made him happy, proud. He nodded. "Yes."

I was thinking how—at an age when most people, Lupe, for example, talk about where they want to live for the final twenty years and how they'd like a smaller place with no stairs or yard work—my dad was planning to live on stilts in sand with no electricity and scrounge for dinner.

"I want to say, Myrna, that even years ago when most people had their hackles up . . ."

What would he say next? I wondered. Imodium.

He said, "I never minded the women's libbers. I saw their point."

No one spoke.

"Early feminists were radical," the art professor said, "but they pioneered the movement."

My dad said, "I've never been prejudiced about homosexuals. You find homosexuals in nature."

I imagined his next spiel would be Indians. The Spaniards called Indian homosexuals *berdaches,* a Middle Eastern word that means slave boy or prostitute, which was not the case in Indian tribes—for instance, the Lakota, who call them *winktes*—where the whole idea was that homosexuals had been granted two spirits, not just one, but this all went underground when someone like Vasco da Gama thought it was an abomination and put them in a pit and had wild dogs kill them. How do I know so much? One of my dad's soap boxes—the Indian way is the best. "Esme's not going to last much longer," I said. "I need to go home and put her down for a nap."

"Are you sure?" Janeway said. "She seems calm. But what do I know?"

"A pleasure to make your acquaintance," my dad said.

"Enjoy your Christmas," Janeway said. And to me, "He's such a character."

Headed home, I felt tense—or in the aftermath of tense. The problem with having gone to college but not finishing is that, hanging around people like Sage and Janeway, you know enough to see you don't know much. Still, no one expected my dad to be an egghead. And Martha had rephrased his ideas so they sounded good. But talking and acting so unexpected, being a character, this is something you'd like at a party, not in a dad. Yet I hadn't seen him in years.

"Who do all the cars belong to?" he said.

I felt like a heel too, giving myself airs. Like I'd expected my dad to be some kind of social climbing aid. "The Subaru Justy is mine," I said. "And I drove that gold car back from Cleveland."

A look crossed his face I couldn't get a fix on. "A Lincoln," he said, "almost twenty-five years old, though." He didn't speak for a minute. "Sorry I didn't go with you—couldn't justify it."

Couldn't justify digging through the past? Spending money? Or flying? He hadn't been on a plane since I'd known him. I unlocked my front door. "Nice place," he said, "but up for sale."

"Believe me, I know."

He looked at me. "I let our house go."

He meant our house on the edge of the reservation he'd been leasing from the state since God knows when. For a while we didn't have front steps, just cement blocks, but one day he got his tools and built steps with beautiful curved branches for railings. Inside was shipshape—everything stowed, even if we didn't have doors on closets. In the kitchen we'd tacked oilcloth over shelves in little pleats. "Are they tearing it down?" I asked. Forever, there'd been talk they would.

"No," he said, "I just can't take the winters."

"When are you going to Belize?"

"I want to spend time with you, because once I get there I don't see myself coming back."

"You're going to just leave?" I was trying not to feel upset. He had ideas like this sometimes. Once, when I was twelve, he wanted to move somewhere warm and live in a tipi, and I put up such a fuss he set it up outside our house and stayed in it all one summer. Once he thought we'd be happier in Canada. But now he'd gotten rid of the house. I wondered if I was mad because I'd miss him. Or I didn't have brain-room to wonder if he was malnourished on a beach.

"That bus that got me here was going to Mexico. I can get there by bus, I figure."

"Do you have a passport?"

"I'll have to find out how to get one. Do you have Web TV?"

"What's that?"

"You get the Internet on your TV."

I said, "If you want to use the Internet, go to the public library." That's what I tell my kids. That's how I'd studied up on how to adopt a baby—and what were the right agencies to contact.

We went inside. I put Esme in the automatic swing.

"Do you mind if I nap?" he said. He sipped the Imodium.

"Do you have diarrhea?"

"My gut hurts."

"That medicine's for diarrhea," I said. "You need something else, Maalox." But I was thinking: where would he sleep? Esme had a big room, and we could make a pallet there. Or he could have the couch. Though I hoped he wouldn't want the couch when my PBS shows came on.

"The floor's okay," he said.

So I lay blankets and a pillow on Esme's floor.

He got a dazed-eye look. "Guess I'll wash up later." And threw himself down fast.

I needed to go to a store that'd be open on Christmas Day and get a can of sky-high-priced formula to tide me over until real stores opened. I got Esme out of the swing to take her, though I did consider I could leave her with my dad. But what if she fussed? Would he know what to do? Thinking about him—that he hadn't set a date for leaving and didn't have a house now, and I'm a schedule-type person and he never was—I was talking to myself, creeping along, rolling up to this stop sign and around that corner. I was taught to drive in a field and on dirt roads. So I sometimes approach real roads like ruts, tire tracks, especially if traffic is light. It was Christmas Day—streets so empty, like a science-fiction movie. Then I glanced in the rearview mirror and saw red lights spinning; I was being pulled over. I stopped the car, reached for my purse, but remembered they think you're going for a gun, so I sat still. The cop asked me: Can he see my license? Sputtering static-sounds came from his walkie-talkie. I said, "Was I going too fast?" He said, "You rolled through two stop signs. And with a baby." He flicked his hand at the back seat. "Can you believe you've been so reckless?" I was thinking: he's having a slow ticket day. I half-hated his guts. He said, "Out-of-state plates. I need your registration too." I was reaching for my purse, thinking: my license. Also: should I rifle through the glove box? That's where most people keep registration. But I hadn't thought to look in my mother's glove box yet and no telling what was in it. I felt my heart knocking on that bone over my chest and remembered Miranda's mother in jail, Miranda with her. I got my license out. All at once the cop grabbed his walkie-talkie and said, "Yup." Someone rattled off words, numbers. He turned it off and said, "I've got a two-eleven I've got to assist. Concentrate on your driving, hear?"

And ran to his car and sped off with sirens.

So I drove to a 7-Eleven in a careful way and bought formula. I stood in line behind a big woman—you see this kind in Texas, lots of makeup, Little House on the Prairie dress, stiff hair. She was buying Kotex, packages of batteries, all sizes, like for toys, four loaves of Mrs. Baird's Butter Bread. She wished the clerk a Merry Christmas. "Put the Christ back in it," she said. The clerk looked surprised. The woman said, "I know God loves me. God's love is huge." Maybe because I was worried about having gotten pulled over—post-emergency stupor—I started thinking I knew God loved me too, but I'd never call the feeling huge, wrong word. Like you were greedy, selfish. I pictured His love like a heel on a loaf of bread, enough to keep you going.

But on the way home I stopped thinking about that and started thinking about the license plate on my mother's car. When it wasn't current anymore, how would I renew it? Would I need the title? I always got titles and registrations mixed up. I'd never even heard of such a thing as trailer house title until the funeral home director asked me to find it, and I looked in a drawer where Duster said my mother kept papers and found it underneath junk mail and old catalogues, a box of rubber bands, a deck of cards, a bag of potpourri that smelled fresh—I remember, because when I found the title, no manila envelope or file folder protecting it, and took it to the funeral director, it smelled like pine and lavender, like a love letter waiting to be sent. Was the car title in that drawer too? Why had I thought the risk was all in getting the car here?

I pulled up at home. The lights were on, and Mike Cleary's truck was parked in front.

I got Esme out of the car and went inside.

He sat on the couch, legs crossed, one shiny shoe propped on his knee. He had a poinsettia in a red pot sitting on the table in front of him, and he was holding the channel changer. He stood—I hadn't seen him since before Thanksgiving, Cleveland. He had that lines-around-his-eyes smile. Droopy mustache. Looked happy, not gloomy. "What are you doing here?"

He winked at my dad. "How's that for a warm welcome?"

"I wasn't expecting you, I meant."

"I rushed out of my family obligations to get here. How's the baby?" He chucked her under the chin.

"What obligations?" I couldn't decide if I should be mad he'd assumed I didn't have any.

"I spent Christmas Eve with my daughter."

The one who used to stand in the driveway and tell him to rot in hell.

"She has a little one close to Esme's age," he said. "Her name is Whitney."

I'd never heard Mike call Esme by name before. I didn't know he had a grandkid.

"But it's weird—I'm used to Esme. Whitney seems pale and sickly compared to Esme."

"She would seem pale." This was my dad talking.

"I got here and saw your car, but your old man said you were driving something else."

"My mother's car," I said. I wished I'd never seen that car. "I got pulled over just now," I said. "I got rid of all her stuff or left it there. I didn't look for a car title." The idea I could keep her car a secret seemed crazy now. The point of laws is keeping tabs on who owns what. Not having owned much, I'd oversimplified. Yet I didn't need the title as long as the registration was current. Just a made-up story about why I had the car. Duster was right, I wasn't better than him.

My dad said, "You don't even know it was registered to her."

Good point.

Mike said, "Go to the DMV and apply for a replacement title."

"But it's not mine exactly."

"She left it to you?"

I said, "She didn't leave specific instructions."

Mike said, "It'd be good to find the original title."

My dad said, "If you want to drive it, just take the plates off your car and put them on hers."

Mike said, "That wouldn't look good if you did get pulled over."

"Too many rules," my dad said. He stood up. "Guess I'll take that shower."

You need one, I thought. Six days.

When my dad came out, wet hair sticking up, white belly plumped out over his belt, he said, "Do you have rubbing alcohol?" He liked to put it in his ears. He also clipped his toenails in a V so they wouldn't get ingrown. He'd done these things since I could remember and tried to get me to.

I said, "I have hydrogen peroxide."

He shook his head. "Not the same." Then, "I have a present for the baby, but I didn't get to wrap it."

I pictured him driving to Stites for a gift—looking out of place in his hunting clothes as he sorted through pastel baby gear. He'd bought me two presents a year when I was a kid: birthday, Christmas. Once, he had a lady from the reservation school take me to town to buy me bras. When he did wrap something, he'd use newspaper. Right now, he went into Esme's room and came back out. He handed me a doll—so I thought—with a big, gray head, wearing a silver jumpsuit.

"Hand puppet," he said. "I ordered it from Roswell, New Mexico."

Mike was coming from the kitchen. "Nice space alien," he said to my dad. "You want a beer?"

"Trying to go easy on the stomach," my dad said.

Mike said, "Did you have trouble with your flight down here, because of the rain?"

"Came by bus," my dad said.

Mike looked surprised. Then shrugged. "Smart. You wouldn't have got here faster by plane."

My dad nodded, like that was the point. And went to bed.

"Thanks for the gift." I wiggled the puppet at Esme who gave it that look she gave the doll—shifting around old ideas, making space for new. She grinned. I folded laundry while Mike watched TV, and I thought how my dad hadn't asked who Mike was or how I knew him. Also how one of my kids, Silvia, said her dad was strict about people she could go places with. I'd told her she was lucky. "He lets people know it's not Open Season." At the time I was thinking my dad never did this because he didn't trust anyone, but he also knew no-trust wasn't normal and so left it to me to sort out who was a bad influence. "Open season?" Silvia had asked. Figure of speech—she'd never heard it. And on TV, *Nova*, they were talking about oxytocin, a brain chemical in mammals that triggers sexual arousal and all bonding, including mother-to-infant. They were interested in female prairie voles who, once stimulated, never bond again.

Esme started fussing. I fed her and put her to bed.

Mike opened another beer. "I know you won't want me here all night."

I did understand his point: but did I want him in my bed a few hours?

I used to drink when I had sex with him—or anyone—but we didn't have time for that. We went to the bedroom and I shut the door, locked it, and turned the baby monitor on. The light glowed green/calm, the sound of Esme's wet, clicking breaths and my dad's snores filling the room. Not exactly some Amore in the Moon song, but if you wait for that, the honeymoon mood, you'd never have sex. But maybe because I hadn't had a drink—and I need it to get in a mindset, hands, bodies, here, now—I was going on about the car. I said, "Maybe I'll call the lawyer and mention to him I have the car down here, and when does he think the estate will be settled." Mike stared at the ceiling. "Your house hasn't sold yet," he said. "Why don't you buy it?"

I made that noise, air emptying out. "I can't afford it."

He shook his head. "People live on credit—the average person is in deep. Borrow it."

"But you have to pay it back. I'd have to borrow the down payment, pay it, and pay the house note too." I wasn't being a tightwad, just sensible. "My babysitting costs as much as rent."

He said, "Most people would have gone in the reverse order—house first, kid second."

I said, "I didn't want a house that bad." I did now though, for Esme.

He was lifting my shirt, putting his hands underneath it.

"But in less than a year," I said, "she won't need formula, which is a hundred bucks a month." He had one hand on my tit now. With the other, he yanked up my skirt. "She won't be in diapers forever, which cost seventy-five dollars a month," I said. "Big co-pay every time I fill a prescription." I was thinking: okay, concentrate on sex. He moved my hand to his dick. I said, "Electricity." Afterthought. Though I did stroke him. "Has it gone up in Louisiana? My heating and AC bill is higher than last year," I said. His mouth— flattened on mine, kissing mine when I said this about electric bills—lost the kissing motion. His teeth rammed against my tongue, my lips, because he was laughing, our breath mixed up. "Keep talking," he said. "This is erotic, the cost of living."

I started laughing too.

And lay there undressed, thinking all I knew about Mike was how he looked, his broad shoulders, chapped-looking skin across his neck most men get if they work outside. The bump on his hip I barely saw anymore, noticing instead a usual-looking, naked man, and then, belated, a second later, the shock of it: curved, knobby. When I was a kid in Mormon church looking at my grandma's old friends with warts or goiters, I thought those were the malignancy the speaker was talking about, the decay we prayed God to clear away. The whole time I was married to Stephen Arco, I looked for outward signs as to what was inside—what dark smear or mean streak?

I'd never asked Mike much. Not about the bump on his hip because it seemed like a bad subject, cold shower. What about his ideas? How far would he go not to hurt someone? Then the phone clicked on, the answering machine. "Little Hoover." It was Dannie, extra-perky even for her. I was thinking of power grids they show on TV because of the energy crisis—strung-out connections between blocks that produce enough energy and blocks that don't. I had the door shut, the baby monitor on with my dad's sleep-sounds taking over Esme's, so I heard bits. "My sister wants to meet you, relieved I have a normal friend." Singing: *wish you a Merry Christmas*. Also, "New job, Tawny. Dancer. Court date. Won't be at work. Landlord. *Pieta*." She said this. I know because it was on the answering machine the next day. The *Pieta* is the Virgin Mary holding the dead Christ. Then Mike Cleary was on top, and the bedsprings creaked, the bed shifting against the window, the window a layer between me and night air, endlessness. Sex seemed like voltage, recharge. Dannie's voice trying to get through would subtract, detract. I let it go on.

ELEVEN

Front porch, New Year's Eve day, I heard Mike going on about a kid he coached in Little League. "Good outfielder," Mike said. "Then he grew up. He's a doctor now and lives down here."

Is that why he brought it up? I wondered. Lately it seemed I worried too much about this—connections between what people say and what might happen, the lurking sense there's overlooked clues and hints all over. I was staring at white puffs of clouds, oleander and monkey grass turned lush because of rain. Warm weather had blown in, and yet I hadn't cleaned the shed. Or gardened, maybe planting some bulbs. Or taking out old bulbs and putting them in a box for when we moved. House-hunting—I should have had a stab at that but was still unclear on when and how. Would I rent a place big enough for my dad, who acted vague about leaving? I looked at him propped in Arturo's chair, hands on knees, eyes closed. I'd figured one day he'd start going on about Belize again, and we'd talk feasibility, or lack of, and his no-funds problem. I should have seen it coming, I thought, my dad's migration from pines in the deep snow to here, me.

My dad said, "They didn't have Little League when I grew up."

"He moved here because of his wife's family," Mike said. "I'd like to have my surgery here."

"What surgery?" I said.

He shifted in his chair. "There hasn't been an easy time to bring this up."

He meant when my dad wasn't listening. Since Christmas, Mike had come by every day after work, and my dad would extend his hand and say, "Well." Heartier than when I came in from the store, which I found myself going to all the time for one box of rice, one cake mix, one tube of biscuits. I wasn't used to not being alone, so I'd put Esme in the car and head out. Today I left her with Dad. I'd showed him her pacifier, her swing. I came in and he was giving her a bottle straight from the refrigerator, cold but she didn't mind. I took it, zapped it in the microwave. According to the *What to*

Expect book, this is hazardous—formula can get scalding hot spots. But not if you shake it up, I figure. I gave the bottle back to my dad, and he was on the couch feeding Esme when Mike came in—talking about angle of drop, EPA standards within two hundred feet of a stream. But on the porch now, my dad all at once was taking deep, sleepy breaths.

"The tumor on my back you've never brought up," Mike said. "It must seem strange—you being young and pretty."

My dad opened his eyes.

Young and pretty? I thought. "How old are you?"

He stared at me. "Forty-eight. And you?"

"Thirty-four," I said.

My dad closed his eyes. "Spring chickens, both of you."

Mike said, "I'd like to have the surgery, and I'd like to relocate here."

My dad said, "An oval-shaped mass between the bone and skin, kind of slippery? My dog had one, fat cell tumor. I had a small one. Vet said it was a sign of age, no need to take it off."

Mike nodded, red-faced. Maybe he hadn't meant to be so detailed, call the tumor by name: fat cell. I was thinking about what he said about relocating. "You'd spend more time here?"

The muscles in his face seemed tight. "Would you like to go for a drive?"

My dad stood up. "I should have been clued in. I'll leave you two alone."

Mike stood up too. "No offense, but she's hard to talk to."

Halfway through the door, my dad turned. "Not her fault, exactly."

Then Mike sat next to me, and I shifted Esme to my shoulder. Mike talked fast. "I tried to tell you by phone. I came early to tell you. Your dad's right, there's no reason to have it removed, but I want to, and I'm one of those people who gets scared about being cut. Jimmy, the kid I used to coach, will do it outpatient, but someone needs to drive me because I'll be loopy from anesthesia. I know you can't. But I thought I could arrange the surgery late in the day, and your friend Dannie would drive, and I'd spend the first hours after surgery here." He paused, exhaled. "This seems a strange way to bring the rest up. I know with a little one you have to go slow and follow your hunches. But I'm getting more work here. I'd like to get a place here. You're sensible. You like sex. That's important to me. I've never had enough. You don't want to get married—I like that too. But if you don't want me, say the word, and you won't have to bother."

So much force seemed behind what he'd said, weeks of planning. Did I want him for sure? That's maybe how you feel after years with someone,

I thought. Yet he'd brought good times and, up to now, no outlay or cost. When I was young I used to pick casual types who wouldn't need much, I figured, but I got conned in small ways: a ten-spot out of my purse if I wasn't looking, or lending my car and not getting it back until I tracked the guy down. Marrying Stephen Arco, I'd had the idea that marriage was more than you or the other person. It was a system to adjust or correct you, good for all. For me, it was a cash drain. You'd have to like the idea of any old person with his promises to cherish you, a hypothetical ideal lover rather than a real person, I thought, to feel upbeat and not nervous about getting hitched. Because a real person was bound to bring trouble. But my qualms were like static I heard no matter who I was with. With Esme looking on, my dad too, I felt pressure to pick a boyfriend and stick with him. Or give it up and be alone. I looked at Mike, his eyes like a surface you can't see past, lake water.

He said, "Your decision."

I said, "Where you live should be your decision."

"If you want me, I'd like to live near you."

For what? I thought. Get what? I should have said this in the past, maybe. But now? Lupe liked Mike Cleary but not Hector. Was that a sign? What I did say came fast and out-of-nowhere. "Affirmative." I don't even know where I'd heard the word except in some TV show about soldiers of war or CB radios. When I said it—I want to emphasize—I had happy wishes, intentions.

He said, "Yes?"

Like my kids say, duh.

"It's okay if I have the surgery here?"

I shrugged. "If you want to, you should."

"You feel . . . ?" He leaned forward.

I didn't wait to find out. "I said yes to you twice already."

He laughed like I'd made a joke. He pushed the porch swing back and forth with his foot. Esme focused on his face in a way that seemed in-the-curve, normal, no obvious developmental delays. "I'll finish up in Lake Charles," he said, "and come back. I put it off until I could find a doctor I trusted. My ex-wife tried to get me a massage once, bought me a gift certificate. Never used it. My ex-sister-in-law cuts my hair. I can't let just anyone put their hands on me."

I've been otherwise. Lax standards for my body. Open Season Outside-Only. "Why?"

He shook his head. "Quirky. Born private."

"I would have never got that." I'd taken him to bed the second time I saw him.

"That's different," he said. His arm, on the back of the porch swing, fell onto my shoulders.

Silence. Birds. Tires on pavement. Janeway raking. I hadn't seen her come outside.

Mike said, "This talk about Belize, how did your dad get started?"

"It's a grass-is-greener fixation."

Mike said, "The grass *is* greener in Belize. And here, compared to Idaho."

Then my dad stepped onto the porch with the telephone. "For you, Delia."

I took it and navigated a three-way conversation. Dannie on the phone, which buzzed and snapped, told me she was calling from her sister's rental car and that they'd talked about getting a car with a TV but decided to be economical. She said, "Who was that, Little Hoover? Your dad?" Pitch and enthusiasm rising on this, *dad*. "From Idaho? My mother was from Idaho." *Mother.* "I have a New Year's gift for Doo-doo on account I didn't get her one for Christmas." I was listening to Esme making chanting, repetitive M-sounds and wondered if this could be construed as the word *mama*. I eavesdropped on the conversation between Mike and my dad:

My dad, "I'd been thinking about getting out of the North, and I met this fellow up there buying easements for oil companies to lay pipeline, working an hour or so a day, time on his hands."

"He told you about Belize?" Mike.

"Lived there. Got in trouble with the IRS and lived there on sixty bucks a month."

"When?"

My dad, "This would have been years ago."

"You planning to spend some time there?" Mike.

My dad, "It sounds like paradise. Good place to end . . ."

"Hoover, you there? We're around the corner. Can we come?" This was Dannie talking.

Did it matter? "That's fine," I said and hung up. I saw Lupe peeking out the window, and she caught sight of Mike and waved a Kleenex like a little flag. She came outside. "Nice to see you."

My dad held his hand out. "I'm Delia's father."

Lupe said, "I saw you and wanted to know who you are." But she didn't talk to me or look at me. Arturo came outside. "We're leaving to look at houses with my niece's husband," Lupe said next, staring at me. "Nice houses and very cheap in Hacienda Bonita Estates North." She was mad, I decided. Because I'd insisted we house-hunt alone. Or I hadn't faced facts, like Arturo. But why all of a sudden was she looking at houses in that *colonia* with tripe in the sewer?

Dannie and a big woman wearing a floppy hat pulled up in a convertible.

Lupe and Arturo headed down the sidewalk.

Lupe made a point of ignoring Dannie and her sister. They were getting out of the car, yelling, flouncing around like those clowns you see in rodeos—supposedly going about their business, but you're supposed to notice them and not the nasty work going on in the corner with a prod.

My dad, standing by the door, frowned. "Like attracts like."

If I had to guess, I'd say he meant that outsiders hang together because they don't have much choice. "I'm Delia's dad," he said, when they got to the porch. "Welcome to the humble abode."

"The porch?" Dannie said. "The porch is your abode?"

Dannie's sister plopped down next to me. "My God," she said, "I'm sweating. It's hot here and it stinks. Dannie said that's Exxon. But I want to thank you for taking her in. I told her I'm so fucking glad she has a normal friend at last. Have you met Tawny?" She made a gagging sound.

Dannie said, "Leave Tawny alone."

Dannie's sister said, "She got a job and moved out. She's a modern dancer. And I'm King Tut."

Mike said, "Anyone want a beer? I've got some on ice."

Dannie took one, I noticed. Though that cop had said not to—people like her shouldn't drink.

Dannie's sister said, "As you know, I live in Atlanta and I have the purse strings. I totally didn't mind she took that trip to wherever. Good investment is the way I see it—you have the training. Next step is getting her out of that house with the wacko landlord. Have you met him?"

Before I could answer—and the thought I had to meet another person from Dannie's life made me feel like I needed to jump up and run away—I saw Dannie laugh hard and loud, wild eyes, laughing at everything my dad said. What could he have said? "Do they have cows?" she asked.

My dad looked startled. "Here and there you'll see a dairy farm."

Dannie said, "I wondered. My mother was from Arco."

My dad nodded. "Delia married into the Arco family somehow."

I'd been married to someone named Arco, for sure. Divorced him, end of contact. But lately I felt evermore blended with Dannie—connected to her, and her sister, mother, girlfriend, landlord, cousin. Crossed over. Meshed. I feel like this about anyone in trouble, that it could have been me having trouble. Except I'd had better luck. There but for the good mood of God go I.

"I have a picture of my mom, black and white," Dannie said, "in front of her house. But you can't quite see it. She's wearing a Peter Pan dress, holding a dog, and what you see is the outhouse."

My dad was struggling to say something. To fit in. He'd probably talked more in the last ten days than ten years, homosexuals in nature, this. Women's libbers okay by me, that. I've raised dogs with the same problem you have, yes sir. Digging deep to find something he knew that matched the conversation at hand. "You saw a lot of outhouses in the old days," he said, finally.

Dannie said, "That's what I figure. We don't have much from when she was little." Then she held up a bag and started pulling out firecrackers and sparklers. "I bought these for the Doo-doo, for her first New Year's. I wanted to buy her a fishing pole. But my sister wouldn't let me."

Dannie's sister said, "I was thinking along the lines of a teddy bear. But fireworks, okay."

Dannie blinked, wide-eyed. I had this idea about her I heard on TV once—it had to do with dogs. An animal like a dog keeps immature characteristics of the wild ancestor, the wolf. Acting like a baby wolf even though he's tough and full-grown is the deal the dog makes to be petted and fed, not hunted down, eradicated. Right now Dannie was telling us about a time she was little and her mother let her hold a sparkler, and Dannie stood there, staring. Her mother said: Now wave. Wave, honey. "And I waved at it," Dannie said, slapping her knee and laughing.

Everyone lit firecrackers then, and I took Esme inside.

I get too many people around me and I start worrying I've let important work slip, like the boy who was supposed to tend sheep or stick his finger in the levee. I looked around the house for signs of trouble. I didn't have to, though. On the porch, I'd been half-thinking already that when I came back from Cleveland I'd had a letter from the lawyer—last week I got another and hadn't opened it yet. Blame this on Stephen Arco, who always got hassled by collection agencies. Or he'd find a new loser who'd give him credit, and we'd get that bill. Once he said he was going on job interviews and needed my Texaco card for gas, and when the bill came he'd charged $249. Gas, also snacks, beer, magazines. The months I tried to stay married, I kept juggling, trying to pay up, stay straight. So I have this feeling letters you don't expect bring bad news.

I was holding the letter, getting ready to open it, and Dannie's sister walked in and said, "Like I said, I want to thank you for looking after Dannie, and I'm going to leave you with my phone number." She held a notebook and pen. "And I want yours so that the next time she calls in the middle of the night because she's in a jam or has picked up another stray, I'll call you." I must have looked nervous, because she said, "But don't worry. I won't call you until the next morning."

Then a series of pops going off outside. Banging on my screen door. "Come on out," Dannie said. "Get out here, because we're leaving. You said we'd go to Houston and wait for midnight."

"Never mind," Dannie's sister said. "I'll get your phone number from Dannie later."

This saved me from answering. From the chance to say no: I can't keep tabs.

I watched the two of them pull away. My dad was in the street, lighting matches, dropping firecrackers, and every few seconds running backward from the bright, loud popping. Mike rushed inside, yelling over his shoulder, "I need to make a pit stop." He looked at me. I was holding Esme and the letter. "You don't want a beer?" He kissed me as he brushed past. "I'll be right there, Ephraim," he yelled. This gave me a chill. The only person I'd heard call my dad by name, Ephraim, was my grandmother. Or someone else, way back. And I had the instant sense I was two—looking at the world with a two-year-old's angle and opinions. Another dusky night, a woman in darkness at the edge of the yard who seemed afraid, saying, "Ephraim, don't leave me out here now." Then she was gone. It was this room again, these duties. I opened the letter.

Ms. Arco,

The notice to creditors we placed in the classified advertising section of the newspaper has run thirty days as required by law, and no creditor has filed claim. I requested an itemized bill for expenses incurred by your mother's funeral and interment. When I didn't receive a reply, I learned from the realtor who first recommended your case to me that Eems Funeral Home has had its license

I hadn't exactly trusted Mr. Eems. Short and talky, dragging his secretary along all cheerful-helpful, like she always went to strangers' funerals. Still, he was the only person who'd talk to me. Indigent Services, someone had suggested. Duster tried that. "I'll work with you," Mr. Eems had said. He suggested cremation, which was economical, better for the environment, and he'd put her ashes in Lake Erie. I wondered if he'd gotten around to that before they shut him down. I read somewhere they're big and chunky—not ashes, more like silt. I pictured my mother's silt in a cardboard box on a shelf. People have been buried in worse places, down wells and in ditches. But it isn't what you'd want. Where was she? I wondered. Nearby, I sometimes felt—in the rafters of the house or high up in tree branches. I looked outside. I hadn't heard any noise in a while. I saw one sparkler fizzling down and someone, my dad, running through shadows toward the porch. I went outside. I heard firecrackers going off in other yards, other driveways.

Janeway was sitting on the swing next to my dad. I stood next to Mike and held Esme.

My dad said, "It's not her fault she was born in that family. Someone needs to be kind to her."

"I'm not saying any different," Janeway said. "It's just the lurid details in that book. They rested the whole prosecution on the fact the family was crazy. Crazy people kill crazy people. The defense tried to make the point the parents were deviant, that they'd raised deviant children."

Mike said, "I wouldn't call her crazy. I guess the cousin had to be. And you never know the whole story—drugs, or money. You'd be crazy too, if you'd lived through that, and all that publicity."

"He did take drugs," Janeway said. "But a lot of people do. He must have been unbalanced."

"Maybe just a worthless human being," my dad said. Like that was an explanation.

"Where were they," I asked, "when they were killed?" The hair on my arms stood up.

"In their bed," Janeway said. "He knew the house. The girls had already left home for college."

I remembered Dannie telling me it was taking a long time to get through college.

Mike said, "You can tell something had gone wrong—that she's living in the aftermath." He looked at me. "What was that she was babbling about on the answering machine the other night?"

Which part? I wondered. Her landlord. Tawny. Court date. "She had a dream," I said. "She has trouble sleeping." What she'd said was she'd dreamed she had a chance to talk to the Virgin of Guadalupe, who's considered good at small miracles and kind to lowly people, and the Virgin had said to relax and enjoy herself, to enjoy Christmas. "I looked away," Dannie had said, "and she'd turned into the *Pieta,* by Michelangelo. That's what I get for studying for my finals."

Janeway said, "You should read the book."

Mike said, "I'm not much for reading unless it has to do with work. Delia's the bookworm."

"She should read it," Janeway said. "It'd help her understand Dannie."

I thought about those pictures. The glaring, splattered crime scene, blood slopped like paint. A bedroom, yes. A blood-streaked bed. "That's not what I need to know to understand," I said. "And you couldn't know all that and not seal off the part of you that's friendly." On the other hand, I thought, maybe I *should* know and seal off the part of me that's friendly. For protection. For Esme. To insulate her. Dannie kept me agitated all by herself, and because she had worse judgment than me, a worse weirdometer, she dragged her rabble through my life too. Not that her sister was rabble. It's just that Dannie's sister wasn't my sister. Where would it end?

Janeway said, "I need to go. Marla's coming tomorrow, and I want to get the house ready."

My dad said, "I thought her name was Myrna."

I said, "You're thinking of Martha. This is Marla from L.A." Marla Martha Sharon Karen, I thought.

Janeway said, "I see the point you've been trying to make all along."

I didn't follow.

"I've been obtuse, projecting my situation. I like Mike, though." Janeway said this in front of Mike, hand on his shoulder.

"That makes two of you," I said. "Lupe would marry him."

Mike and Janeway laughed about that. She headed across the street, and my dad and Mike and Esme and I stayed on the porch. My dad said. "Do you get fireflies down here? I like fireflies."

"Not until April," I said. "You planning on staying?"

"Well," he said. And nothing else.

Mike said, "I've got an early morning—I thought I'd head back." He was sitting down. I was standing. His hand climbed up the back of my legs in the dark, under my skirt, and stayed there, cup-shaped, on my ass. I felt unsteady, holding Esme. He was waiting for my dad to turn in.

My dad said, "I guess I'll wait up for midnight. I haven't done that in years."

Mike's hand fell away. "I'll go back to my motel. Say, did I tell you I found a place to rent?"

"Already?" I said.

He said, "But it won't be available until the first of February."

"Where is it?"

"Off Blevin Street, a little house tucked in between all the big ones."

Different price range from places I'd been looking at, I thought. I said, "You own your house in Louisiana?"

He nodded.

"What will you do with that?"

"I'll leave it for the time being. My daughter and her husband might need it."

He has three houses, I thought. Owned one, he'd rent another, and a motel room he could afford whenever. Some people don't have one. Of course they're homeless, not exactly mainstream.

He was kissing me good-bye in front of my dad. In the dark, but still. Squishing Esme between us.

"I'll see you in a few weeks."

He drove away, and I sat there pulled two ways, two ways multiplied by everybody. Because everybody, besides Esme and maybe a kid or so at work, made me feel contradictory. People need patterns, guidelines, categories. *Friend. Lover,* which for most people is the short track toward spouse. *Family member,* that category. Everyone else stays outside these lines. But I've always been on the brink myself, or maybe outside, and I get confused, for instance, about Janeway, who seemed well-adjusted but warped. Mike, I wanted him near, but not too. Dannie I cared about, but I didn't like what I learned when I peered hard into her life: the debauched know-how she'd pieced together, the ABCs of getting by. Yet I couldn't help watching out for her. There's no ignoring bad news, warnings, but you can't spend your alive-time in misery either, on guard. I said, "Dad, what did you say about some-one has to be nice to Dannie?"

He stirred. "What? Yes. Golden rule. Do unto others. But you're asking the wrong person," he said. "You know more about that. I haven't been much help to anyone, when it mattered."

Who was he talking about? "Who?" I asked.

He winced and rubbed his stomach. "I used to be afraid of what I wasn't yet, or hadn't managed to do. I saw other people as pulling me back, drag-ging my thinking about myself down a slope."

"Right," I said. "You have your chance, and you can't think about some-one else's bad luck."

"Depends," he said, "on who that person is to you."

"How do you know that?" I asked.

He wasn't listening. He was in the dark, snoring.

T W E L V E

I was blinking awake in the morning, hearing my dad's snores, Esme's delicate breaths. I'd been dreaming I was in a house with a porch, a sewing room, a nursery, a kitchen. A realtor—not the man in Cleveland putting a lock-box on my mother's trailer, but the woman who'd told me I couldn't live in Pesquera—said, "There's a room here for everything a family does." She opened a door to what I thought was a closet but turned out to be crawl space filled with people—shoving, cringing, so at first I didn't see the pale cords like tendons, like dried-out rubber cement stretched from one person to another, webbed around someone to someone else. The realtor shut the door, and for some reason I hoped my mother had found privacy, leeway, in her last moments, that she hadn't gone toward death with Duster throwing his weight around, giving off scorn that comes from people you've lived with too much in small spaces. Stephen Arco used to say I was a pit bull. "You get a hold of an idea," he said, "and can't let go." He said so early in the relationship, admiring my stamina. "It's how to get ahead," I said. "You feel desperate." I was thinking it wasn't just that you held on to something you were afraid to lose but that the past snapped and snarled behind you. Every time we had a fight after that, he'd call me names: Pit bull, he'd say. Raging cunt pit bull. I hoped my mother's last minutes weren't like that.

Or this, overcast skies.

I lay in bed trying to remember the Hebrew word for wind, all Rs and vowels, a sound like moaning. God exhaling. Today was the day of Mike Cleary's surgery. I felt half-sad, and it took me a minute to remember why—house buyers yesterday, the woman with her navy blue purse, bumping into the door frame with her elbows and purse, nodding her dyed, shiny head as she looked around and said, "Perfect perfect," each syllable a hurrah, a cheer. My dad glanced at her, then me. I introduced him to Chuck, landlord, and my dad said, "I'll go sit on the porch, if no one minds." Then the house-buying woman said, "I like the way she's kept the cottage motif throughout."

Chuck said, "You can do the same on the other side. It didn't cost Delia much, just elbow grease."

"He's starting his job," she said. "He can't live over there while we renovate. He'll live here first. If you want your apartment," she told me, "you can have it back after we remodel that side."

This would be impossible, of course.

Chuck took up for me. "Delia can't live in limbo while you remodel."

"I guess not," the woman said.

The husband—first time he spoke—said, "It wouldn't kill Trey to live with a little construction."

The woman said, "Absolutely not. He needs to get off on the right foot at Exxon."

Chuck said, "You won't have trouble finding a place to live, Delia."

The woman said, "Maybe you could consider this your thirty days' notice?"

Chuck said, "Legally, you have to put it in writing. And you can't do that until we close the sale."

Now I don't understand the kinds of things Sage understands—logic, for instance, which her dad teaches in college. It's also the name of a fire ant poison. But I do think the words *sane* and *sanctuary* come from one idea, that you can't feel sane without walls to keep the world out. There's you and what you know. Everything you don't know, right or wrong, stays on the other side. Of course prayer is supposed to do away with that. You ignore the margin between yourself and everything. If that's so, a house has the same nullifying-of-fear effect as prayer. And you can't pray twenty-four hours a day; you need a house some of the time. Mike had pulled up as I stood in the living room thinking this. Chuck and the house buyers meantime fingered my walls, my woodwork. It was Mike's first day back—the day before his surgery. I introduced him to Chuck, who shook his hand. Mike gave me a rankled look, like: how could I not manage to keep my house? I was thinking about money. To move, you need two months' rent. One for deposit and one for the first month. Some landlords want the last month too. If a landlord takes a shine to you, he might let you in on rent alone, and when you get your deposit back from the old landlord you hand it over. But that was rare. Maybe my dad had money? He'd been handing me fives and tens lately when I went to the store. He wouldn't have much, just a few hundred from selling his truck before he moved down here. My emotions were swerving, heave and ho, swamping down when I considered it was my house they wanted, then the hurtling-forward worrying about where to get money, time, a moving van, someone to lift big pieces.

That's what I was thinking about the next morning, lying in bed.

I got up and went to the kitchen. I was making coffee when Mike knocked on the door. He looked nervous, pale, his eyes too-bright and darting around. He pointed at the handwritten sign on a piece of paper—Contract Pending—taped over the For Sale By Owner sign. "Bad timing."

I couldn't tell if he meant it was bad timing my house was being sold on the day of his surgery, outpatient, big deal. At the moment, my lost house seemed worse. Be a man, I thought. Was this the warning I'd waited for, he didn't have courage? He wanted some of mine, but I couldn't have his back? Or bad timing picking today because Dannie wasn't free to take him to surgery this afternoon, just this morning? We sat on the porch with Esme, who was eating a tortilla.

My dad came out, shirtless. "Do you want coffee?" he asked Mike.

"Nothing after midnight. The anesthesia—I might drown on what's in my stomach," Mike said.

My dad looked puzzled.

I said, "He's having that tumor cut off today, remember?"

My dad nodded. "Right."

"Why did you ask Dannie to take you?" I asked Mike.

He said, "Who else? You have to work. She'll leave me alone, I figure. No fussing."

"Good luck with that," I said. Dannie was careless about commonsense things—like he might need water and she wouldn't think to offer that. But she'd scurry around and never shut up.

"She should be here by now." He stood. "I'll go find her. Where does she live?"

I started to explain. I'd never been there. Four blocks from here, Dannie had told me, where the neighborhood starts to turn. It's just like your duplex, she'd said, two shotgun apartments joined down the middle. I told Mike, "It's behind that bar, Justa Beer, and on the other side of that muffler shop. I don't know which house exactly, but you could look for her truck."

"A little black Ford, right?" He stared at me, fingernails clicking the porch railing.

"I'll go," I said. "It'll take me two minutes." I wanted out of here, alone-time.

I got dressed. I got Esme's car-seat carrier. She was almost big enough to need the new upright car seat, I thought, eighty bucks at Wal-Mart. I went outside, and Mike was pacing. My dad had removed the door on the driver's side of my little hatchback car and set it on the sidewalk. I'd been driving the hatchback since I got pulled over in my mother's car, but the door on the driver's side was stuck shut, which meant I not only had to load Esme in the back of a two-door car but also had to climb in on the passenger side and over the stick-shift to drive. It wasn't good timing on my dad's part either. "I'll take the other car," I said. I went inside for the keys.

When I came out he had the license plates off both cars—my mother's gold car and my hatchback—and was making the switch. "Until I get your little car up and running," he said. "It could use an all-around tune-up, points and wires. I might look at that air-conditioning problem too."

I said, "And the lights." They'd go out for ten seconds, headlights, dashboard, then blink on.

"Leave the baby here," he said. "I'll watch her."

I found Dannie's duplex right away. It was exactly like mine, a clone. According to Janeway, native stone was once the main-style, cheap way to build here because of the tree shortage. Two doors led onto her porch in the same configuration as mine. The difference was we had silvery green window trim that made the stones look necessary, beautiful. Dannie's was mustard yellow. They had no yard—a bulldozed lot with a mailbox smack-dab in the middle like a lawn ornament. Dannie's truck sat in the street. So did another truck, except it was high in the air with big tires—a monster truck—and smile-face fog lights. On the side of the porch that would have been mine, a towel hung in the window for a curtain; it shifted and someone peeked out. On the side that would have been Lupe's, lights glowed yellow in the overcast morning light. In front of that door sat a pair of boots I'd seen Dannie wear. I banged on it. No one answered.

I could hear the TV going, a morning talk show, brisk forecast—windy, but fair.

I edged around to the window to look inside.

Like Stephen Arco used to say, I'm so clean I'm weird. But this was disorder. Not the housekeeping. Mental disorder: treatment required. The living room was knee-deep in not garbage exactly but newspapers, paper bags, Styrofoam carry-out containers, plastic cartons, water jugs, paper towels, old phone books, discarded clothing. An electric can opener sat on the end table, plugged into the wall. And yet there was an end table, also a couch, a footstool, a lamp, a TV. Everything was turned on full-tilt, lights, TV. Dannie's dogs sat on the couch, watching TV.

A door creaked open behind me. "She didn't come home last night." I turned around.

A guy—black hair, spade-shaped beard, jeans, no shirt—said this from the other doorway.

"Thank you," I said and left.

I got home and told Mike, "She's not there. I'll have to take a sick day and drive you myself."

My dad wiped his hands on a rag. He'd carried Esme's wind-up swing outside and set it on the sidewalk, and she was swaying back and forth, smiling at the sky, early sunlight blurring off the edges of roofs and treetops. Somewhere, a dove was cooing. "I can go," my dad said. "Just let me clean up." He propped the door against the side of the car and started picking up tools.

Mike said, "We have to leave real quick, though."

"Before you say Jack Frost," my dad said.

A beige, low-slung car pulled up. The door opened, and Dannie hopped out and all of a sudden was walking up the sidewalk, combing her hair, tucking her shirt in. The car squealed off again. I said, "Where were you? You're late." I caught a whiff of alcohol—a scent from her pores.

She said, "I said I'd be here and I am." She looked at Mike. "Ready?"

"Ready," he said.

I said, "Mike has to drive on the way there." She'd be sober by the time it was over maybe.

I got Esme ready for Luann's. "Can you drop me at your local grocery store?" my dad asked. "I need some supplies. I can walk home." I did drop him off. And drove the ten miles to Luann's.

When I pulled up in her driveway I heard music, banjos and fiddles. I knocked. Luann's mother saw me through the window and waved. I knocked again and Luann's mother waved again. I pushed the door open and went in. Luann was in the kitchen, sitting at the table next to a man with a ponytail. On the table were two plates filled with scrambled eggs and fried potatoes, also a pitcher of tomato juice. I walked over to the stereo and turned it down. Luann jumped when I did this. She was holding a joint—a roach. She tamped it out in a saucer. Now I'm not one of these people who thinks marijuana is worse than alcohol. Worse legal problems maybe. Still, you won't see me getting in an altered state during breakfast. "This is Drew," Luann said. He

146 |

smiled, charming enough. "He's leaving," she said. "I had a little tiny toke, sorry."

"I can vouch that's true," he said. "See you later." And he left.

"Are you going to the reform school today?" Luann asked me. "Or the high school?"

"High school this morning," I said, "and reform school later on—Project Promotion, I mean."

"I was just curious. We're taking Mama for a drive when you get done working."

When I got out of my car at the school parking lot, the first people I saw were Sean and his mother. We were late, all of us. They had another kid with them. "Miss Arco dresses like a Goth," Sean told him. Sean's mother extended her hand. "I'm JBD. Do you remember?" Then she said to him, "Sean, shut up." To me, "He likes you, probably has a crush on you." Sean rolled his eyes. His mother said, "This is his friend, Conrad. I want to compliment you on what you did, brought Sean out of his shell so he made a friend. Just in time, because work has picked up."

"I'm glad." I looked at Sean. "So you've made friends?"

He stared at me—eyes narrowed, tumbling ringlet-hair. "I've learned one fact I can arrange my life by. If you have a friend who thinks exactly like you do, you won't need anyone else."

I wished Sean was right—that there were friends like this. That's why God's so important, the idea: our sins and griefs to bear. "As long as he never changes," I said, "or you don't."

But JBD agreed with Sean. She said, "Sean and Conrad need each other. Conrad just moved here. His mother, who works in that balloon bouquet shop, told me how she'd planned to move to a suburb of Houston, and the realtor actually took her aside and said not to. They're a mixed-race family." JBD said this in front of Conrad. I watched his face for signs it bothered him to be talked about point-blank. Eyes: an indicator of self-control. Lots of self-control in Conrad's eyes, I thought. "His mother's white," JBD said. "The father, who's not in the picture, is some other race. Maybe Filipino. I haven't the vaguest. But the realtor said he wouldn't be able to live with himself if he didn't tell them that they needed to find a more tolerant place to live."

"Port Town?" I didn't mean it wasn't tolerant. It's not the tolerance mecca either.

"I don't know why they picked Port Town," she said, "but the other day his mother told me she felt grateful the realtor had been candid, because

Conrad is happy here. And Sean's happy because Conrad is happy. They have a secret club or something. Sean is a joiner." She paused. "And a loner— if you can be both at the same time. Conrad is at our house all the time, which is good for Sean, because Sean's sister practically lives with her boyfriend." JBD checked her watch. "I'm catching a plane," she said. "But Sean finally has a friend, and we have you to thank."

Sean bowed. "Thank you, oh Great One."

Conrad's face split open for a minute into a laugh. Then he stopped laughing.

At least Sean isn't looking up white supremacy Web sites anymore, I thought. Or Pussy dot com. Believing in a Siamese-twin best friend who'd never misunderstand you seemed harmless by comparison. I should have stayed and talked maybe. Or called Conrad into my office. But on what grounds? Besides, someone was already there—a girl who said her mother's husband abused her but wouldn't say how. The girl's mother said she wanted attention, that she'd gotten the idea, the word *abuse,* from afternoon talk shows. The girl's mother and state social worker were in my office too. Having turned the case over, which is the law once a kid makes an accusation, I have to let go. It's not my place now, until her grades sink. But letting go is hard, because I know from experience you need evidence, not rumors, to get a kid out of a house like that. Out of a frying pan into what? How do you know you're not sending her into fire? I held her hand as we said good-bye. "Let's talk about your grades once a week," I said.

I left and drove to Project Promotion. I parked and went inside.

Sage stood in the main office, reading mail, dunking a tea bag in water. She pointed out the window. "Delia, what are you driving? How many miles a gallon do you get, twelve?" She started laughing. I got the drift—the side of the exchange I was meant to keep up. I should laugh too, act comic but self-righteous about my fetish for gaudy cars. But this wouldn't have been true. I'd rather be driving my own car. Lately I'd realized I didn't know if my mother's car was insured and, if it was, if I'd be covered. "How do you like Delia's car?" she asked Mason Pratt.

He said, "It used to be a symbol you were upper echelon. In a Third World country, it still would be."

Sage said, "I know. But we're not in a Third World country. We're here."

"Supposedly getting paid to work." This was Hector, from the corner— in front of filing cabinets. "I'm running out of room. Do either of you have space in the filing cabinets in your offices?"

"I do," Sage said.

I said, "Me too." So far I kept protein shakes in mine, and a sweater.

"We need a computer," Hector said.

A few minutes later he was stuffing file folders into the cabinet in my office—breathing hard. He'd run up the stairs, I thought. He was big. He smoked. Never exercised. Touchy on the subject of exercise—sneering once when Sage had asked what he did for a workout. As if exercise was high-tone and pricey like golf lessons. Not within Hector'sæwhat do you call it?æken.

I got a phone call. Even before anyone spoke on the other end, the air seemed full of want, grabbiness. "Delia, what's up in Texas?" Duster. "I called your house and got this number."

I couldn't believe my dad gave out my work number. Dad who says: Don't volunteer anything.

Duster said, "Will you drop the charges, please."

I thought about this. "What charges?"

"Trying to write a check on someone's account, forgery."

"My mother's account, you mean. I didn't file those charges. The bank must have."

"Will you testify for me? Say I was her common-law husband?"

I was thinking: No way. But I needed something. I said, "Why not?" Then I asked, "Do you happen to know where her car title is? Was it in that same drawer where I found the trailer title?"

He said, "Car title? I have no idea. Did you look for a safe deposit box?"

Hector had left the room, tactful. Or busy. I was thinking my dad might be right, my mother didn't own the car. Also that there was a safe deposit box at the bank—a letter had said so. But why put one title in a drawer and another in the bank? I said, "Duster, I'm working. I can't talk."

He said, "Are you willing to write a letter saying I'm your mother's common-law husband?"

"When rats fly," I said. And hung up. I sat there thinking that one of the letters from the bank for sure said she kept a safe deposit box, but I'd spaced this out that nightmare morning I emptied her accounts. So I picked up the phone and called Information, got the number for Cuyahoga Credit Union. I dialed, waited for them to answer, and explained I'd been named payee. I'd come to Cleveland, done the paperwork, got the money, but forgot her safe deposit box.

"You want the contents shipped to you?" the woman said. "You'll need to sign a release."

"I already did," I said. "I flew up there. I can't afford to fly there again. I emptied out her accounts already. It was your mistake, not mine, that you didn't give me her safe deposit box."

"Can I put you on hold," she said, "while I talk to my supervisor?"

So I listened to Muzak. "Wichita Lineman." "Yesterday." "Theme from *Star Wars*." Then Hector came back with more files. I tried to get work done too, but we don't have mobile phones, so I was stuck with what I could accomplish tethered to the wall, the receiver under my chin. I reached for a stack of test scores and brushed up against Hector between my desk and filing cabinet, our fronts pressing together, and he let out a sigh that turned into a laugh so young and faraway-sounding compared to his usual gruffness, his clipped words and moods. I saw Miranda in the hallway. Also Betty, who used to be friends with Veronica, who ran away. And Nelly—I needed to talk to her because she'd gotten into a fight in the women's restroom. Her mother encouraged this. "I don't want no one mad-dogging her," her mother said. "I tell her to stand up for yourself." On the phone, a man picked up. When he spoke I knew who it was, the teller who'd acted superior that ice-cold winter morning. "Miss Arco, do you want the contents insured?"

"Is it a lot?"

"The insurance?"

"Is there a lot in the box?" I said.

He paused. "No."

"Send it priority mail," I said. I gave him my PO box number, all that.

I'd barely hung up when the phone rang again. Caroline Blakely: "I'm trying to find Dannie."

"I haven't seen her since this morning," I said.

"Will you tell her to call me? She's got a few gaps to fill in if she wants to graduate."

I said, "Can she get it all done in time?"

Caroline said, "Delia, this is a minor emergency. We'll deal with it. Believe me, she'll graduate."

She hung up. Hector left. I asked the girls who'd been hanging around in the hallway to come in. I told Miranda she was at Project Promotion a lot—more hours than we'd agreed on. When I set her up over here, I meant for her to learn office skills. Now she was hanging out with kids who were sweet, all of them, even if you had to look hard to see this, but they were also dropouts, some on probation, some violent based on what they'd seen. I wouldn't say: I don't want you hanging around the not-good-enoughs.

I didn't want her to act unkind, exclusive. Still, she needed to have standards for herself. "Are you keeping up with your classes?" I asked Miranda. "How are your grades?" I said this in front of Nelly. We do pass/fail at Project Promotion, but it was hard to get Nelly to think about passing because she was having a baby in a month. Yet I'd promised Hector I'd talk to her. I was also thinking I needed to phone home—they'd be done with the surgery. And that Miranda could tutor Nelly. Then I heard tapping on the door.

Luann stood in my doorway, holding Esme, who let out a happy yelp when she saw me. Luann said, "Am I interrupting?" She stepped all the way into my office. Her new boyfriend, Drew, was behind her. "You get off work in a half-hour," she said, "right? We decided we want to go to a seafood restaurant south of here, and if we're not going to eat at midnight we need to leave right now. I wondered if you'd be able to take the baby in your office for the last half-hour?"

I was floored. But I wouldn't say, No, you idiot, she has to stay with you. If someone was trying to drop off your baby—had decided they'd already put in a long enough day—you wouldn't insist they keep her. It was all headed south, I thought. Luann in a car with Drew. Were they taking Luann's mother to this seafood restaurant? My babysitting situation was headed south. You can get scared, looking for a new sitter. I remembered a woman in the doctor's office waiting room going on about visiting a babysitter's house to see if it'd be good enough, and the babysitter didn't turn the TV down, let alone off, and it was pay-per-view, X-rated.

I'd have to talk to Luann later. Fire her. Or something.

I held my arms out for Esme.

Miranda and Nelly were all over her. Miranda said, "Miss, is this your baby? She's so cute." Hector stood in the doorway, arms folded. Creola Wheat stood next to him. "At last I get to meet Miss Thing," she said. "What a prize, what a fat chunk of answered prayer. You're living with an answered prayer for a roommate, Delia." Esme sat in the middle of this, laughing, batting at people. "You're doing a good job, Delia. Look at her," Creola said, "she's sure she's perfect."

"Can I hold her?" This was Miranda.

"Has your mother had her baby yet?" I asked.

Miranda said, "Soon, April."

I watched Nelly, hands in front of her belly, the look on her face, scared, happy. Close to crying.

We spent a half-hour like that.

Then I drove home, thinking how convenient it was not to have to drive ten miles into the swamp, past half-finished houses, to pick up Esme at Luann's, then ten miles back again. At home I took stock of what seemed like a parking lot in front of my house: my mother's car I was getting out of, my hatchback with its door leaning against it, Mike's custom cab truck, Dannie's little Ford. And I remembered that landlord dressed like a gym teacher who wouldn't rent to me and Lupe because he thought we were immigrants who'd squeeze a half-dozen people into a small apartment. I shut off my car and went inside. What happened next? I'm set in my ways. I need my house orderly. Not because of hygiene. Nothing else is orderly, see? Not life, your future. Or it is, and I can't grasp the pattern. I stood in the doorway, holding Esme, looking at newspapers on the floor. A flung-down heap of groceries in the living room looked like an accident too. In the kitchen, someone had spilled pretzels and walked on them. Mike looked up from his spot on the couch, my dad on one side, Dannie on the other. "I hope you don't mind I'm watching some TV," Mike said, weak smile. On TV, electric guitars wound up, and Hank Williams Jr.'s face stretched like putty, like a bad dream, and he yelled, "Are you ready for football?"

All three of them on the couch, I thought. Born in a barn.

Dannie said, "Mike is fine. He's already been doing business on his little cell phone. He's a trouper. I loved it. He never flinched. They cut a slice in him, put a tube in, suctioned it out."

"A vacuum pump," Mike said. "New technology."

"See?" Dannie said. "Tough as nails. He's like my dad."

"He's not," I said.

"Your dad is too," she said. "Together, a composite dad. And you're like my mother, or sister."

"And your dogs are my grandsons and nephews," I said, "and your landlord is my son-in-law. Listen, Mike Cleary and I are not your family. If we were, I would have kicked your ass for staying out all night." I shocked myself, being this mad. The expression on Dannie's face crumbled.

My dad and Mike stared. "No reason to be upset," my dad said. "Do you want a beer?"

I couldn't tell who he was talking to. Dannie took the beer. "You're drinking," I said.

"Mike wanted some." Dannie said this soft, apologetic.

"You're drinking beer with anesthesia?" I looked at him. "Are you nuts?"

"One or two," he said, glazed eyes. "I asked Jimmy first."

Dannie said, "I'm sorry, Hoover. I didn't know. I'm sorry I was late this morning."

"I thought you had somewhere to be this afternoon and that's why he had the surgery this morning," I said.

Dannie said, "I did. I got stood up."

"I'm tired," I said. "I want to eat and go to bed." Then someone scored a touchdown. I don't know jackshit about football, but I understand there's a leap forward in points—one side scores seven—when a football goes through the white H at the end of the field. Mike yelled, "Cowboys."

My dad was clapping his hands, low, rhythmic. He said, "Good, good, good." This has always annoyed me. It's what he says when I tell him about my life. He says good, good, good, I imagine, because if I'm talking a lot he assumes I'm happy and busy and he's off the hook. Who knew he liked football anyway? On the table, next to a bag of pork rinds, sat two bottles of Imodium, one still in its cellophane seal, the other cracked open, chalky fluid dripping down its side.

It was the Imodium that did it, maybe. I left.

I had Esme's diaper bag with me, stocked up. Anything else I'd need, I'd buy. As for me, I didn't take anything. As for where I was going, I could have gone to the public library, but it would close in a few hours. I drove down the highway, thinking about those apartment buildings someone threw together five years ago, six buildings built foundation-to-top-floor by an out-of-town crew in a span of weeks. Hector had paid his deposit before they were done. When he moved in, the place smelled like carpet glue, drywall, sealer, paint. Knocking on the door, I could smell those smells, faint, toxic, but also Hector. He opened the door in his stocking feet. I heard meat sizzling. He cooked his meat into leathery strips. "Come in," he said. "Pull up a chair."

He had the good sense not to talk. We sat and chewed.

Esme drank a bottle and slept.

I looked at his apartment, disorganized but clean. He had a lot of what you'd call ornaments. A piece of wood carved into a bear. A poster of the singer who got shot, Selena. A picture—bright, cheerful—of stick-figures, hordes of people, related no doubt, cooking food together.

"Do you want to watch TV?" He handed me the remote control.

I switched to PBS, where I knew what was on, *Antiques Road Show*. They were in Seattle, looking at leggings an Indian chief had worn, and when he died his daughter gave them to a Lutheran minister. I started thinking about my dad at home in a half-stupor with his stock-piled Imodium and beer in his veins: did he think I was mad at him, that I'd walked out because of him? But I'd expected my dad to be there. And Mike. Nearly perfect now, he must have thought of himself, tumor on his back gone. Only Dannie had surprised me, and the mess. So had ending up with Esme at work, the nagging feeling I needed to be figuring out where to live while my babysitter acted unreliable, fly-by-night. I felt like crying. Trying not to, I got a runny nose. I needed a tissue or something. I went to the kitchen, got a paper towel, blew my nose.

From the living room, Hector said, "Try to get some sleep." Stern. Bossy.

We made Esme a bed—thick towels, sofa cushions circling around her. In the bathroom, I found my toothbrush I'd left there years ago. I got ready for bed, then went to Hector's room, hung up my dress and got under the covers. When he came in, I didn't turn over. I lay still until I heard him snore. He thrashes and fights for air, sleep apnea. I thought how I'd heard a kid at work, Bree, telling Vanessa: "Girl, you don't mess around with no more than one boy a semester. No way should you do two at the same time." I didn't interrupt because—even if we're supposed to act like kids don't have sex and Bree's advice was too simple, no why or wherefore—the gist was right: you break up with one before you sleep with another. Still, I wasn't fucking Hector yet. And I didn't feel like I'd ended up in his bed by my own willpower, more like some compulsion, big and powerful as God with His arbitrary plan, had pushed me. With all the changes, I was having trouble knowing my part, my portion, fending off bad habits, the escape-way I sometimes used sex— Hector?—to forget my worries. Sometimes I want the hit, a boy at Project Promotion, a crack addict, supposedly recovered, had said. I felt mad at people who didn't see how hard it had been to find my place, this gap no one else claimed, and to keep it, save it. Speaking of people, I thought of Sage and wondered if it helps to take Paxil or Elavil.

Peace of mind doesn't come because you earn it. I try not to do wrong but, all the same, only once in a while do I get the delirious sense I'm right. The rest of the time? Unlit passages, collision, blunder. So I thought, lying near Hector—his breathing an engine, his body a bulwark, a dam.

THIRTEEN

Four days later, Hector said, "Damn." I was lying on his bed wearing my coat, and Esme was scrabbling around the floor. I took a second look. She was rolling over and over like a barrel. And laughing. "Look," I said, "a developmental milestone, almost on schedule. And she's good at this, no amateur." Hector didn't answer. He was looking at Esme's packed-up diaper bag—bottles, rags, diapers, clothes. The three of us were going to eat dinner at Luby's, and then I was headed home. "You're doing it a third time," Hector said, "making me into a fool."

We'd been impersonating a family. Hector made the coffee. I washed dishes. Every night after dinner I'd walk to the coin-operated laundry room wearing his bathrobe and put a load in, mostly my clothes and Esme's. At 10:30, I'd go to bed and he'd follow. The second night he rolled onto me, conjugal right. I didn't go rigid like the dead man's float, but I didn't say no. I made love back barely—trying to send the message, okay, but don't get attached. Hector might have missed this hint. Or hoped it was sex I all of a sudden felt different about, shy and ladylike. In the morning, he held Esme while I showered and dressed. No one at work noticed I was wearing the same outfit again and again. I wear black most of the time because I get nervous if I think people are paying attention while I'm figuring out what to do always, what tactic.

We left Hector's and went to Luby's, where they serve food family-style. We got a few double takes: people looking from Hector to me to Esme, wondering how we'd ended up as father-mother-kid. I had the urge to tell them: "We're just friends." Though technically this wasn't true. But that's what I told my dad. I called and said, "For a few days I'm staying at a friend's."

Hector set his coffee cup down and stared. Like this was work and he was still the boss, see? "You're too attached to that house," he said. "Home is not a physical place, unless you own it."

I felt like rolling my eyes. You don't own your place, I thought, and you seem attached. I didn't say so. I fed Esme red Jell-O, not because it's a nutrient but you don't get a lot of choice at Luby's.

"It's a three-bedroom unit," Hector said. "Your dad could have his own room."

He was talking about an apartment in his complex that would be available in April. He thought I should put down a deposit now, stay where I was as long as I could, and if I had to leave my place before the new apartment was ready, I'd put my furniture in storage and live with him. In about fifteen minutes I'd go home and find a note from Mike Cleary with a similar offer: stay in his house on Blevin Street. "Not a problem for a few weeks," it would say, *few weeks* underlined.

I looked at Hector. He's handsome and tough. He takes you over because of his height, his jutting cheekbones and angry eyes, his pachuco clothes, jeans and black leather. I'd be alone with him and feel privileged, let in on secrets, his sad sighs. His skin—arms, legs, shoulders, the backs of his hands—silky as a baby's, as Esme's. When we made love, I concentrated on the harsh look of him and then the surprise, soft touching. Maybe I'd seen that outside softness as a sign.

"If you stay in my apartment awhile," Hector said, "your dad could sleep on the couch."

"He'll be in Belize by then," I said, hateful. Melodramatic even. My dad hadn't mentioned Belize lately. One less problem, his harebrained retirement plans. But he had to live somewhere.

Where?

Esme was gnawing on one of those heat-and-serve dinner rolls.

Hector said, "We have a lot in common—commitment to work." He had a way of breathing out, deflating. Last night he'd leaned over in bed and said, "I'm too nice. Is that it?" Men say this. I've heard it enough to wonder about it. If someone dumps you, they don't seem nice, but cruel; you want them back just not to feel like a loser. By contrast, someone you're leaving seems sad. Was this the same as "nice"? In my lifelong, rescued-into-normal daydream, I'd be happier with someone like Hector. I'd love him, marry him. But I couldn't. And it's not like Mike and Hector were interchangeable, not exactly. Hector tried harder in the world than Mike, making his way. But this makes you defensive, deprived, worried all the time someone else got rewarded who didn't try as hard. I could be talking about myself. One house can't hold two people this spooked, angry. Hector said, "No one will care more about you." Esme started choking.

Her face puffed up, eyes wide. She made this sound like air pushing against a rubber stopper. I remember each detail because she almost choked quite a few times until she was four, and I finally found a doctor who looked down her throat and said those are the most abnormally large tonsils and adenoids I've ever seen and scheduled surgery, and Esme's throat never clogged again, and she was never sick again with breathing problems, but I didn't know this when she was still using the nebulizer three times a week and the fact she inhaled and exhaled, sustained life, seemed miraculous. That day in Luby's was the first time she nearly choked. I leapt up and did the baby Heimlich, which involves holding her facedown, neck and chest cradled in your left hand while you strike her diaphragm with the heel of your right. Strike hard, harder, but make her breathe. I taught this technique in Expect-ant Mothers class, which is not to say I didn't freak out, that my heart didn't stop beating while Esme's was threatening to, her face mottled, purple, and then the bread chunk flew across the table in a stream of liquefied red Jell-O. I spent the next few minutes mopping up and said, "I can't talk about rela-tionship problems now." A shortcut, yes. But who could argue with it? I left Hector in Luby's and went home.

When I got there I stood in the doorway, holding Esme. My dad didn't notice us at first. He was vacuuming. In the kitchen, plates and glasses gleamed in the dish strainer. The plants on the porch had been watered. A bunch of flowers sat in a vase on the coffee table, where, when I'd left, the Imodium and pork rinds had sat. I did see a bottle of Imodium on the kitchen counter, though. My dad switched off the vacuum. He saw us and smiled. He really smiled at Esme, who laughed and held out her fat arms to him. As he took her, I thought his color looked bad, worse, pasty, his eyes glassy and small. I said, "Dad, it can't be good for your liver to keep taking that medicine. It says on the bottle to consult a doctor if symptoms don't go away in ten days."

He said, "I never exceed four doses in twenty-four hours. Back home I did talk to Dr. Burke."

"He's a veterinarian. Retired too."

"Well, I'm a mammal," my dad said. "By the way, you have a note from Mike. And flowers."

I looked at them. Not gladiolas. Wrong time of year. Lilies

My dad said, "I told him to let you cool off for a day or two, that you had PMS."

Apparently, he'd been watching TV. "Thanks a lot, Dad," I said, "great excuse." And Mike was speaking lilies. Janeway's line. She and Marla had a fight and Marla sent tulips. "I don't speak tulips," Janeway said. I opened Mike's note: "We got in your space, I respect that. I need space too. If you don't want me, I can fade out. But I did sign a six-month lease. Whether you want to be in contact is up to you." Then the offer to stay in his house for a few weeks, his phone number. He has himself posted, I thought: Room to Let, Not Much, Temporarily Only. What kind of a racket is it that, every time he thought I was mad, he offered to vanish? Maybe I'd implied I want that. Once, in Cleveland, I told Harriet Mosley I didn't want to be married, and she said, "You haven't met the right man." Nice thought, right man. Right-size plug in the right-size outlet, won't fade out when he doesn't get the reception he wants. Offering to leave—is this a polite-martyr method of getting your way? I don't burn bridges, though. Thanks for the flowers, I thought, a meditation, telepathic communication. Over and out.

My dad said, "Are you going to look for a place to live?"

"Why? Are you moving with me?"

He looked evasive. "For the time being."

I said, "I didn't want to burst your bubble, but your idea about Belize doesn't sound practical."

"Maybe not," he said. "But I have to live somewhere warm and cheap."

"There's thousands of places like that, and you won't need a passport."

He said, "What do you think of that housing development your neighbors are looking at?"

"Who?"

"The couple next door."

Lupe was looking in a housing development—for a rent house? How hard up was that? I said, "It's a *colonia*. A developer threw some sand in a swamp. It doesn't have city water or a sewer."

"Regan thinks we should stay here."

"Regan?"

"The lady across the street."

"That's her last name," I said. "Her first name's Janeway."

"It isn't," he said, "it's Regan. She told me. She says the values here are going up."

"That's good advice if you're buying. We can't afford to, remember. Do you have three thousand dollars?"

He did his standard blush, cheeks and forehead patchy red. "I could throw in a few hundred."

I looked at him. "That's what you meant to retire on?" Unnecessary. Rubbing it in.

He said, "I thought I'd get a job once I was there."

People like my dad get by and get by and forget they won't always—that someday they'll turn up old. "I might need to borrow a couple of C-notes," I told him, "for a deposit on a new apartment."

He nodded. "I'm going to the store. I got your car running—fixed the AC. It was the switch."

I got suspicious. "Are you buying more Imodium?"

"I'm stocked up," he said. "I thought I'd get some catfish for tomorrow's dinner."

I said, "Fine." He left. And I got Esme ready for bed.

I got ready for bed too. All of my problems—where to live, the legal jam my mother left behind, Hector acting earnest but mad, Mike aloof and transient, and my dad's bad gut—I set aside.

I slept hard.

Until morning. Then I crept into Esme's room and got her out of bed. My dad didn't wake. He slept with his hands folded over his chest. He always has. When I was a kid I used to stare at him sleeping—especially on weekend afternoons—and will him to wake up cheerful and take me somewhere. He never did, except to the lumberyard or feed store. I fed and dressed Esme.

And drove to Luann's and gave her a talking-to.

I should have sooner—the day after she dropped off Esme. But that was the morning I'd woke at Hector's, shocked I'd revved up the combustion between us again, and he was cooking breakfast, and I was rushing to buy myself the time and camouflage to figure out how to tell him I appreciated the food and shelter, and him, but not forever. In the end, I didn't figure out anything. I masqueraded for four days as reunited lover, then walked out. But that first morning I drove to Luann's and made small talk, I couldn't think of doing anything so unfamiliar as bossing her around. I can't give orders. With Esme I won't have to. We're building habits together. Unlike in grown-up relationships, for instance, marriage, we're not patching together unrelated lives, all the wires and jerry-rigging continually straining. But today, I thought, Friday, I could lay down the law with Luann, hurry when I picked up Esme after work, and have the weekend to cool off. So I sat with Esme in my lap and told Luann, "I'm not in a position to not get much done at work." Maybe I should have just said: It was wrong to bring Esme to my office. But

I didn't. "I'll be looking for other sitters for backup," I said, "but I have to find a place to live first, so let's coordinate our efforts and make sure Esme has a stable environment for now." This must have been vague because Luann looked puzzled. She showed me shirts she was making by taking cast-off shirts from the thrift store, cutting off collars and sleeves for a scoop-neck, sleeveless look, then trimming them with rick-rack. "They're so cute you could sell them," I said.

"I know," she said, "at a flea market."

"I'll see you this afternoon."

And I went to Port Town High. The first kid in my office was Michelle Millay, a great-great-great-niece of a famous writer, she told me once, though I'm skeptical. Not the first or last person to say she was related to someone famous. This woman apparently wrote poems about love affairs. "What lips these lips have kissed and where and why I have forgotten," a line Michelle told me once. This poem ends with the woman saying she can no more remember men she'd been with than birds can remember trees they'd lighted in. Big deal, I thought. A few people could write that. Michelle always drums up reasons to see me, like she thinks she won't have a real adolescence if she's not troubled. She always does research on her proposed problem areas. Then you find out what she wants: dirt, dish, gossip. "I think I have an unrealistic body image," she told me today. I gave her a pamphlet on anorexia nervosa and bulimia and said, "There's a quiz in here and if you mark Yes enough times, we'll tell your mom to phone your doctor."

"Why was Amber Brown in your office on Monday," she said, "with those other people?"

Amber Brown was the girl who said her stepfather abused her, and her mother said she made it up. I didn't think so though, a hunch. Michelle wasn't Amber's friend, different social rank. The whole idea of this—the fixed, petrified, defended cliques—made me think of the year I transferred from my last year at the reservation school, eighth grade, to Stites High, and no one except a girl named Vernice, famous for being a slut, and the janitor, spoke to me. I wasn't an outcast. I was a no-fit, invisible. I'd watch the social life, the grid, people you envied because their lives looked easy, people you envied because their lives looked hard and they seemed stimulated by this, charged up, the easy-lives and hard-lives brushing against each other, now ignoring, now antagonizing, like countries who've fought each other so long the point is to keep fighting. I sat on the sidelines, thinking I'd get asked to join one or the other, and which did I want, not realizing there's a lifetime of not belonging. I looked at Michelle who'd never hang with Amber. I could say: I'm not allowed to discuss other students. What I did say: "None of your beeswax."

And Coach walked in. It was his office too. And I hadn't hung the sign on the door, Conference In Session, because it was just Michelle Millay. That wouldn't haven't stopped him though. Today I was happy for the interruption. "Long time no see, Coach," I said. "What's new?"'

He made a noise. I had a college class once that actually talked about this kind of communication, phatic, it's called. Coach was making a disdain-signal. A sigh with consonants: "Ffff."

Michelle perked up. If she sticks with this, I thought, she could be a gossip columnist.

Coach said something like: "My honeymoon."

"What?"

"I got back from my honeymoon, the fiasco," he said.

"I didn't realize you got married." Or used to not be, I thought.

He said, "A man without a wife is like a dog without a leash, which is to say not quite allowed. But she wants to talk all the damn time, this pure-D foolishness about being married. I tell her, Honey, you keep working on the marriage. You're doing a fine job. I can tell from over here."

Michelle gave me a thrilled look. Inside scoop. "You need to go back to class," I told her.

Michelle left and Coach started talking about Sean. "I know you've met with him. I can't put him on any of the teams—he's not an athlete. Can't make a silk purse out of a wimp. But that friend of his? Conrad Kamikaze. Lots of pent-up something. I can't wait to get him on the field."

"Who?"

"Conrad somebody, Oriental, just moved here."

"Okuda," I said.

"I call him Kamikaze. Send him on suicide missions, right into the thick of it."

"You don't call him Kamikaze?"

"He doesn't mind. These kids aren't politically correct. They get that from their parents."

You better hope he doesn't, I thought. But didn't say so.

Coach said, "Too much of this intermarriage nowadays—if they ever were married. Have you noticed that if you see a kid, half-Spanish, half-white, and so on, one parent has bailed out?"

I hadn't noticed. I said, "Divorce rates are high all over."

Coach was unpacking his lunch. "I've got a great lunch," he said. "Beef brisket sandwich with those bread and butter pickles. Now this is the part of marriage I like. You want some?"

"I'm thinking about eating at home," I said.

I didn't usually, but I wanted to check on my dad. When I left in the morning, he was asleep. Most of the time, he got up with Esme. I tried calling him. No answer. I got in the car and headed that way.

On an average day I drive from my house to Luann's, then to Port Town High, then Project Promotion, then back to Luann's and home. So I don't usually drive from the high school to my house. But that day I did and ended up on a street that had been hit hard by rain from Hurricane Melissa. Not that they got more, but you could see it had washed down slopes, and the street pitched downhill, then curved, and two houses in a low spot, one Easter egg pink, the other with brown shingles, had stood in the way of what must have been ten feet of water. The brown house had missing window panes. One corner of the pink house was gone, gone, and a waterlogged white crib hung off the foundation, a kitchen chair rammed against it. The people who lived there must have escaped, I thought, because I hadn't heard of fatalities. But if you're poor and move a lot, your chairs, tables, pictures, and beds become your home, transportable. It looked sad, a wrecked household. I'd been lucky, water seeping in and eviction pending, that's all.

At home I found my dad on his pallet. He was dozing, pen in one hand, newspaper over his chest.

I shook him awake. "Why didn't you answer the phone?"

He opened his eyes. "You probably have the damn thing turned down. I was circling ads so we can house-hunt."

"Why are you in bed?"

"Must be the flu." He fell back asleep.

I went to the store and bought 7-Up. I brought it home and set it next to him on the floor.

Then I went to the post office to get my mail. New insurance cards. *Newsweek* I get for free, JC Penney good-customer bonus. A letter from Brask & Greenstein. I breathed deep, opened it.

Ms. Arco,

As you know, in December we asked Eems Funeral Home to submit an itemized invoice for expenses incurred by your mother's interment. We also placed a notice to creditors in the classified advertising section of the newspaper which ran thirty days as required by law. I have now notified Eems Funeral Home that they must submit their invoice in the next seven days, one week.

And then what? We were off the hook?

On the way back to work, I was thinking Esme could catch my dad's flu, and she should sleep in my room that night. I remember this specifically, because when night fell I wasn't home, not under the same roof as Esme either, first time since I'd been her mother, worst night of my life. But I knew none of this—worst and best, my empty arms—as I drove back to work, my mind tumbling along full of junk, dailiness. It was the day I first realized my dad could be my babysitter. That when he got over the flu, I wouldn't be high and dry if Luann quit, because he acted jolly and agile with Esme, and she'd pull his beard and laugh. As a dad, he was lacking in the Big Ideas department: advice about ethics, survival. He was remote. But safe and careful. I was thinking I'd solved one problem and could focus on the next: *where* he'd do this, where to live.

At Project Promotion I sat down and concentrated on PGV, Parent-Guardian Visit, a one-day open house. The hardest part is getting parents to come. Most kids who turn up at Project Promotion—last-resort except it could be worse, jail, or where they are now, home—don't have the showing-up kind of parent anyway. Yet, like Hector says: you don't know if it's the tenth or twentieth time you try, but once in a while you get through. I'd already sent letters. I gave Miranda a directory and a phone. Follow-up calls would help—we'd get one or two more parents. I've made calls like this myself. The parent no longer lives there. So you ask the uncle or grandmother to come. They get angry that they can't or don't want to. They yell at you for waking them. Miranda sighed and hung up. "The number is no longer in service, Miss. What is that?"

"Disconnected."

"They didn't pay their bill?"

"Probably."

"We did that once. It costs even more if you have to get it hooked up again."

"Exactly." This was a life lesson right here.

She said, "Do you have a boyfriend, Miss?"

Two halves of a boyfriend, I thought. The part of Mike that knew how to kick back and escape—hard liquor, hard sex. The part of Hector that was ready to pledge himself but was too sad. Could I keep them both, zig and zag balancing into direction, progress? "No," I said, "I don't."

She leaned forward. "Mr. Jaramillo looks at you all the time like a *chiflado,* a flirt."

"Right," I said. Before I realized I'd answered her. Then I said, "No." And I worried about Hector, working with him. How I'd taken care of myself for the short-term, getting in and out of bed with no regard for how this swindled him. I could have slept on the couch, but the bed was warm. So was the feeling, big and wordless, just his breaths, breathing, radiant heat of skin.

Sage walked into my office and said she was headed for the high school to start prepping teachers about getting students ready for TAAS tests. "I hate dealing with Mrs. Martin," she said. "When she teaches evolution she tells the students it's a much-disputed theory and that there's scientific proof the world was made in seven days. Why major in biology if your interest is mythology?" she said. "Delia, how do you stomach it? You go to one of those holy roller churches."

I hadn't been lately—not since that rainy day. I said, "Evolution doesn't come up much." Most talk from the pulpit was cloudy, uncertain. But once in a while a parishioner stood up with a private theory. I knew what Sage meant— propheteers, I call people who think God talked to them but not you. I get wary. For example, a woman at church said to me, knowing I'm single and not rich, that I have to work: "I choose to stay at home with my children." And because that's all I know about her besides that she believes in God, I wonder if she thinks God thinks I'm wrong and it's her duty to warn me. Or it could be bad word choice on her part. Paranoia on mine.

Creola walked in, and Sage kept talking. "I've seen Christianity used as a blunt object."

Creola said, "There's people everywhere who think they run things, but they run their mouth."

Sage said, "I do my spiritual work at home."

You have to, I thought. And everywhere. This walking toward a lit speck, and then the glimmering somewhere else. I always wonder: Do other people sitting in pews swerve this much?

Sage said, "Mason's already over there with a busload of boys. I'd better head out."

She left.

Creola went back to her office.

Miranda said, "Miss, I've been thinking about your baby. My mother is a good mother, I think. Even if her dad messed with her and her mother didn't stop him, my mother still loves her mother because she otherwise took good care of her. I think your baby will think you're a good mother."

This was a strange compliment—the comparison to the mother who didn't save her child from abuse but the child loved her anyway and turned out to be a good mother herself, sort of. Miranda's mother cried all the time and was obsessed with Miranda's virginity, her cherry. Do you have your cherry? she'd ask. But I started thinking about what Creola said the day Luann had dropped off Esme at work: "You must have had a loving mother because you have the touch." That a textbook in her psychology class had said this was a telltale sign. Creola walked past my door. I waved her back in. I said, "Tell me more what you learned in that class about touch."

Creola said, "It starts with the hands-on when you're a baby. You either get on that bus, or you never get on it. I was watching you the other day with your baby, things you probably don't know you're doing, rubbing her skin with your thumb while she sits there, lapping it up. I say this because my mother died when I was four, and I have just spooky memories, nothing clear-cut. But my own doctor said I must have had good mothering, lots of it, because I had the instinct to do the same for my children. Of course it was over too soon for me, but I got that—touching."

I started thinking how Creola's memories were spooky. And I hardly had any except that time at my grandma's when my mother came and left again. Because she was looking for a better party, my grandma had said. What my dad said was that my mother gave up. She'd been pulled out of her home early, gone through five or six foster homes, then hooked up with my dad when she was eighteen. Look at the nest, my grandma said. If the nest is foul, the bird won't fly. My grandma had rules, a slew of them. Less said sooner mended, was another. I stopped asking her about my mother. I'd ask my dad. He'd open his mouth to answer and you'd see big winds blowing. Nothing. A door opening like a door, closing like mountain. But I wanted to ask him if what Creola said was true, that I'd had good hands-on care. I'd learned love: giving, receiving.

I heard Hector come into the building. I can tell by the way he walks if he's sad, happy.

Or mad.

The phone rang. It was Caroline Blakely. "I still haven't heard from Dannie Lampass about her new application for graduation, which was due yesterday. Do you think she's coming in today?"

I checked the schedule. "She'll be here in an hour," I said.

Caroline said, "Can I leave a message for her?"

I said, "Sure thing." I hung up and was taking down the message, one hand still on the receiver when the phone rang again, vibrating. I was about to answer it, but Hector did in the next room. Then he shouted. We heard this. Miranda. Creola in the doorway. Students up and down the hall. "No," he said at first. Then louder, but higher, treble-pitched, "No, no." My first impulse was to go get Esme. She's with Luann, I told myself. She's fine. My dad, at home. My family, fine. I was listening to Hector. "What are you saying?" he said. "Then it did . . ." I could tell by the way he paused he was searching for English, the right word. "It did," he said, "detonate."

F O U R T E E N

Detonate, a word we started using. Also *blow up, go off, explode.* My family, I thought. People think of family in an emergency. I read in a book that families survive emergencies but not the aftermath. We stood in my office, aware of our bodies, their uprightness so temporary, this crooked pitch we sustained as the world spun. At least I was aware. Hector told us a bomb had detonated at Port Town High, two students arrested, no deaths because it detonated half-ass. They'd used pipes stuffed with black powder. What's black powder? I wondered. Turns out I'd said so out loud. Hector didn't know. Creola said, "You use it for fireworks, honey. You get it at the hardware store." But they'd used plastic pipes, not steel. "Polyvinyl chloride," Hector said, by rote, automatic. Because the bomb didn't go off correctly, there'd been flesh wounds only, he said. I imagined white arrow-shards of plastic flying through air. Would it have been different, lethal, I wondered, if they'd used steel— more force? A slipshod detonation, thank God. If you had to suffer through one, let it be sloppy. "Who was that on the phone?" Creola asked Hector. "Hal Hollie," he said. This is our district superintendent, who always gets his picture in the newspaper, the *Port Town Sun.* "We're evacuating," Hector said, "even though they have the two students in custody, who said it was just one bomb. This is a precaution until the police search schools." So we decided to go to an abandoned greenhouse across the road. "Unsafe structure, possibly," Hector said. "We don't have a choice," Creola said. "Round them up."

I went up and down the halls. "Come on," I said, "everybody this way." We were herding students across the parking lot, ditches, culverts. "Where are we going, Miss?" someone asked.

"We're in the middle of a bomb scare," Hector told him. He sounded like a big dog. This is why students are afraid of him. He seems mad when he's just scared and can't help fast enough.

"Some of our kids are at the high school," I said. No one answered. "Using the shop tools."

Creola glanced at me. "No one's dead yet."

"Sage is there," I said.

Miranda was beside me. "My mother doesn't know I'm here. She thinks I'm there."

We got to the greenhouse, and one of the boys lifted a window, climbed in, kicked the door open. "I'm going back to see if we have everyone," Hector said. I waited in the greenhouse—hot, stuffy. Some kids raced around on those carts they use for hauling plants. Creola and I watched Hector walk back across the road. First, he went to the old hangar that was the boys' dorm. Then the pole barn, the girls'. He was in the office when cop cars pulled up. He came out, talked to the cops. They went in. Fifteen minutes passed. Or one. Or fifteen hundred.

Hector came back out then, crossed the parking lot, the road, huffing. Trying to run in those boots, I thought. Panting, he said, "Delia, on the telephone, your father. He said to come home."

"Why?"

"He's sick," Hector said.

Creola reached into her purse and handed me her cell phone. "Call him. And when you're done, I'll start calling some of these parents. Everybody who has a home to go to ought to be there. You, and you," she pointed at kids. "You," she told Miranda. "And I'll keep the rest with me."

She had one of those flat phones, numbers like the head of a pin. I dialed three times because I kept hitting wrong numbers. The phone rang. I heard my answering machine. "Please leave . . ." Would he pick up? Then my dad's voiced mixed with mine, "message, *hello,* after the tone."

"Dad?"

"No reason to shout," he said. "I'm shitting blood here."

"Hang up and call 911." I was still shouting. "Go to the hospital. I'll be there as soon as I can."

Creola interrupted. "We'll handle this," she said. "There can't be more than thirty students."

I looked around—the kids were so fidgety. Girls laughing. Boys wrestling.

On the phone, my dad said, "I'm not in pain, just weak."

"Can you drive," I said, "in the white car?"'

He said, "Where's the hospital?"

Creola said, "Delia, we'll probably be back in our building in an hour."

I looked across the road. The police were outside now. To my dad, I said, "Get dressed."

I drove home but hardly remember. I got inside and got him into the car. As I drove, he kept his eyes shut. He doesn't take baths as much as you'd like, but he smelled different now, worse, sour. I pulled up outside the door that said Emergency Only. He said, "I can't piss either."

They checked him in fast.

I sat with him in a room. The nurse used a thermometer that beeped in his ear, then the blood pressure arm band. She moved us across the hall to take blood. She glanced at me, mouth pursed. I was filling out papers. "How old are you?" I asked him. "Sixty-three," he said. "He doesn't have insurance," I told everybody. "He doesn't have money either. I wish I did, but I don't." I thought—my mind drifty, sporadic—that he was my dependent and I couldn't afford him.

"Don't worry about money now," the lady in the Plexiglas window in charge of money said.

"We have a full house," the lady next to her said.

What did they mean—they had room for a freebie?

"There was a bomb at the high school," the first lady explained, "three people injured. Mostly cuts. One we thought might lose his eye. But I guess not, or they would have sent him to Houston."

I wanted to ask her who was hurt, if they had the names. But a nurse was wheeling my dad into a cubicle surrounded by curtains. I sat with him for ten minutes, twenty. A short doctor walked in, looked at the chart. He said, "I'm going to cut him open and see what's up. Now," he added.

A nurse gave my dad a shot to relax him. My dad was talking. "My father," he said.

"Are you praying?" I didn't think he was religious.

"For Christ's sake, no," he said. "I'm saying it's a shame I never met my father."

Never? They'd wheeled him away.

I went back to the waiting room. I sat and watched TV, Rosie O'Donnell talking to Julia Roberts, who was saying she didn't like to prepare for her roles. "I'm not a research nut," she said.

Then I used the pay phone to call Luann to tell her I was in an emergency, ask if I didn't get there right away could she hang on. She didn't answer. She could be outside, holding Esme, I thought. Or maybe giving her mother a shampoo with the phone turned off while Esme took a nap.

I sat back down. On TV they showed a man with a beard, an earring. He looked like a pirate, I thought. The print on the bottom of the screen said: A. J. Martine, SWAT, Houston Police Department. Then they flashed a picture of Port Town High, except it looked smaller, angular, cops milling around and students thronging like at a pep rally. "They're talking about the bomb," I told the ladies behind Plexiglas. They didn't look up. A woman in a chair—knitting, her yarn inching out of a paper bag on the floor—did. Two other people looked at me, then at the TV. It showed the SWAT man again. He said, "A pipe, closed at one end, a nipple on the other." "A nipple?" the interviewer, a perky blonde, asked. "A stub-out," the man said, "plumbing equipment. You stick a wick in it. Terrifyingly simple." Then the interviewer said, "A special report about a town forty-five miles southwest of here, Port Town, that lost its innocence today." Then back to Julia Roberts, talking about yoga now. She said, "I do it for my butt, not my soul." I thought: the Houston TV station is having a slow day and muckraking over here. No one had died. How was that news? But people in Jasper said the same thing when those boys dragged that man to death and the press showed up: this is a fluke in your average town.

I decided to call Mike Cleary.

I didn't have his numbers with me. But I called Information and got the number for his house on Blevin Street. His answering machine said he wasn't there but interested customers could call his cell phone. I called it. He answered—"Hello"—in the middle of noises, people talking.

"What's that racket?" I said. "Are you in your truck?"

"Where are you?" he said. "I heard about the bomb at Nick's Cafe when I ate lunch. I'd been over on the other side of the county. But a guy at the cafe said he heard it at Exxon—a mile away."

"We didn't hear it at Project Promotion," I said. "I'm fine. I'm at the hospital."

"Are you hurt?"

"My dad—they're doing surgery on him."

"What's wrong with your dad?"

"They're trying to figure that out." Then I told him I was supposed to pick up Esme at Luann's, and Luann wasn't answering. "Could you drive out there?" I asked. "Explain that I'm at the hospital—ask her if she can keep Esme a little longer. Or you could bring Esme to me here."

"You want me to pick up the baby or not?"

I considered it. "Pick her up." I didn't know how I'd feed her, though. I gave him directions.

"Hold on," he said. "I'm writing this down."

I was hanging up when a lady came out from behind the Plexiglas and asked if I wanted to see the chaplain. "He can be such a comfort," she said. "But right now he's with the football coach."

"Coach?" I didn't know his name, I realized.

"Two teachers got hurt. The other . . ." She pointed at the lady knitting. "That's his wife."

"I work for the school district," I said.

"Really?" She went back into her booth, then slid the Plexiglas open. "Tommy Melton—that's the coach's name." She looked back at her clipboard. "Gregory Mason Pratt is the other teacher."

"Mason Pratt is here?"

The knitting woman looked up.

The Plexiglas woman said, "Do they know who did it yet?"

Did I? Me, social worker? I should have seen it coming. I heard someone yell. "Who's that?"

The woman listened for a minute. "That's that coach—he's been like that since he came in."

I tried to hear. It sounded like he was saying, "Port Town High Loves God."

This seemed odd, reversible. Like you could also say "God loves Port Town High."

Then Mike came through the door without Esme. The look on his face, empty. He said, "No one's out there except an old lady sitting by herself at the picnic table. I made her go back inside."

"That's Luann's mother," I said. "What did you do with Esme?"

"No one's there. The old lady doesn't make sense."

"Did you check to see if Esme's things were there, her diaper bag?"

He looked confused. "No."

"Maybe Luann brought her to my office," I said. "I'll try calling." I stood up and called Project Promotion. I let the phone ring and ring. No answer. I looked up Creola Wheat's number in the directory and tried calling her at home. I wished I had her cell phone number, I thought. I dialed my own number, I don't know why, but hung up when I heard my answering machine.

Mike, standing behind me, said, "What happened to your dad?"

"He's shitting blood. They're operating. We need to find Esme." I stood next to the phone.

"Stay with your dad," Mike said. "I'll look for the babysitter."

We're not looking for the babysitter, you dunce, I thought. We're looking for the baby. I didn't say this. I said, "You looked for her already and came up short, remember? I'd better go now."

Mike said, "If you'll excuse me for saying so, you seem too upset to drive."

"I'm not going to sit here," I said.

"The babysitter probably took Esme somewhere."

"And ditched her mother?"

Mike sighed. "Can someone from the hospital call my cell phone if they need to reach you?"

"I don't know."

"Ask," he said. "Then I'll drive you."

So I went to the women in the Plexiglas booth and explained I needed to locate my babysitter, and could they call me on the cell phone if I had to get back to the hospital pronto? I tried imagining this: I'd be in Mike's truck and the phone would chime—not good news—and I'd show up for my dad's last five minutes, deathbed revelation, or they'd need an organ donation. Ideas I got from movies. I'd never been around someone alive but this close to dead. The lady I talked to looked surprised. She said, "I'll ask a nurse." She talked to a nurse, who talked to another nurse, who said she'd walk to Surgery and talk to that nurse. I could have located Esme by now if they'd walk and talk faster, I thought. "Take it easy," Mike said. "It's like you're on speed."

She came back. "They found what's wrong. A surgical nurse will explain."

We waited for that nurse. "Diverticulitis," she said when she showed up. "The small intestine diverts—creates its own space, a pocket away from the general flow. And this can rupture."

"Blow up, you're saying," I said.

She said, "They're patching it back together, but the trick now will be surviving the aftereffects. Basically he's poisoned, toxemia. Heart damage is possible. Brain too, if it goes on."

"He has that?"

"Not necessarily. The doctor will talk to you."

"He can die?"

She said, "His condition is very, very serious."

"But not critical," I said. Also an idea from movies: serious, not as bad as critical.

"Worse than critical," she said.

I couldn't help him from the waiting room, I decided. I'd worry about him in Mike's truck. I gave the nurse the cell phone number. "I've got another problem," I said as I left. Mike followed, silent. One of those, I thought. I'd been down this road. Some men see a woman this upset, they nod and obey her. Afterward disappear. Can't sleep with someone they've seen so altered.

"Where to?" Mike said, opening his truck door.

"Luann's," I said.

It took too long to get there. I'd think for him to hurry, drive faster. But I'd look at the speedometer and he was doing sixty-five, on gravel. When we got to Luann's, her Jeep was in the carport. No other cars. I knocked, no answer. I went around the back and knocked on that door. I spotted her mother in the kitchen. I went inside. Mike was ten feet behind me on the porch. The expression on his face? Blank, vacant. "Where did Luann go with the baby?" I asked.

Luann's mother said, "Luann." Except she said Lew-un. "She lives in the country."

"I know. Where's the baby?"

"They took the brown baby with them."

"Who did?"

She didn't answer.

I looked around—at the shelf in the living room where Luann usually stashed Esme's toys and clothes for me to carry home. No sign of this. "Did Luann go somewhere and take the baby?"

"The man."

"Drew?"

She said. "I don't know, and I can't help it."

"Fine," I said. I hurried to Mike's truck. "Go to Project Promotion," I said. I told him how to get there. I staved off a hundred thoughts. Or tried. When we got there, Project Promotion was deserted. Depopulated. No human trace except a jacket in the parking lot with the sleeves cut off, a picture on the back: Mickey Mouse holding a gun, gang insignia. Kings. Or Hispanics Causing Panic. I couldn't remember. Here, we had nephews and little brothers of gang members, wannabes talking about their uncles and brothers in Houston. "My house," I said.

Mike drove there.

No one was there of course. I wanted to check the answering machine. I did. Two messages. One of them, Dannie saying, "Hoover, Hoover," and hanging up. "Why does she say that?" Mike said. "It's the name of a vacuum cleaner her mother used," I said. And realized it didn't make sense for Dannie to call me Hoover. The other message was my own hang-up when I'd called from the hospital. I banged on Arturo and Lupe's door. Lupe opened it. "Delia, nice to see you."

"Has Dannie been here?" I said. "Have you seen the baby?"

Lupe shook her head, worried. "No."

"If someone shows up here with Esme," I said, "bring her to me at the hospital."

"The hospital?" Lupe said.

Mike was standing behind me. "Her dad's sick. It seems like Dannie has the baby with her."

"The *lesbiana*?" Lupe looked horrified. "She won't know what to do."

I saw Janeway getting out of her car. "If you see Esme, bring her to the hospital," I yelled.

Janeway was holding a bag of groceries. "What?"

I gave up on explaining, too complicated. To Mike, I said, "Hurry."

"I'm stopping to get something to eat," he said.

"We don't have time."

"Whataburger will take five minutes," he said, "and it won't kill anyone."

Bad choice of words, I thought. But maybe he was being sensible. And I wasn't.

He pulled up at a drive-through. "What do you want?"

"I don't give a flying fuck."

"Two cheeseburgers," he said into the speaker, "onion rings on the side." He turned to me. "There's a chain of burger joints in Louisiana that has carhops," he said, "and cold beer in mugs."

Who cares? I thought. I couldn't look at him.

When we got to the hospital, he carried the food inside. I went to the Plexiglas window to say: Is my dad okay? Did someone show up with a baby? But a new lady—she didn't know who I was—sat behind the Plexiglas. She was checking someone in, a woman with a little boy who had bronchitis maybe. I wanted to take him. Do what? Hold him. I thought how if you break or lose something—a car, an heirloom piece of crockery, your house if it blew or burned down or floated away—the next step is figuring out how to find or finance a new one. But a person isn't replaceable. Not a big insight here. But at the time my heart stopped. If I lost my dad or Esme . . . I can't, I thought. I was talking to myself. People stared. All of a sudden I remembered I'd given the nurse Mike's cell phone number to call if my dad's condition got worse. I walked past the Plexiglas window and asked a nurse eating a sandwich, "Is my dad okay?"

"I'll check." She wiped her hands on a paper towel and walked away.

When she came back, she said, "The doctor will be with you in a minute."

I sat next to Mike. He had a food wrapper spread over his knees, onion rings in a pile on top. He was chewing his burger slow, steady. "Do you have your cell phone turned on?" I asked.

He glanced at me. "Last time I checked."

I looked up and Creola Wheat was coming through the door. I stood up. "Why are you here?"

"I came to sit with Mason's wife. Is your daddy here?"

I never called him that—even when I was little.

Creola said, "The police closed everything—I sent some kids home. The rest are in the basement of First Baptist. Hector's there. I'm supposed to relieve him in an hour. Is your daddy okay?"

"I sent someone to get my baby," I said. I didn't sound like me. I forced myself to go on making sentences, telling Creola. "My babysitter's not at her house. I don't know where Esme is." I sounded old, weak. I wondered if I was mixed up about time, like now was morning, be-at-work-time, and I wasn't supposed to have Esme; Luann had taken her for a walk, and that's why Mike was calm, worried about food and not Esme. And, if she were gone, gone, how would I survive?

Creola said, "Your babysitter does have the baby, or did. She gave her to Dannie."

Dannie had Esme? "Why?"

Creola said, "We were loading everyone to move out. Maybe I shouldn't have let it happen, but I was responsible for thirty kids. She did take the car seat, honey. The baby's somewhere."

Somewhere. With Dannie? I never thought I'd be awake and saying: she's got to be here somewhere, somewhere. I wasn't asleep, was I? "Mike," I called out. Everyone looked up, families with kids. "Mike," I said. He looked at me. "Stay and talk to the doctor. I have to find Esme."

I rushed out the swinging doors across the parking lot to my mother's car.

I drove to Dannie's. Her truck wasn't there. The other truck wasn't either—the truck belonging to the landlord with his evil-shaped beard. I pounded on Dannie's door, banged until my fists ached. I banged on the other door: the monster-truck, spade-bearded doorway. No answer. Could the landlord be with Dannie and Esme? My breath fell out of me, thinking this. I stood there. It's like a cliché in a five-hundred-year-old song, that the sky was blue but I was changed if the world didn't have her, Esme—the sky a sky, trees still trees, but I would never be okay.

When I got back to the hospital, Creola was gone.

The knitting lady, Mason's wife, gone.

The doctor hadn't come out. "Go put a note for Dannie on my front door," I told Mike.

He said, "Why are you worried about Dannie now?"

His panic level was off, wrong. Or mine was. I said, "A lady I work with said Dannie has Esme."

The doctor came out, reading from a piece of paper, "The family of Ephraim Frigein?" Mike stood up, waved him over. He shook Mike's hand, then mine. He sat down and said, "The next twelve hours will be touch and go. If he lasts through the night, his chances improve exponentially. Hell, if he makes it through tonight, he'll be fine." I was thinking I could call Janeway and have her put a note for Dannie on my door—she'd have to just walk across the street. I should have left a note on Dannie's door when I was there. Maybe Mike would? He didn't know where she lived. This made me remember the morning of his surgery, and I had an upsurge of hate—a sin, I realize, when you're tunnel-visioned like a mole in blackness, dead-sure your hard time trumps someone else's. Still, he'd stirred us up with his worries about anesthesia, a ride to the doctor, beer. Why was he lazy about leaving notes for Dannie now? He doesn't feel my urgency, I thought. Sees it as less than his. I should leave a message on Dannie's answering machine, I thought. The doctor was talking to Mike like he was the son-in-law.

Mike said, "You had a busy day. Out of the ordinary."

The doctor said, "About average. We got a few at once because of that school bomb. But I was a medic in Vietnam—this was nothing. Not much of a bomb, really. Everyone's fine."

Mike was rubbing my back in slow circles. "Delia works at the school." My muscles felt spring-loaded.

The doctor looked at me. "You're the one who had the bad day."

I said, "I float between the regular school and the vocational-residential."

"You did your best," Mike said.

Was he talking to me?

"We'll keep our fingers crossed," Mike said. "He's a tough old bird."

The doctor said, "Had to be, living with that."

"He took Imodium all the damn time," I said.

The doctor nodded. "That would have masked pain."

Then the front doors banged open, and I saw Hector, big entrance. Click click, his heels on tiles. He should have a posse, I thought. He glanced at me, then away. Then back again—studied the situation. The doctor in green scrubs, standing now, flexing, and talking to Mike, who was sitting down, one ankle over his knee, creased pants and shiny shoes. He must polish his shoes a lot, I thought. Mike's hand on my back ambled around, now up my spinal cord, gentle, then from one shoulder blade to the other. A good way to rub a person who was worried stiff, but his mind, his conversation, somewhere else. I thought all of this in the flash-freeze second Hector stared at me, then Mike, Mike's hand on the small of my back now. Hector spun around on his heel, changed direction. For a minute, it looked like he'd go outside. But he made a right turn and walked up to the Plexiglas. "I'm here to inquire about school bombing victims," he said.

"Someone will talk to you in a minute." The lady was checking in a man with a cut hand.

I disentangled and stood up. I walked over. "Were you at work when my babysitter came?"

I don't know if the afternoon had taken its toll—he was tired, used up. Or the afternoon had taken its toll on me and I was tired, used up, projecting. Or he hated my guts. He said, "Yes."

"Did Dannie take her? Who has Esme?"

He breathed deep, and in a loud voice, his work voice, said, "You need a new babysitter."

"That's something to fix later," I said. "Right now I have to find Esme."

In careful, staccato words, he said, "Creola said you were here. That's why I came."

I nodded. He'd rushed to help, he meant. I'd made him into a fool. Fourth time.

"And you've met someone. You're having an affair," he said.

I was Mike's girlfriend—that's how I saw it. And I'd had the affair with Hector. I'm not trying to justify this affair, either. You're supposed to live by the rules not so much to get to heaven but because you'll have a better life, less grief and confusion, if you do. "Not exactly," I said.

Hector said, "Dannie told me she'd bring the baby to you. Maybe she couldn't find you."

The lady in the Plexiglas booth turned to Hector. "Can I help?"

It was the lady I knew—like she'd had dinner and come back. She smiled. Hector said, "I'd like to see Mason Pratt."

She said, "Oh I hoped you'd ask for the coach. He can't locate his family."

Family? I thought. His new wife?

"That's making him real nervous," she said.

Hector said, "I don't know him. I'm not a football fan."

Odd thing to say, I thought. Like hobbies mattered here. But she worked in the ER and was probably used to addled conversation. She looked at her clipboard. "Mason Pratt is with his wife."

Hector said, "I'll come back."

He walked off. I waited for him to turn and give me a look, a communication about how to hope, what to want. If this problem was small or insurmountable. By way of problem I meant finding Esme ASAP. Not trust and commitment, our relationship, that. The doors shut behind him.

I walked back to Mike and asked—slow, careful—would he put a note on Dannie's door.

"Dannie's?" he asked. "Not yours now?"

"Right," I said. I told him how to get there.

I stood up to make phone calls. A message for Dannie on her answering machine saying I was here and could she bring Esme to me, though this would be redundant with the note on the door unless she called home to check her messages. It crossed my mind that I should check mine. I never did learn that code, dialing in, dialing home. I ran outside and told Mike to stop by my house—I gave him the key—and check my messages. I went back inside and called Janeway and told her to put the note on my door for Dannie, though I could have told Mike to do that, I realized. When students act this confused, I tell them they need to eat, low blood sugar. I looked around for the McDonald's bag and started eating. On TV now, the ten o'clock news was talking about spring break, how it arrived like a weather front here, college kids from the North invading.

Then a new segment, a picture of two men—boys—wearing prison suits.

The newscaster was talking. I didn't hear her. I stopped eating. Then the picture blinked away. They were gone. But I'd seen Sean, his yellow hair, his thin frame handcuffed to Conrad Okuda's.

Siamese twins. A friend who thinks exactly like you so you don't need anyone.

I understood why even a remnant of family—last-known, living, ragtag shred you find yourself left with—is a safeguard, a regulator of impulse, yes, and fear. You need people, and it's best if they're not crazy and need you back in equal measure. Your family maybe gives off misery and you try to be alone but people seep in, default family, and need you to be theirs in return, the missing mother, father, whoever, and it's hard. On the one hand, you're a match, ideal. On the other, you drag each other down, strength multiplying strength, weakness heaped on weakness.

All this time I used to think I'd been on the sidelines because I didn't have money or fancy manners. I'd hid myself, thinking everyone could tell I'd started out without a regulation family unit, a core, and my fallout was shame, a residue, I'd thought, like ashes everywhere. So that people who were happy gave me a wide berth, I thought, sent the signal they had their own families and I shouldn't think they were available to stand in for mine. Or pitied me, which meant they weren't like me, wouldn't go to the same strange lengths. I began without the usual beginning, a nuclear family, and felt shoddy, contagious. The idea I had an aura—Warning: Hazard Here—might be a delusion, I realized. I'd kept secrets, felt close to exploding, and people noticed this. Yet most families were in some kind of mess. Still, there are blow-ups and blow-ups. On a scale of one to ten, Dannie's was a ten. Mine, maybe a four. The upshot? I didn't want to go to my grave without love having attached me to my one or two best chances, one or two people still living, after I'm dead, and the memory of me: perpetual. Afterlife, *that* kind.

But whose love? You had to be fussy. If I'd figured this out sooner, could I have told Sean?

"You have a message." The lady from behind the Plexiglas gave me a note.

Mike, it said. Cell phone. #361-851-7197.

I went to the pay phone and called him.

He picked up, first ring. "I'm at your house. Listen to your answering machine. I'm going to hold my phone next to it." Then, scratchy but I could hear it: "Hoover, Hoover, it's me and I have Doo-doo and she's vomiting that green puke, you know, like she does." I did know. I'd sent peas with her to Luann's. Pease porridge. "I want to know what to do about the puking, and where in hell you are. I'll try back." She didn't leave a number though, or say where she was calling from. But Esme was alive. Had been. Mike was back on the phone, "This isn't ideal," he said, "but it sounds like you'll have her back safe soon. Now what do you want me to do?"

"Go to Dannie's," I said, "and leave a note."

"I did."

"Can you sleep at my house," I said, "stay by that telephone?"

Mason Pratt's wife was sitting across from me again, untangling yarn.

"I'll call if I hear anything," Mike said. And hung up.

Then it was me and Mason's wife alone in the waiting room. And I was remembering that time Dannie showed up to take Mike to surgery at 7:00 a.m., drunk. A nurse tapped me on the shoulder, saying I could go sit in my dad's room if I wanted. "But you need to be ready," she said. "He's taking a drug, prednisone, to flush toxins out of his system. He doesn't look like himself."

"How so?"

"He's puffed up like the Michelin man," she said. "It's temporary. But it does throw people for a loop when they get their first glimpse. I'll move a chair in there and come back for you."

When she left, Mason's wife looked at me. "I wouldn't let myself see someone who was chockful of prednisone," she said. "If he died, I'd worry that's the only way I could remember him."

I couldn't think what to say.

"I've known a lot of people chockful of prednisone," she said.

This seemed far-fetched. "Who have you known full of prednisone?"

"People," she said. Her voice trailed off. She kept knitting. "Who've undergone things, trauma."

That covers everyone, I thought. She was shell-shocked from Mason being here, I decided. Or one of those people fascinated with sickness and death. The nurse came to get me. I hesitated. I wanted to be near my dad in case he called out. But what if Dannie tried to find me in the waiting room? Mike would know to ask a nurse. But Dannie? I told the nurses and the ladies in the Plexiglas booth to look for a white woman carrying a black baby and to help her find me.

The nurse brought me to my dad's room. It had a sign on the door,

ICU. He didn't look bad—like a healthy, sleeping man, size 50, whereas my dad wore 42 Long. I looked at his face. Not his. Not his cheeks or chin, too puffy. Only his fingernails looked right. The hands pumped up, inflated, but the fingertips: his. My skin started to crawl. Because it was like looking at a corpse, embalmed. Not that I'd seen many. But this is what you say—so natural, but not quite him.

He opened his eyes. Did he? "Dad," I whispered. "Are you awake? Can you hear?"

"Make that rattling stop," he said, hoarse.

"What?"

"Dead leaves," he said. "Is it the baby making those noises?"

"She's not here," I said. And I don't know why I asked then. Or if I expected a coherent answer. But I might not have forever, I thought. So I said, "Who took care of me when I was a baby?"

"Your mother. But not really. No one taught her."

"She tried to care for me?"

"She hugged you." Seemed like he was done talking now, asleep. "Kissed you," he said next. "But left you in the car when it was cold. Once in the bathtub all alone. I tried to train her."

What a strange couple. Him seeing catastrophe around every corner so he had to be incognito, a blender-in. Like me. My mother so unguarded that the idea of protection—a wall, a set of skills—didn't figure. I had the same idea about Dannie: she hadn't seen protection, couldn't conjure it. Did I have both—wariness from my dad, willingness, reception, from my mother? "What else?" I asked. He was out, sedated. I wondered if I'd half-imagined his answers.

I went to buy a soda and got lost, walking down dim, connected corridors—east, south, right—into a hall they were cleaning, I guess, because the floor was wet. The hospital was a maze—had probably started off small, got added onto. I got back to my dad's room and thought of places I'd been that day, Luann's, school, home, Project Promotion, greenhouse, hospital, Dannie's. You can't know what a day will hold. You improvise, intuition a light, illumination, strapped on.

I started praying, the Lord's Prayer, all-purpose, good for stress, emphasis on Thy Will, acknowledging lack of control, shock ahead likely. Thy Kingdom Come. Heaven Exists. Deliver us from evil evil evil. I switched to a new prayer. For All that has Been (picture it), *Thank You*. For All that is To Come (you can never picture it), *Yes*. In the old days people put spires on churches to help prayers rise up. I remembered my dead mother in her trailer, pushing herself on me. *Nightmare,* a medieval word meaning night, as in *night*, and mare, as in *female of species*. A nightmare sits on your chest as you sleep. When I'm afraid of the dark, I walk around, grope this door, that corner. I asked my mother to sit on my chest again. Help her, I said, your granddaughter who's lived like you, bumping from home to home. Except she's found me. Tandela-Esme, one of those double names, no middle name. My last name is Arco. The baby should have all our names, Tandela-Esme Hope Stoner Frigein Arco. I prayed past the night.

Toward day. At some point I slept.

A nurse came in. "These numbers went up," she said, pointing at one display on the monitor next to this bed. "And these are coming down." She pointed to another. "That's what we want."

She left and I looked out the window at the pale sky, traffic on the highway low and steady, everywhere people riding to work in rows, like brainwashed. I wasn't afraid of the dark anymore, because day was here and I had no idea how to survive it: light, but no Esme. My willpower started to drain. I stood up, left my dad's room thinking I'd check for phone messages. As I passed the Emergency Room entrance, I saw a van outside. A person got out, her back facing this way. Then the passenger window opened and someone handed out a bundle, a baby. The van backed up, then ahead, back, forth, back, like a preposition lesson on *Sesame Street.*

She turned. Creola Wheat, carrying Esme. They could have been related, a woman, her daughter.

I ran out the doors in my stocking feet.

Creola said, "We thought you might be here. How's your daddy?"

I held Esme, squeezed her solidness. She laughed, pulled my hair. "Where did you find her?"

"Miranda Gutierrez had her."

Miranda leaned out the van window. "Miss, I saw that dyke teacher at H.E.B., and she was asking the man at the *farmacia* how to take care of your baby, yelling at that man to tell her how to make the baby stop throwing up. She gave me your baby. She said, here, you understand babies."

I went around the van to thank Miranda's mother. She looked angry and so pregnant. I said, "*Gracias.*"

Her eyes narrowed. "*Miranda no es juvenil delincuente.*"

Esme twined her fat, palpable arms around me. "What?" I asked Miranda.

"She's mad you took me to the reform school."

FIFTEEN

We sped away, Mike driving, Esme in her new car seat in the half-seat behind. It was the second time I'd been in Mike's truck, I thought. The first time was that day we'd looked for Esme: driving to Luann's, to Project Promotion, the hospital. I'd thought he was driving slow. Now I thought he drove too fast. "Slow down," I said, "you have passengers." He said, "I have to get gas," and pulled over at a filling station on the outskirts. We were headed for Port Aransas, that town on an island, to spend a weekend at the beach, which would be crowded, people had warned, drunk college students everywhere. It was spring break. Projection Promotion had shut down, skeleton crew. Port Town High, closed. Lee College, closed. Dannie was in Port Arthur— with her sister, whose photography class in Atlanta was on spring break too— and finishing her incompletes in time to graduate. Mike had the nozzle in the gas tank, the door open, ding ding. He leaned over and pulled out the keys. He looked good, crisp clothes, springy hair. He must use a blow-dryer, I thought. He jingled the keys in front of Esme's face. "I hope it doesn't rain." He pointed at our luggage in back, one suitcase for him, two for me, three for Esme if you count the portable baby bed I'd borrowed from Lupe's niece, also a satchel full of Gerber's, another with wipes and diapers. "We could have taken my car," I said. I meant my mother's.

"I sure wouldn't," he said. "You're asking for trouble if you get pulled over."

I said, "I did find the title."

I'd found it by haphazard luck that morning—looking for the registration. We'd been in front of my house, packing Mike's truck. Janeway, who'd wandered over, had said, "Why don't you take the ghetto cruiser? You'd have room for yourselves and a few hitchhikers down the pike." Mike answered, "Hey, don't call it a ghetto cruiser. It's got only thirty-five thousand miles on it." They were standing around in that southern way, taking twice as long to get tasks done as you would in the North because you'd be freezing, worried about stowing gear before snowfall. Mike leaned forward, one foot on the bumper. Fine, I thought. I had Esme's food to pack, peas, pears, beans, peaches, chicken, yams, beef. I'd also need to pack Zyrtec, a new medicine to keep her airways open. I'd told my dad I'd swing by the hospital—Rehab/Recovery ward, where he was learning to eat fiber. He was supposed to come home in three days. He'd been arguing with nurses. Janeway called out, "He's a bit of an intellectual, Delia." I'd thought: Mike was? Mike said, "It's Delia who reads. She'd read a phone book or placemat if she didn't have anything else." I thought: I should pack a book for the beach. But didn't. I was getting into my car with Esme.

At the hospital parking lot, holding Esme, reaching back into my mother's car to get a bottle I'd fixed before I left home, I decided to open the glove box. I felt profane doing it, prying into the zone of the dead. I'd felt the same way opening drawers and closets in her trailer. But her registration was maybe here. I'd been thinking if I had that, and her death certificate, and papers from the probate court, letters of administration, which freed me to sell the trailer, I could probably get a title. I opened the glove box and saw an ice scraper and car manual. I started to put them back, and a piece of paper slid out of the manual. Registration, I thought. But no. Who knew where her registration was, in her purse? I'd never seen her wallet or purse. Duster probably took them to write those checks. The piece of paper turned out to be the title, State of Ohio. Hope May Stoner—her middle name I'd heard maybe once. When I went inside and told my dad I'd found the title in the glove box, he pounded on the food tray they'd wheeled in. "I told her never to do that." This would have been decades ago, I thought. How long did they live together, two years? "Haven't I told you not to put the title in the glove box?" he said. "Perfect setup for some lowlife who'd drive it away." Duster, I thought. If he'd only known. "We'll be back on Sunday night," I said. I gave him Mike's cell phone number. "Call if you need me. Please don't harass the nurses." He said, "They're just fascists." But he pronounced it his way, fassists.

At the gas station, Mike was hanging up the fuel pump. "You found the title?"

"In the glove box," I said. "But the license plate is wrong. My dad switched them."

He shrugged. "We're all packed up here anyway."

Then Esme sneezed three times. "I forgot her prescription," I said. "I need to go home and get it." Mike drove back to my house, parked behind a trailer pulled by a truck. Arturo and Lupe's niece's husband stood on the trailer, tying down a sofa. Lupe waved at us from the yard. I got out. "How's your dad?" she asked. If she'd ever been mad at me, she was over it. "Full of piss and vinegar," I said. I could tell by the look on her face she didn't know what I meant. "Grouchy," I added. She said, "And your mother died last year, so sad." I explained I'd never known my mother, so it had been a relatively easy version of a parent's death. She looked offended: How could a parent's death ever be easy? How could a mother set a child aside? I didn't know which angle offended her and decided our ideas right then were too complicated for our small overlap of words. "Yes," I said, "but my dad is fine." Lupe was talking about her new house they were buying, not renting. Wal-Mart didn't have curtains she liked. And she'd had Mike inspect the house and he'd told her it was overpriced. But she'd already paid the developer twenty-five hundred dollars. By law he has to return it, Mike told her. But she and Arturo didn't have papers, so the law didn't matter. "When we live there," she said now, "your father, *la bebita,* and Mike—you visit."

"We will," I said.

I went in and got Esme's medicine. Also the breathing machine—though she hadn't used it in weeks. I was on the porch, coiling up the cord, and Lupe asked, "When will you move, Delia?"

"At the last possible minute," I said. Chuck had come by and removed the contract pending sign. The buyers had backed out. Their son turned down the Exxon job. They'd almost bought him a house and he didn't want it, I thought, amazing. I was hoping that by waiting for a new buyer, also the time it would take to close, and the thirty days' notice the new buyer had to give me, I could stay in this house until the end of the school year, May. "I'll find something," I said.

"Look. *Soy muy llorona,*" Lupe said. "I cry too much."

Cry? I thought

She held out her arms. "We have been a family."

We had been?

"I'll miss you and *la bebita.*"

I hadn't realized. I hugged Lupe good-bye. "We'll visit, I promise."

I got back into the truck. Janeway was leaning in through Mike's window, waving at Esme. "Fuzzy wuzzy, bye-bye," she said. Fuzzy wuzzy? I thought. Was she talking about Esme's hair? Not exactly, I decided. I remembered how I used to think Janeway was a cricket—a member of a species who didn't like kids. Or understand them. Maybe she didn't, hadn't been around many. But that didn't make her bad, just not someone you'd leave your baby with. "We're off," I said. Also: "I've called you the wrong name all this time. Your first name's Regan."

"But I've loved being called Janeway." She smiled. "It made me feel like a different person."

We pulled away.

I told Mike to go to the post office. "My mail," I said. Four days had passed since I'd checked.

He turned the air-conditioning on. "Is Dannie watering your plants?"

"Janeway is," I said. Even if Dannie were in town, I thought, I wouldn't ask. When I'd talked to her after that night she took Esme from Luann (decent impulse), palmed her off on Miranda (careless impulse), left disjointed messages so we couldn't find her (recklessness), she was standing on my porch returning the bucket-style car seat she'd forgotten to give to Miranda. I said, "You should never consider a career in child-care, and you might not want to have kids yourself. Stick with dogs. Where were you?" How did she answer me? "Hoover, I flipped out in that store when that man asked where I got the baby. He told me to prove she was mine, because I'm butch, not likely to have a baby, and also white, and the Doo-doo, you know, is not. I already have problems. I'm like a kid myself." I was thinking: yes. And Luann's excuse? She'd saved me from having to be angry by calling, angry, and saying: "It's time for me to take care of me. All my life I gave to others." She'd put her mother in a nursing home and was going to flea markets with Drew, selling her hand-sewn clothes next to his scrap from houses. I could have told her she'd been unreliable, caused hours of fear, but it wasn't all her fault Esme ended up with Dannie and Dannie lost track. I said, "If you ever babysit again, never give the kid to anyone besides the parent." She'd said, "You should have made that clear," snippy, and hung up.

I went in the post office and got my mail. A priority mail cardboard envelope from Cuyahoga Credit Union—safe deposit box contents, I figured. And a catalogue. Junk mail. Bills.

I got back into the truck. Mike pulled away, and I started to open the big envelope.

Esme was crying.

I moved Mike's toolbox away from her leg, popped her pacifier in. I studied the envelope. Not much here, I thought. Mike gave me his pocket knife, and I opened it. Five snapshots—some black-and-white, some color (faded greens, rusts, ambers)—fluttered out like leaves:

She had on a bell-shaped dress and boots, hair bouffant
but long, looking like Jeannie C. Riley, Harper Valley PTA,
I thought. I was wrapped in a blanket.

Sunburned, cloudless sky behind, wearing a swimsuit,
a strap sliding off one shoulder, she held me.

She looked out a dim window, her hair short. A Christmas
tree twinkled. I rolled around in wadded up wrapping
paper.

In front of a fountain that dripped icicles, she wore a parka.
I faced the camera, reached for whoever held it.

My grandma's house, I realized, the pink stucco, Astroturf
on the front steps. That house smells like mothballs, I remembered. My mother squinted. My dad held me. She
must have been picking out his clothes because he had on
white shoes.

Were they all taken in Idaho? Did we live in the reservation house yet?
She'd kept these photos in a vault in the bank, I thought, but not the
title to her car or trailer.

I was struck by how happy we looked. Or normal. Every family that
later on blows up and scatters probably has five normal photos, I thought. I
wondered if the reverse is true. If normal families have five bad photos. "These
pictures were in my mother's safe deposit box," I told Mike.

He glanced up. "You've never seen them?"

I hadn't told him about not knowing my mother. "I was raised by my
dad. I don't think he had a camera." I was remembering Harriet in Cleveland
saying my mother had showed her my school pictures—one with short bangs,
missing teeth. I knew which one. My dad used to cut my hair. That year, first
grade, a few days before the photographer got to our school, which wasn't
often, not every year, I had one of my dad's hunting dogs on a leash, pretending he was a pet, and he pulled me down a gully and I knocked out my
baby teeth. My dad must have mailed her those pictures, I thought. Where
was the copy Harriet had seen? In my mother's lost effects, I decided.

We were at the ferry then, waiting in a line of cars and trucks to board. A man directed us to our spot and Mike put the brake on, and I woke Esme by shaking her gently, and we got out. The gulf wind whipped. Gulls screeched, and the sun made the blue water and white boat ultrablue, ultrawhite. "I have a camera," Mike said, "so smile." It was one of those disposable ones you buy at the grocery store. Esme and I posed, the railing behind us, the gulf beyond. "Wave, wave," I said. Esme raised her hand. I tilted my head toward her. A man and woman stopped to watch. The man said, "You want me to take one of the three of you?" So Mike posed near us, arm over my shoulder, and the stranger snapped that. "Thanks," Mike said. The man handed the camera back. His wife said, "Your baby's precious." The man said, "I like her hair." And touched it. Esme instinctively jerked her head back. She'd been in white-only settings too much, I thought, already sick of it. "Give me five," he said to Esme, like she was Michael Jordan or something. Mike said, "Thanks a lot. You folks have a nice day." A few minutes later another lady said Esme was beautiful. "So exotic," she said. Mike said, "She's a good eater too."

The ferry pulled close to the island. We got back in Mike's truck and waited to drive away. I looked around and remembered the hurricane. If you didn't know, you'd ask: What blew through here? Because stacks of lumber and cinder blocks sat next to buildings enclosed by scaffolding. Here and there you saw a wall gone from water and wind, another gone on purpose: demolition. Oiled-up young people in bright swimsuits milled through rubble. Mike was driving while reading a scrap of paper. "I found this on the Internet," he said. "A family rents it out when they're not here, and they don't take college students, which is why it was available." He pulled up in front of a clapboard house, and we unlocked and went inside. It was full of their be-longings we were allowed to use: linens, towels, Tupperware, brooms, pots, pans, toys, wine glasses.

We ate in a restaurant that night, Esme clapping oyster shells like cymbals. We went back to the house and put Esme in the portable baby bed. Mike and I drank vodka on the porch, and it wasn't long before his hands started roving, rearranging. We went inside to the bedroom with the biggest bed, and Mike made love like he did, like I always want, steady attention at first so that by the time he'd have at me I'm thinking: hurry up, get to me, please please. And I thought how we didn't talk, or trade ideas, on the porch or in the restaurant or driving down the road as easily as we settled, admitted, accepted, cleared the air here. No talking. Would it be enough?

I decided to say something. "Have you always liked sex? Seems like you've had some practice."

He smiled, too good-looking. "Hell, no," he said. "I spent the seventies reading *Playboy*—you know, really reading it, the how-to part. Most men my generation needed that. But I was married to my wife, who thought any kind of foreplay was perverted. It's been nice to run across someone with the same interests." He slapped my ass. Then turned over and went to sleep.

It was my first overnighter with him since before Esme.

I'd revised my original plan a few times. First, not to have a man. Then not to have a man for a whole night. Then I'd stayed at Hector's with Esme on a pallet on the floor. And Hector wasn't talking to me now, or Esme, though he'd had the chance—waiting for my dad to get well, come home and be Esme's sitter, I'd taken her with me to work. I needed someone who'd be decent in the long haul, because I didn't want Esme growing up with my ever-changing, serial boyfriends, fake uncles. Pretty soon she'd start calling one daddy, then another. Maybe I should just quit? I'd said so to Creola, who'd answered: "If you send clear signals, Delia, she'll know who is and isn't daddy. And if you quit, you'll never meet a man who could be."

Was Mike good enough?

I didn't blame Hector for being mad.

And almost understood why Dannie in a tight squeeze had sex with so many people, including her landlord. She'd been lonely too long, though it was complicated with Dannie, who'd had sex with three men, not two, in a shorter period of time, one night, and she was a lesbian. Everything about Dannie is complicated. But it seemed clear you can't give up on finding high-quality love, because if you do you get lowered standards, second-rate, and worse, bad love.

When Mike had asked me to go away for this weekend, a house to ourselves, room for Esme, I wanted it. Him. This. I'd never been on vacation before. A getaway from work and worry.

This made me think about Sean's spring break, permanent. He was at home, waiting to be arraigned. He had a beeper on his leg. Creola Wheat watched Esme for a few hours while I went to see him. His sister had moved to her boyfriend's. His mother lurked on the edge of our conversation, now in the kitchen, now the hallway. The temper Sean once flaunted, trying to be edgy and surly, was gone. He flicked through TV channels. His computer was gone. It, and the record of emails and sites he'd logged onto, confiscated. "Would you turn the TV off?" I'd asked. He did. He said, "You want to know why? It's because he mad-dogged us, talking about Conrad being a gook, me a mama's boy." It seemed possible, I thought. Some coaches—not just Coach—think anger is a steroid. "We didn't want to kill him," Sean said. "We wanted to scare him so bad he'd piss on himself." What did I say? "I understand you were mad." I did. "But you hurt yourself and other people." Mason Pratt, I was thinking, who was retiring now. Anyone else who'd been scared—Sage, for instance, in a nearby room when the plastic shards flew.

She came back after the two days the superintendent had shut down all schools and said, "Every day I'm driving to work, and I think I'm giving too much. I know that you, Delia, believe in God, so maybe you'll be repaid." That wasn't how I saw it, though. More like that lady who helped me get Pell Grants gave. My boss, who got me accredited, gave. I couldn't give to them, only the next people. She said, "Face it, I haven't helped anyone anyway." I told her what Hector once told me: You try to help and don't see progress, but ten years from now a kid might be in a hard spot and make a better choice based on something you did. She said, "Delia, the profession's out of touch with the times. Everyone's talking about self-help, not other-help."

True enough, I thought.

That night in Port Aransas I got out of bed to make myself a drink, sit on the porch. But when I turned on the kitchen light I saw baby cockroaches, palmettos, scurrying. No one likes bugs. I've never had many, superior housekeeping. I turned the light off, then on, to see them come out again, count them. Mike all of a sudden stood behind me, naked. "What's going on?" he said. I turned the lights back off, and on—to let him see. His eyes went wide. He looked a little crazy, gray hair poking up like he was that famous genius. "Get the baby and get outside," he said. "Get on the porch."

He put his pants on and went to his truck. I was getting Esme up when he came back in carrying a plastic jug of bug spray. He stopped. "Maybe we should just move to a new place," he said. "But I don't think we'll find anything tonight. Everything is booked because of spring break."

I said, "If you spray, what are we going to do afterward?"

"I'm working that out," he said.

Esme flopped her head, sleepy.

Mike said, "You have to understand I've fought this my whole life."

"What," I asked, "cockroaches?" I was also thinking how weird he kept spray in his truck. And was so scrubbed clean all the time. His septic tank business, drainage this and that. A fixation?

"You didn't see the house I grew up in. My mother was no house-keeper, let me tell you. This is a recent hatch-out, though," he said. "They've sprayed recently, I can tell." He pondered this. He went outside and came back in wearing glasses I'd never seen before. He read the back of the jug. "Okay," he said, "I'll spray, then open the windows, and we'll drive around for a few hours."

I said, "Spray the kitchen and shut the door, and we'll go to bed. I don't want to drive around."

"I guess not," he said.

And in the morning it was over, a nightmare. Mike's.

We spent the day at the beach, taking more photos.

Esme and me in the sand.

Esme and me in the surf.

Esme and me walking the shoreline.

Mike under the umbrella, reading a book.

"What book?" I said, setting the camera back down.

He held it up. *The Fall of the Bingo King.* "Janeway's—about Dannie's parents."

I must have had a strange look on my face. I wouldn't want people reading some take on my dead family, I thought, reading and shuddering with pleasure, gratitude, thinking they're luckier, safer than us. And it was dark business—we have darkness already without looking for more.

Mike said, "Janeway palmed it off. I got curious. I used to work around Port Arthur."

I said, "But you know these people, sort of. They're not strangers in a newspaper."

"It's a book, Delia. Reading it doesn't make me bad."

No, but . . .

We were getting sunburned.

We went back and dressed for dinner. Mike poured glasses of champagne.

I was having a glass in the bathroom, putting finishing touches on my makeup. I looked like someone else, tanned and hardy in a house that seemed cush, luxurious. Mike was in the living room like head of household. I heard him. "Easy, girl. Watch for corners. That's it." It's hard not to let a man in the next room talk to your daughter and smile at her, I thought. How soon would they get attached? There must be people who look across a room at an adult playing with their kid, I thought, and don't immediately see the adult as potentially removed, unnecessary. I walked out there, and Mike was in the kitchen, closing the freezer fast. "What?" I said.

He said, "It's nothing."

I looked in the freezer, vodka. "So you had a sip," I said. "Don't be paranoid."

He said. "I'm not."

"You were hiding it. Why?" I had this feeling we were in an old pattern again, his.

"I thought you would mind. My wife did."

"I'm not her," I said, "calm down."

But by the end of the night I saw her point.

He took us to an expensive restaurant. Waved and talked to people at other tables who'd nodded hello and said something noncommittal like: hope you're having a good time and what a cute baby. To all outward eyes, hale fellow. But his attention flitted. I had to remind him to take his credit card back after he paid the bill. I left him wobbling by the front door and went to the bathroom to change Esme. On the way back out, I heard someone say, "Miss, Miss. Over here."

I turned. Outside the kitchen doors in a white apron, a kerchief over her long hair—Veronica. She smiled. Her skin had cleared up, I thought. I hugged her. "I thought you went to Utah."

She said, "I did go. It was too cold. I saw you eating dinner tonight. Was that your husband? Is this your baby? I wanted to talk. The lesson you gave us on job applications, that was good. My boyfriend, he's my old boyfriend's little brother, he got a job too and helps me out."

"I'm glad," I said. "What does he do?"

She looked confused.

"Where does he work?" I said.

She said, "I don't know. Something near the video store."

"Delia, are you all right?" It was Mike, not lurching exactly.

"I have to go," I said. I gave her my work phone number. "Call me collect if you have to."

She smiled. She wouldn't, I knew. I felt sad and helpless, like I was her.

In the parking lot, I put Esme in her seat while Mike stared at the sky. "My dad saw a UFO when he was plowing an onion field," he said. "Your old man and I think they're there, Delia, and everybody else will miss out on the biggest news of the century. Have you seen those fetus mummies they found inside Egyptian pyramids? They look like that Roswell thing, or E.T."

Because that Roswell thing or E.T. look like us, I thought. A creature from out there, like us, but smallish and kind. That's what people say about religious saviors too. I thought: Do you break up with someone because he thinks space aliens came and are still coming? "Mind if I drive?"

"What?" He did stagger.

I took the keys away from him. "Get in."

When we got to the house, he poured himself another. "Three fingers," he said.

"Do you need it?" I was thinking that before I got Esme I used to get a little drunk with him. Had I seen him this drunk then? Was I just sober now? I'd been full-tilt drunk only once since I got Esme, and that was last fall, the first time I saw Mike after I got her, a backsliding kind of one-time night. But I didn't do it again. My circumstances had changed and his hadn't, I realized.

I wondered how people fit their lives together. And keep them there.

"You said you don't mind," he said.

"But this is too much." I put Esme to bed. When I came out, he was sleeping in an upright position. I took his drink away, led him to bed. He made a few clumsy grabs like we were going for that. Not this: him on top of the covers, fully dressed, snoring. I decided to sleep on the couch. And couldn't sleep, thinking he'd lost some of his gloss, promise, and might not get it back. He'd think this about me someday—maybe he did. This next phase was going to be harder.

Giving up on sleep, I checked for cockroaches. I flicked the light off, gave them time to creep out. Then on: nothing. One small problem gone. When I'm trying to sleep, I try to think of problems-solved and not go near the long list of problems-unsolved, mine and everyone's. I can never fall asleep away from home, I thought. I got on the floor to pray. At home, I hold a small cross. But here, itchy from sunburn or humidity, thinking of bugs, I couldn't pray. I stood up.

There wasn't a TV here. Or books.

Mike's book—Janeway's, about Dannie and what she'd survived—lay on the table. I picked it up. I decided to somehow hook the photo pages together so no one flipping through would accidentally see black-colored blood. But I couldn't help myself. I did look. At corpses. At Dannie on the witness stand, her fixed expression like she'd been quivering, trying to stop. Another shot of the family in front of a camper—Dannie a skinny kid who looked ADHD, her sister already gruff-looking. I wondered if the man who wrote the book bought these photos from people who had them lying around, non-family members to whom they weren't sacred, because no one would give them up who cared how the past was, cared how it had once seemed likely to move forward into possibility and quickening force, into a future in which Dannie's dad lets go of her shoulders and she squirms away, and Dannie's mother lets go of her pose, her arm over the sister's shoulder, and they sit down somewhere and eat ice cream. And all stay alive for the next twenty years. Dannie revisits this past, I thought, and can study it, make up a new ending, but can't ever go back to the stillness of these photos, so alive and poised, go back to the stop-action and restart it. I dug around in the kitchen and found a clip for closing up bags of potato chips and used this to pin the photos in the center together so all you saw was a first happy, jinxed shot, the parents. And the last, the frantic-faced cousin. *The life story of a dispossessed man made us sad*, the caption said. On second thought, I covered these too, with print pages, sealed them.

As a reader, I'm fast. When I finished up at the reservation school and switched to Stites High, I got accused of faking results, cheating, on those standard tests that assess speed and comprehension. Because I'd read a lot already. But I didn't want to read this whole book, this *Fall of the Bingo King* seat of horror. I'm not sure what I wanted, a swift insight to settle at last the question of how to help, and what's the next step when helping starts to hurt or threaten you, the helper. Or anyone else. Maybe I thought I'd get the answer soon and fall asleep, peaceful. Or I was morbid and curious, like Janeway. At any rate, I wanted wisdom fast and easy, moral turpentine. I skimmed. The book said Dannie talked high-pitched like a cartoon, and her motor coordination was jerky, irregular. I thought how she was after a night of insomnia, doped up on remedies from the health food store and whatever else. She was pretty, "gamin-like and sloe-eyed." The ancient plantation house on the bayou her parents owned was threadbare. The cousin who killed them was a fourth cousin twice-removed who'd been scuttled around to every imaginable relative before he'd moved into their spare rooms. He was a drug user, possibly schizophrenic.

I read for hours, getting wider and wider awake. I got up and checked Esme.

Sat back down and read more.

Which came first, the book asked, the cousin's drug habit or his hallucinations, chicken or egg? He killed the parents because he thought they caused Dannie and her sister to turn bad, lesbian. This is only shades away from Caroline Blakely's idea, I thought. He'd spent time in prison, a breeding ground for groups of people who drum up scapegoats: someone out there so different it's a simple relief to blame him, or her, that type of person generally, for the fact you don't fit in either. If you're a misfit you'll likely be picked on or picking on, the book said. But maybe the real reason he killed Dannie's parents was for money they'd made running nine bingo parlors.

After reading the book, did I understand Dannie better?

No.

I understood her that split-second when I thought Esme was gone—what staggering effort it takes to ride out the aftermath when an essential piece of your happiness has been done in, purged.

Did I understand better who killed them, who done it? I didn't know more than what Dannie told me that first day. Did I understand why? No one ever would. As for why Dannie had arrived in my life, in the web of people around me, and what I should give her, I'm still understanding.

The family you're born into feels holy. It's the first pattern you know. Patterns that include you seem right. Patterns that don't seem like conspiracy. Conspiracy theories aren't new—people who have too much hardship have always speculated about God's motives. They want to know why. If they stop believing in God and still feel helpless in the face of trouble, they want to give trouble a name. Faraway mindsets unthinkably treacherous. Foreigners with weapons of mass destruction. Church's Fried Chicken Corporation setting out to make your race sterile. Homosexuals rising up. Broken homes breaking up the national character. And me, thinking people from intact families are putting the rest of us, losers and loners, down. When you feel left out of what other people call normal, it's hard to concentrate on yourself, what you should do instead, your alternate plan, the shape of your life you're making from scratch, because you end up with all choices and therefore no clear choice. I worried about Dannie, her breaking and entering, the instant way she found new people and places to live. Myself too, with my sense that no one is enough like me to attach, so why bother. We could go too far toward endless choice.

Then with that moaning slump you hear when all appliances in the house shut off at once—the humming refrigerator, AC, ceiling fans—all lights everywhere blinked off. Power failure. I waited until my eyes adjusted and gray settled. I looked out the window. Darkness was general all over the island. But down the road, across the way, scattered spots on the grid flickered, boxy towers speckled, glowing. Hotels probably, with backup generators. You lose power a lot on an island, I thought. But everywhere else, doors opened, flashlights pinpricked their way out. I was thinking about Dannie and me, that we had hunkered down in rifts and leftover spots, and what you find there, apart from rule-stripped confusion and unlimited choice, is permission to improvise, make a new way. But you have to keep your wits sharp, no days off, no sliding by. It hit me all at once that other people checking fuse boxes, staring into neighbors' blank, black windows, running around in darkness like serfs, weren't different. They were probably kowtowing too to a tyrant-idea of what normal is, an idea I'd never seen for real, but just the same I gave it the power to keep me lowly. No one had how-to manuals for surviving change.

Veronica, Miranda, Bree, Nelly—they thought I was steady, wise. I'd kept my worries secret.

This is a good strategy, if only because most people do.

I'd remember this later—though I couldn't foresee how I'd someday remember myself that night in the beach house. But five years later, when Project Promotion had more funding, community support, an award from Washington, DC, for the highest GED scores in the Southwest, we made a float for the Fourth of July parade, a school-spirit float I was riding on to keep my daredevil kids from jumping off, tipping it over, pelting people in the face with candy. Esme was riding with me. My dad stood on the side of the road with a video camera he'd bought and become obsessed with: filming Esme riding a bike, dressing a doll, hunting Easter eggs, climbing trees, now riding a float and flinging candy. She blew him a kiss. A new teacher—fresh out of school, no experience, reminded me of Sage with her talk about ideals and purpose—said: "The bond between your daughter and dad is great. You're close-knit. This will keep her safe from so much." I laughed, thinking of my dad's Chief Joseph hang-ups and Mormon tics, the paranoia he must have got from *his* dad, a Jewish shepherd in Idaho, fish out of water. Also the idea I'd patched together a family structure that kept us partly exempt from risk. But that dark night in Port Aransas, the town that smelled like water, I watched a few more people scurry around unlit yards and went to sleep near Mike, who, beginning to stir now, seemed less stupefied and inert, more living.

By the time I woke because Esme was calling out, Mike was on the couch with a glass of water on the coffee table, a bottle of old-timey pain reliever, Bayer or something. "Morning," he said.

I'm not a talker in the a.m. I was measuring powdered formula.

"I went out for a paper," he said. "Would you like to hear your horoscope?"

Did he know what sign I was? I wasn't sure, Capricorn maybe. I told him my birthday.

He read: "You realize goals by inducing people and shaping matter. Tend your own back yard only."

Was this a plea for mildness, to go easy? "Did you make that up?"

He blushed. "No, it's right here. Read it yourself. Do you want to hear mine?"

"Fine."

"Apologize for recent excesses." He smiled.

We drank some coffee, packed up and left.

On the way home, Esme slept.

We passed through a small town, Refugio, and I said, "Did you know the lights went out last night?"

Mike gave me a careful look—like I was talking in code.

I said, "When you were asleep, I was still up. Electricity went out all over the island."

"And came back on again, I guess," he said.

We didn't talk much the rest of the way home.

"Can you stop at the post office?" I said when we'd pulled around the curve and I could see Port Town—a swampy town with twisting roads and Exxon's blinking towers. I wondered how it got its name. I asked Mike. He shrugged. "Maybe some founding father was named Port." He pulled up at the post office. I went in. I'd made a resolution not to let my mail pile up. My mother's out-of-the-blue way of materializing, then dying, was done, I told myself. The sad work she'd left behind: endured. I hadn't been married to Stephen Arco and his spending habits for years. I didn't sleepwalk into malls and run up bills. What bad news could arrive through my mail slot now? I grabbed everything, two days' worth, got into the truck and went home.

Mike unloaded luggage. I lifted Esme out of her seat. I unlocked my door, aware of Lupe and Arturo's vacated apartment, its hollowness too tangible to have been caused by just a missing porch chair or Arturo's slippers gone from the mat by the door. The glass in the front window seemed sleeker, repelling light. I felt half-gone myself, ready to stop living here and yet not-here. I went inside, checked my answering machine, two messages. Creola: "It's Friday, you're probably out to dinner. I got out of a meeting with Hector and Hal Hollie and wanted to run ideas by you." The second, my dad: "It's Sunday, Delia, and you can pick me up any damn time."

I called Creola. "What's up?"

She said, "Hal Hollie finally put the money together for a full-time social worker and two guidance counselors over at the high school—people finally see the need. So next year, you'll be at Project Promotion full-time. But that's no piece of cake. We're having a lot of turnover right now."

"Mason's talking about retiring," I said.

"And Sage Hearttsock turned her resignation in."

"Is she going back to Fort Worth?" I asked

Creola said, "She's going to work for AA."

Work for it? I didn't know they had paid positions. "Do you mean Triple A?"

Creola said, "I have no idea. Point is, we've got to hire. I'm the new director. Hector quit. "

"Hector?"

"He's going back to school in the valley—Pan Am U. I want to move you up into my old job, Delia, which would mean a raise for you. But you've got to finish your degree or at least be enrolled."

So she knew I hadn't finished college. Hector always made it sound like he alone knew. But no way could I afford school. "I'm happy at this level," I told Creola. I wondered if it were true.

Creola said, "Hollie's got a fund that'll cover your tuition. You complete six credits a year."

"I could," I said. I was thinking about Hector. Wondering if the bomb scare drove him off, the knowledge, undeniable, we were stretched thin, exposed. Or the bomb scare combined with me, my turncoat treason. I'd worried about this last week, standing next to Sage at the Xerox machine when she'd said Hector was hard to work with but she liked him better than Creola. I told her Hector acted most grouchy when he was worried. "I've gotten a little too tied up over there," I said, deliberately vague, "a boundaries problem." Sage had looked at me and laughed. "You mean because he stares at you with his tongue hanging out? I don't see why boundary-keeping is women's work. I don't see many men worried they've gotten too close to women."

The only time I saw Hector again was four years later, at a state colloquium on education. We met in a room with tables, people handing out pamphlets. He tipped his head to one side, said he was teaching college now. How was I? Fine, I said. I made enough money. Esme was starting kindergarten. My dad seemed happy. I had a boyfriend I liked so much I thought I'd marry him and so had the tremoring high hopes and doubt that went with that. But I didn't tell Hector about my boyfriend. He said, "My mother has tormented me about you—why we didn't last." We were alike, I thought, afraid at the first complication. I couldn't take on someone *as* afraid.

"And," Creola said on the telephone now, "that hard-headed woman from Lee College called to thank you for handling Dannie, and she's sending you a new intern who's the cream of the cream this time. High grades, good attitude. Only thing, she's gotten into trouble with her parking."

"Parking?"

"Parking her car in the wrong lot on campus, I guess," Creola said, "you know, where professors should park. But that won't matter to us. Name is Flores. I have it written down. Melissa."

Same as the hurricane, I thought. "It'll be fine."

"Usually is," Creola said. And hung up.

I went back outside, set Esme on the porch floor, and sat in the swing next to Mike. I could smell Lupe, her household—*comino,* also this mint-scented hand cream she used, Dr. Bell's Pomade. I wondered if these smells had always lingered around the porch or if they'd wafted out with her furniture. I said to Mike, "I need to go up to the hospital and bring Dad back home."

"Look at Esme," he said.

She was standing up, holding porch rails, yelling.

I reached for the stack of mail I'd set on top of a suitcase. Junk mail. Bills. A letter from the lawyer. I opened that envelope and a pale green check fell into my lap. I picked it up. $8810.47. Typed, neat. Made out to me, Delia Arco. I stared at it. I read the letter that came with it.

> Ms. Arco,
>
> The realtor you contracted to sell your mother's mobile home found a buyer, Barbi Zehm, who made an offer of $13,000 contingent on her ability to take occupancy quickly. This was a reasonable offer on property in less than ideal condition. As your resident agent during the probating of this estate, I have accepted the offer on your behalf. Our firm completed the title search expeditiously. Enclosed find a settlement statement where I have signed in your stead, also an invoice that reflects expenses deducted from the gross sum.

It didn't sound quite legal. On the other hand, maybe it was just blunt—like I was a small-fry client and they wanted this case off the desk. And I was $8810.47 further ahead than I'd been before and had my mother's car, which, technically—lawyer's word—was part of what they were entitled to take a cut from. And the funeral home scam was maybe over for good. $8810.47 might not change *your* life. But it was already changing mine as I sat next to Mike, my brain zinging like a calculator, subtracting, estimating, reserving this over here for rainy-day spending.

Janeway crossed the street, wearing a gardening hat. "How was the mini-vacation?"

This made me think of mini-bottles on airplanes. I said, "A little boring after Mike passed out." Rude to say, but that's what I was thinking. Seemed like progress I'd said so aloud, instead of just thinking it. Either we'd face the problem, work it out. Or break up. Why not? In fact, how much he drank did level off. But how drunk he acted got worse. We broke up six months later.

Mike said, "Delia, that's not a good way to handle this." He looked annoyed.

I wanted him to feel not too bad about himself but at the same time try to do better. A contradictory urge. I'd feel like this a lot, I realized. I said, "But you're not drunk now. That's headway."

He rolled his eyes.

I went back to considering the check in my lap. Harriet Mosley had said that a married man bought my mother her car. Did she get her trailer house the same way? If so, I'd ended up with profits from her hard-earned home, her price-dearly-paid zone of protection. I thought about the pictures she'd kept in her safe deposit box and remembered waiting to adopt Esme—my paperwork completed, my two-thousand-dollar deposit on impending legal fees paid, waiting, waiting for a baby I knew in time would get here, staring at the phone thinking, *will he call?* meaning the social worker with the face lift who'd supervised the adoption, but I never called him because I didn't want to seem frantic, desperate. Even if I could see the outward signs that I'd be a mother soon, I couldn't imagine how it would feel until I held Esme that first time. My mother must have had the same feeling she couldn't be a mother the whole nine months I was inside her, and then they put me in her arms and she was one. A few years later she wasn't again. The pictures were the only proof she had. She'd kept them safe, saved. She hadn't made a will, but she put my name on her papers, called me before she died. She wanted me to have what she'd gathered, earned.

I was comprehending this precise instant of change—when I went from being a person who couldn't own a house to a person who could. I thought about telling Mike and Janeway my plan. Chuck wanted three thousand dollars down, and that left plenty to buy paint, floor covering, furniture. I'd move my dad into the other side. All I had to do was walk into my house and call Chuck, maybe put up my own "contract pending" sign. I listened to Mike. He was handing *The Fall of the Bingo King* back to Janeway—minus the clip that had held the photos together, I noticed—telling her he'd read some of it. "How'd you like it?" she asked. He shrugged. "Same old story," he answered. She looked disappointed. How odd, I thought, that she had that sign about divinity, *Namaste,* in her front yard, also this gloomy, prying bent. I wondered what divinity meant: The freedom to figure it out? The sure feeling you could? As for Dannie and how her life turned out, she still calls me late at night. Her voice comes on the answering machine, barking at first, pretending to be her dog Jackson leaving a message for Esme. The last time we talked, she said she was getting married in a Unitarian ceremony to a divorced woman with teenage sons. "As you can imagine," Dannie told me, "that's been good preparation for dealing with me. I fit in."

But sitting on my porch that day, I looked at Mike, Janeway, Esme. I couldn't yet imagine my next phase. Janeway stood up to walk back across the street. She said to Mike, "It's a good thing she lives in L.A." She was talking about Marla, I guess. "The distance keeps us together," she told him. Mike nodded. Esme climbed onto one of the suitcases. "Ga ga," she said. I was starting to see I'd confused two ideas. The saved and damned categories in the afterlife were one thing—you were or weren't and, depending on what church you went to, you might not be able to change your status. But I'd been operating like there were saved and damned categories in this life, people who are fit, and those unfit, thwarted from the start and sidestepping pitfalls. Direction, as I far as I'd seen it, had shown up as movement away from dark places I didn't want to reenter, running away, not forward, this sense of hurry hurry because you get only so many chances and, once gone, they vanish, evaporate, and our time in the world runs down. I'd navigated blind corners, steep circumstances. "Ma ma," Esme said. She was hanging on to the railing and grinning. I'd never be able to explain to Esme or anyone else, I thought, how I got to this split-second when for the first time I felt fixed, not transient, *invited.* Would this moment lead to others like it? *Probably.* At the time, I didn't know more than that.

ACKNOWLEDGMENTS

My first and best thanks to Cindy Chinelly. Also to Leticia Jasso, for her stellar suggestions throughout. To Frederick Busch, for advice and friendship. To Kathie Lang, Lee K. Abbot, and Carol Lee Lorenzo, for making the novel better. To the editors of *Prairie Schooner,* where sections of it were first published. To Mary Powell, for keeping it alive by reading so carefully that long, hot summer. For technical expertise in probate law, John Powell. For technical expertise in bomb making, A. J. Martine. For great child care, Joan Rothelle. For understanding what it was about before I did, Sidney Burris. For giving it a title, Ralph Tejeda Wilson. For encouragement and insight in all phases, early, late, and suspended: Shen Christenson, Scott Blackwood, Melissa Falcon, Susan Anderson, John Dufresne, Jim Magnuson, Jonis Agee, Dick McDonough, René Leblanc.

And of course to Marie, whose enthusiasm (for everything and everybody) is unstinting.

.